THE ROAD TO MATAPALO

RODNEY SMITH

littlepondpublishing.com

THE ROAD TO MATAPALO

Copyright © 2015 by Rodney Smith
ISBN: 978-1-940720-15-9
First Published 2015 Printed in the United States of America
First Printed 2015
Originally published by Little Pond Publishing, Inc.
Cover Design and Book Production by Laura Kelly
Edited by Mark T. Bradbury

All Rights Reserved. No part of this book may be reproduced or transmitted in any form or by any means, electronic or mechanical, including photocopying or recording, except for the inclusion of brief quotations in a review, without written permission from the author.

Disclaimer: This is a work of fiction. Names, characters, businesses, places, events and incidents are either the products of the author's imagination or used in a fictitious manner. Any resemblance to actual persons, living or dead, or actual events is purely coincidental.

*Dedicated to the women
in our lives who dare to walk
to a different beat.*

Prologue

Smoke lifts wistfully towards the heavens as darkness embraces the edge of light. The fire's embers dance like spirits seeking peace from the flames. The flame slowly hugs and caresses each splinter of wood, silently fondling its bark before devouring the core.

The smoke and flames start as one, escaping together as the embers float upward into the sky. Dancing and swirling their way out of the fire, they drift up and away; there one moment, gone the next. The universe opens to its warmth and peace; the fire is perfect in every way. It provides the light, and then the darkness to the physical and spiritual world in unison. Its message is clear. Look to the beginning to find the end; first the light and then darkness.

The fire's keeper, Hephaestus, sits and watches, and then stands, pacing the perimeter of the fire's warmth and light. He fears by morning the fire will be nothing more than a cold heap of lifeless ashes, but for now he sits and watches, and prays for peace.

All would be good if he could only find this peace within fire. The fire is everything, and he knows that as long as he is close to the fire his knowledge is strong. He is mesmerized by its captivating finality; he sits and worships the smoke, ash and embers and idolizes its flames.

His mind wanders, but he remembers the importance of his task. Idle thoughts occupy idle minds. Feed the fire and the fire will feed you, Hephaestus. You must sustain the fire!

Peace is his in the moment, if only he had a moment for peace. Looking beyond the flames, he sees only emptiness and sadness as smoke gets in his eyes, stealing his serenity. His vision returns to the present and power returns to the fire. He feeds it; it feeds him. Hephaestus waits for darkness to return, because his fire is brightest at the darkest moments.

THE ROAD TO MATAPALO

The Road To Matapalo

Cheyenne was engaged in a serious cell phone conversation with her soon-to-be official fiancé. A touch of dramatic flair had crept into her voice. "You see I have to go! I'm the only chance my grandfather will have to complete his last dream." On the other end of the line, Sidney ignored her demands and started questioning her statement, "to complete his last dream," but Cheyenne avoided his query and moved to close the conversation. When she put her mind to it, she had a special knack for dodging Sidney's personal investigations.

Handling Popi would be another story in itself, and she'd need to employ a completely different set of skills. She knew, in his own eyes, he was old and tarnished, silently praying for years to join his life's love Virginia for their eternal afterlife. Virginia's death nearly a generation ago had helped her escape the bonds of this increasingly material world. She was one of those rare types who never placed herself above anyone, and in her time here she had been an angel to Popi and a saint to many others.

But Popi had kept going, outliving most of his immediate family and all of his mentors he had ever cared about throughout his life. He had been born a dreamer, but one day he dreamt what he feared would be his last dream and somehow over time the dreadful nightmare became part of him, and each day it came closer to defining him in life and death.

He realized he must return to Matapalo to alter his destiny and to reshape his legacy. Matapalo was a place he had forcibly and regretfully removed himself from years before, but Matapalo's good and bad spirits and its dark secrets had followed him for much too long. Now it was time to take care of unfinished business; it was time to return. This magical, mysterious place, Matapalo, had driven a metaphysical wedge between Popi and his family all too often for so many years. His unfinished business there had returned again and again, haunting both his dreams and his waking moments. Murder had frazzled his impression of paradise and tainted him to the core. But, like the rest of us, Popi reacted in his own way to get beyond it.

Somehow Cheyenne fully understood her responsibility. She would be Popi's final helper, and if all went well, his apprentice. She was prepared, knowing since childhood that this was her destiny. She was also a dreamer, and she understood his dreams. And even though it had been too long since they had spent time together, she remembered the warmth and security of his hand in her hand.

Traveling with him would be challenging, and listening to him at times perhaps painful. He had the reputation of an old codger who'd spent too much time talking about the good old days, and about the ignorance of modern culture desecrating the planet, God's sanctified creation. It wasn't her cup of tea, but Cheyenne was no wimp; it was his last request, even if he never requested it of her, and she embraced the role.

Her cell phone rang again; it was Sidney, and she defiantly responded. "I won't be gone too long, dear. Yes, dear, I know, dinner with your parents at the Chart House a week from Sunday. I know how they love the stuffed tilapia and the view of the Lagoon. That might be pushing it, however.

Yes, yes, I know dear, we'll have a safe trip. Anyway, it looks like I've found his address. I'll see you in a week or so. Yeah, well, a week, maybe. Popi is getting too old to travel well. I have to go now."

Cheyenne didn't always pay much attention to what Sidney had to say. He was a semi-sweet Jewish boy from East Beach she'd met in school, and they'd been mostly hanging out while doing both college classes and part-time work, but now they'd been happily dating for close to three years. In his parent's eyes, it was time to tie the knot; grandchildren were an important commodity. They were a cute couple, happy most of the time, but their relationship had been born of convenience. Sidney hadn't proposed, or anything like that, but the two of them had talked about it for months, and a mutual understanding had been silently agreed on that it was a reasonable time to move forward.

There was no traditional proposal between them. They had come to terms on an agreement based on a mutual common law understanding of commitment. They had a harmonious symbiotic relationship; it neither suffered crosswords nor had to endure contentiousness. In her mind, Cheyenne mostly thought they were a perfect lifetime match; together they would pursue a life of love and honor laid out before them. But in her gut, she knew convenience wasn't all it was made out to be; deep, lasting love came from hardship. She had learned this from her own family's experience.

She often judged Sidney to be too predictable, formal, meticulous, and boring. He lacked a killer instinct and had no heart for adventure or conquest. Yes, he was an ample provider of precious security; his family tree came with strong financial roots. With his deep pockets and polished demeanor, he provided her a level of comfort she had rarely experienced as a kid growing up in her middle-class Florida neighborhood. "One man can't be everything" she mused.

The sun rose on the eastern horizon, hurling razor sharp rays of light and shadows in a brilliant burst, tucked behind a towering dark lavender thunderhead erupting with billows of white puffy clouds. The reflected light from the high sky illuminated Popi's humble old brick house. The house was nestled in a ring of fruit trees, surrounded by lush vegetable gardens and leafy tropical plants; it sat near the edge of an old Florida Gingerbread-style neighborhood.

Cheyenne hadn't been to Popi's home for a long time. Now she had grown into a young woman, and she wondered if he would even recognize or remember her. A childhood fiasco had nearly pulled one side of their family apart, and they had rarely seen one another since then. Deep inside she knew it was wrong that she didn't see him more, and at times the thought of their relationship clawed at her stomach.

The waxing sun was hugging the upper edge of the thunderhead, casting a shimmering silver glow on the humble house sitting at the southeast corner of Schrader Drive and Hartmann. The house sat directly on the edge of two conservative beachside communities, and even though she hadn't been to Popi's house for years, she remembered many of its peculiarities.

How could she forget the plank of mahogany driftwood nailed above the garage door, elegantly crafted with seashells, sea beans and other ocean debris announcing 1957 Schrader Drive. Or the yard's uniqueness compared to the others around it, without a single blade of grass on the ground. The old grass had been replaced with beach sunflowers, aloe and Indian blankets years ago. She could still see it all with her eyes closed; the crab traps with their red, white and green buoys, and shrimp traps made of rusting galvanized wire piled high in one small corner of the yard.

A solid wall of head-high pink, red and yellow crotons interspersed with splashes of dark green and yellow speckled plants lined the curvy sidewalk leading to the front door. A majestic Canary Island date palm, with its giant fronds and their nearly foot-long stiletto-like thorns, dominated the center of the yard. Off to the right side, a pathway of flat coquina rock slabs wound its way towards the street.

There were two brightly painted chartreuse sitting benches positioned across from each other on either side of the walkway. Two cats occupied the benches; there was a massive twenty-pound taffy Maine coon in one, and light gray and white one in the other. Neither paid any attention to her return.

It seemed as if there were always cats in the front yard. She had tossed them scraps of fish as Popi cleaned the ones they kept from their fishing trips many years earlier. She and Popi did quite a bit together back then. She recalled helping him plant the date palm in its very spot. The walk added to a warm and inviting feeling brewing within her as she made her way towards the house, and with each step her confidence grew. But before she could knock on the door, she heard his firm voice say "Who is it this time?"

A living room and a small foyer at the front door faced north. The light in the house was low, but she could see him sitting in a wicker chair, silhouetted by the green light coming through the window from the backyard. Popi looked ancient; his shoulders slumped, and his red, blotchy, bumpy head sprouted a few meager puffs of silver-white hair here and there. He looked much too thin for his clothes.

"It's me, your granddaughter Cheyenne."

"Please come in." It was the same tone she recalled.

His eyes gazed up and down her length. He didn't think it was possible, but Cheyenne was more radiantly beautiful than he had remembered. Her jawbone, well pronounced and rigid to her chin, established a well-defined border between her face and abnormally long smooth neck. Her nose was neither large nor small; it was perfect considering the largeness of her eyes and the fullness of her strawberry-blonde eyebrows and lashes. Like his were many years before, her shoulders were square and well balanced, and her figure was like an hourglass, shapely at the top and bottom, and slightly thin in the middle.

To Cheyenne, his stature was one of a proud man, a bit past his time. He stood in the doorway with his shoulders squared and his jaw firm and straight away. She was pleasantly surprised by his firm, comfortable handshake. His hands were a testimony of use; his voice that of a sage. Before he released her hand, he reached out to hug her; it was a little awkward, but warm and caring. Guessing his age or estimating his full size or power was no easy task. Even though his shoulders still looked as though they had once been mighty, his body was only a shell of what it once had been. But his blue eyes still shone like a crisp spring morning sky, and a warm smile stretched across his face.

He maintained steady eye contact with her and asked "Why are you here child?"

He was setting her up; she had expected him to try such nonsense. "Popi, they said to come get you. I'm here to take you to Matapalo."

"Why did they send a girl? Go away. Don't come back!" His words trailed off as he turned away from her.

His once loyal sons had sailed away years earlier, never to return. The female side of the family had been afraid of him; they believed they had been offended, dishonored and disowned by him. Their lack of ability to clearly communicate had proven to be a two-way street, and they had severed their ties with one another over time, content to let open wounds fester.

Thankfully, Cheyenne was not affected. "Popi, please don't give me a hard time. I'm a woman now, and I'm just as capable of making this trip with you as any man. On second thought, you would be hard-pressed to find a man who could take my place or put up with your nonsense."

She almost broke the news of her marriage plans, but instinctively refrained. That would not be advantageous. Popi might use that as an excuse to beg off. She needed to come at him from a position of strength and independence, but her most valuable asset was her ability to listen to him and understand his needs.

"No!" he said, "They've sent a young woman to do the job of a full-grown man. Please, just go away! You don't know what you are asking for! There's more to it than meets the eye! It is no easy task!"

"Regardless, there's no one else to go with you, Popi. No one else has the time or desire, and I'm taking the time. Who else do you think cares? You're old, and nobody has time for the old, the weak, and the infirm. I'm the only one who can go, who can help. I volunteer, so let's go to Matapalo! I know a little about dreams, too. To Matapalo, Popi!"

He knew her words were true. It sapped his spirit to hear them. It was difficult being so old and at the whim of a girl following the family's directions. They didn't empathize with him, understand him, or even know him. What did they care if he got to Matapalo? It was as it often was the case with families; there was more to it than met the eye.

When he was twenty, he worried about what people thought of him. By the time he was forty he didn't care what people had thought. Then when he turned fifty he realized no one was thinking of him, and now that he was over sixty it occurred to him everyone was only thinking of themselves. He knew Cheyenne was very special to think of him, but all the same her words disarmed him. He would have to overcome the past and overlook her youthfulness to create a synergy between them.

He internally referred to his very last dream, the only dream he could now recall, as The Strangler. He knew he and Cheyenne would have to go back in time to set the course straight, but how on earth did this young lady know about that? He had never mentioned his dreams to anyone. Was she a dreamer, too? For sure, she could raise a welt with her words. She might be a worthy travel companion after all. He'd formulated a plan of retribution in his mind, and it was now becoming clearer.

He yearned to expedite the matter and to end his pain. Those who died young were lucky; they would be remembered as young. To grow very old one must watch friends and family die, and in some tragic cases, children and grandchildren, as well. He had been dubiously blessed by Cheyenne's willingness to help him. He was ready to leave this material world, and there was only one thing left to do. Facing his fate he'd go with her to Matapalo to endure the daunting task of resurrecting his murderous memories. He would accept her offer; he knew it was time.

He pointed towards the dining room table where he had placed some refreshments. "Please Cheyenne have a glass of iced tea. I have some walnut sesame honey roll, too." He smiled.

Cheyenne was glad he seemed to be coming around to the idea of the two of them completing his journey. "Why thanks, Gramps."

"Don't call me Gramps. Remember when you were a little girl? I called you Che and you called me Popi."

"Sorry, Popi, I was just pulling your old leg!"

"So, it will be an old man and a sassy girl going to Matapalo, after all," he said.

"Popi, I promise I'll make you proud. There will be no regrets."

Cheyenne had no idea Popi had liquidated his life's savings for their journey, but she would soon find that material things had little value to him. As he prepared his things to go, her eyes scanned the front room. Its furniture was sparse and simple, but its art was expressive and lifelike. Her imagination was sparked as she inspected the many images. She liked what she saw; there was a beautiful print of bonefish and permit cruising a shallow, pristine tropical grass flat, while across from it there was a mesmerizing watercolor of a mystical sailboat somewhere in the Abacos, bobbing in a brilliant island sunset. There was also a signed print of a much younger and less defiant Popi releasing a rogue-sized snook against a tall shoreline thick with black and red mangroves. Her eyes lingered on this image; to her, his eyes were a pathway back into their history.

The art's collective energy touched her, but not as deeply as a lap-sized, cherry wood glass display case sitting on the table beside her. It was full of beach treasures; she instantly remembered well how she'd spent hours investigating its stash as a kid. She lifted the lid and brushed her fingers lightly over the collection of tiny shells, crab claws, sea beans, shark teeth, and other prized beach-combing relics as if they were family heirlooms. Her memories of the box and its contents were good ones; she wished all her dreams were as gentle and sweet.

Popi returned with his backpack much quicker than she had anticipated; he had their plane tickets ready in his hand, and he was eager to leave his refuge and close a twisted segment of his past, a fatal fragment standing in the way of their future. Once out the door, he said a fast goodbye to his feline friends as they continued their way to her car. "Little Gray and Mommy Kitty, we'll see you when we see you!" They were heading towards the airport within minutes. The man-made causeway leading away from the barrier island over the Banana and Indian River Lagoons had been flooded again. Two of the three lanes heading west were closed due to recent high water, and traffic moved at a tortoise's pace.

Speaking expressively, with his hands as much as with his lips, he passionately described some of the damage and costs caused by a recent visit from Hurricane Zelda.

"Not only did three relief bridges collapse, but the waves scored large trenches through the Causeways on both Lagoons. Mother

Nature, with help from Zelda, dug herself a new inlet a quarter-mile wide just a couple of miles north of here. Heck, before the Army Corp of Engineers could arrive to close the new inlet the ocean came and sucked away billions in waterfront homes and properties. You should see all the real sand it deposited on the beach!"

Waving his right hand out the window, he pointed north "She came and took down Patrick's main runway; it was sitting right over there!" Cheyenne's jaw dropped when she saw the damage. "We were lucky Zelda didn't hammer our neighborhood; other homeowners living north and south of us didn't fare as well."

Before reaching the top of the bridge, they came to a dead stop, and it didn't take long for the fumes of hot pavement and traffic residue to engulf them. The toxic brew seemed to lubricate Cheyenne's imagination; she was performing one of her cute childhood acts, fiddling with a lock of her hair with her left hand. It had slipped out from under her Ray's ball cap. The cap, a gift from her grandmother, was her only memory of Virginia.

Thinking back, she remembered the many times she crossed over these Lagoons with her family. Usually they'd search for breaching bottlenose dolphin, or maybe a manatee, osprey, or some other marine creature cruising on or near the Lagoon.

She assumed the chances of seeing them, here again, were slim to none. Marine mammal sightings were no longer a common occurrence along the Lagoon; they were much more of a freak thing since its rapid demise. This thought drained her, and it provoked a series of deep reflections. She recalled the time her grandfather first took her wade fishing along the causeway's shoreline. It was just before sunrise one morning when, hand-in-hand, they methodically did the stingray shuffle as they made their way from the shore.

"Remember how we heard the sharp airy sounds? You told me not to worry; it was a pair of bottlenose dolphin breathing in and out of their blowholes. There was a full moon waxing at dawn; it was warm and no-see'ums were eating us alive. You said the dolphins had been chasing, catching, and eating ladyfish, mullet and spotted sea trout all night."

Cheyenne sat up in her seat and moved closer to the steering wheel as the cars ahead of them started to roll. Watching her bulging eyes and expanded expression, Popi could see her excitement level rising.

"As the sun began to appear their attention turned to our escapades. They came in from the deeper water side-by-side, slowing down as they moved into shallower water." She hesitated momentarily as she recalled catching a glimpse of their dorsal fins melodically slicing the water. "One dorsal was hooked raggedly to its right side, while the other's fin was perfectly curved and symmetrical. They were only a stone's throw away when they turned towards us. It was magical to see them coming to greet us. Even though the water was only shin deep, it didn't slow them down."

Looking out the car's window, she continued reminiscing. "We stood dead-still until they were close enough to touch with the tips of our fishing rods. I was scared!" As the car stopped again at the top of the bridge, they turned their heads until their eyes made momentary contact. He thought, "She is growing up."

He looked away and said "As they got closer to us the big one started veering away while its mate kept coming, using its fins to push himself to your feet. I was stunned when it turned its face sideways, peeking its eye at you. I'll never forget; it used both its flippers to slowly back away and then disappeared. You said goodbye, dolphin." Cheyenne shook her head in agreement, and he was sure he saw a tear trickle down her cheek.

"Popi, I'll never forget what you said to me next," you said, "We live to fish, and the dolphin fish to live."

The traffic speeded up, and without another word they both realized how they shared a similar spiritual course; Nature was their savior. As they drove their way west past the sea walls and over the next tall bridge above the empty water, Popi started a story she felt she had heard before. Not because of his words, or their meaning, but in his tone. His voice was true and commanding, and Cheyenne sat back and listened to him return to his childhood as she tried to take everything in.

"Ignorance must be bliss; those words sprang out and over the sound of the screen door double slamming behind me. There on the old wooden pine floor sat a string full of the biggest bass I'd ever seen. There were at least six of them, and they were sows. I walked around them, showing great respect as I made my way towards an ancient red and white steel cooler. It was one of those with two sliding doors on top, where cool moisture always collected. It held ten-cent bottles of ice-cold pop on one side, and cans of beer on the other. It was a real blessing in a neighborhood where air conditioning hadn't showed up yet, and indoor plumbing was a recent luxury for most of the establishments. Hard to believe Florida was once the backwoods and swamps of our nation.

In our tight-knit rural community everybody brought their best catches and kills to Day's Grocery. A two-story, white-washed, wood-framed house, Day's Grocery was located on a gray, gravel road across from Garden Lake. Day's sat on the north side of Gunn Highway in the heart of Odessa. No more than a little rural region back then, Odessa was dominated by cattle pastures, lakes and woods, and was dotted with a sprinkling of houses. Showing up at Day's with dead fish and animals was a long-standing tradition no one cared about in them days.

Looking back, I couldn't understand why Mr. Day, the sole proprietor, stood behind the counter, slowly shaking his graying head in a display of negativity and disapproval. Standing in front of him was Mr. Martin, who lived only a few hundred yards away on Garden Lake's north shore in a house with a fancy lawn and few trees. He was from somewhere else; everyone knew it by the odd way he spoke. It might have been a place named New Jersey, New York, or New Delhi, as far as I could recall.

One thing for sure was Mr. Day was giving Mr. Martin a stern talking to well after I'd placed my shiny, mercury dime next to the cash register. He kept shaking his head and saying something about how that man, Mr. Martin, should have never killed all those big female bass. He was saying it was, 'A real waste of future fish killing those bedding beauties!' At the time, I didn't understand what he meant by that.

On my way out of the store, just as the screen door swung shut behind me, Mr. Day reminded me about returning the bottle 'cause, 'There's a two-cent deposit on them now.' A little later on in life I made a fair amount of pocket change collecting them bottles. As I crossed the street, I heard Mr. Day start up again at Mr. Martin, 'Ignorance is no excuse. You types are going to ruin Florida's fishing.'

A couple days later, Mr. Day shared his unique theory on Florida politics with me. I was drinking my usual, a cold soda, and he was standing in his normal spot behind the counter. He seemed concerned in the most serious kind of way.

Here in Florida we need a political party of Crackers. We'll soon need one of them labor leaders to organize us into a strong group of home-grown Florida people, who share the same values; individuals who worship our Sunshine State, not the almighty dollar! It wasn't until years later that I began understanding what Mr. Day truly meant by Cracker.

I met another man later on in time from that place they call New Jersey; his name was Peter. One day when Peter's girl couldn't join him, he offered me a chance to go see 'The Boss' in concert. I'd never been to a concert or a live performance of any type, except at the circus or in a church, or to see Pastor Billy Graham. That certainly wasn't a concert, but it ended up making me feel the same listening to both those men. They shared a spiritual way about them.

That 'Boss' fellow and his band were amazing; at one point he asked the stagehands to turn up the lights and then he told everyone from New Jersey to stand up and be counted. The whole place went wild, and it seemed like everyone but me stood up screaming. All I could think about while sitting there was 'Where's New Jersey? There sure are a lot of them!'

A few years later I met and married a woman, your grandmother, from there, but by then we called it Jersey for short. She would be the only woman I'd be with the rest of my life. As difficult as it was to understand her Jersey accent at times, it was easy to like her. To me, she was like milk and honey. I'd found the Promised Land, and I didn't plan on leaving.

But back to my story, Day's Grocery was part bait shop, part beer stop, part hardware store, part grocery and part City Hall. Of course, my favorite part of the place, besides the soda cooler, was where Mr. Day stocked all the fishing tackle and fishing magazines.

At the back of Sports and Field, I'd seen a mail order ad for a tackle box stuffed with fishing gear. 'All the gear you'll ever need to tackle any fish in the sea for only $9.99!' was the way they marketed it. The ad claimed the box held a thousand pieces of tackle, including hooks, weights, snaps, swivels, bobbers, fish stringers, lures, rubber worms, etc. I wanted it, but I had no money.

I never had ten dollars in my hand until Donny Watts gave me a ten-dollar bill in seventh grade. Unknown to me, Donny had stolen it from his grandmother's purse, and I had to give it back when I found out where it had come from. It was as close as I ever came to buying that tackle package. Who'd imagine one day I'd have more tackle than I'd know what to do with?"

"Which reminds me of the first time I smoked pot, Mon," accentuating his words like a bad Bob Marley impressionist. He was doing his best to protect his storyteller legacy and establish a foundation between them in the only way he knew how; through his words and passion. She did her best to keep her eyes on the road and let him run on a bit.

"Lester, my best friend, had spent the summer between ninth and tenth grades picking tobacco in western Massachusetts in 1972. Lester got in with a cult of hippies. His hair had been a bit long before he left, but when he came home it was hanging below his shoulders.

Lester hadn't much interest in music before his introduction into the counter culture, but when he returned he had a duffle bag packed half-full of eight-track recordings from the likes of Jimi Hendrix, Janis Joplin and other purveyors of rock music. He had also changed the way he dressed, switching from more normal wear to flip flops, tank tops and blue jeans. You can bet eight-tracks and blue jeans weren't the only things in that duffle bag he returned to Florida with either!

As clearly as though it happened yesterday, I remember him

tossing a heavy plastic bag to me. 'Take a whiff of it.' he told me. I did, 'cause Lester was nearly a year older than me. Mom had taught me well to respect my elders, and besides, Lester was the smartest kid in all of the school. If you wanted to get smart, you listened to him. The bag smelled like a place where we'd go digging for earthworms, but sweeter, a little less wet and earthy.

Next thing he threw my way was a pack of Top's rolling papers. I knew what to do with them papers 'cause we'd been wrapping up our own cigarettes since third grade. Smoking wasn't new to us, but this stuff was.

After I had been done rolling, which ended up being a more difficult task than I had anticipated considering the seeds and stems, Lester suggested we head down to the Hole, the neighborhood's favorite swimming place. We did. On the way Lester explained how the weed, as he called it, came from a place called Colombia, somewhere in South America.

Lester said 'In Colombia you can see snow-capped mountain tops from the ocean.' Then he mentioned the pot cost twenty dollars an ounce, which sure sounded like a load of money back then.

In the beginning, we'd roll joints with buds, leaves, seeds, stems and all, but soon after we learned to clean the byproducts away. The pot burned much smoother, and tasted less harsh by not burning the seeds and stems, and by then you could buy a quarter-ounce for five dollars.

When we got to the swimming hole, we incondoobiated as we liked to call it. Lester must have asked me twenty times if I was feeling anything strange or different, and each time I answered truthfully that I wasn't. I always had a high tolerance for pot's effects, but coffee kicks my butt. Anyway, we sat contemplating the water for a spell. After a bit, the sun's rays bounced off the lake's surface at a perfect angle, which sent shimmers of brilliant silver light blasting in all directions in front of me.

Then we got up and walked home through the woods and past a maze of little pink and white houses and some vacant lots, in middle class suburbia. When I jumped Lester's back fence I could reach home a little quicker, but instead I decided to walk the long way back, going east up Waters Avenue and north down Gomez Avenue.

When I got home the house was dark and I was alone. Mom and Dad were at work; nothing new there, and my sisters were still at afterschool care. I went into my bedroom without turning on the overhead light and stretched out over my bed.

Within minutes, Mom was home and at my bedroom door, flipping on the lights. She looked at me on the bed and firmly said 'You've been smoking pot.' Mom had a sixth sense about these things. For this reason, and a couple of others, she was a real pain in my butt for the next couple of years. However, you got to give her a lot of credit, she did give me my first fishing pole, and fishing has been very good to me.

Lester, his brother Albury, and I did a ton of fishing together. The two of them had the best equipment money could buy. Their dad was a highbrow Tampa lawyer, and he'd divorced their mom. Feeling guilty about leaving the boys behind with her, he gave the pair anything they wanted. Lester and his brother loved their dad, but he never spent much time with them, which was all they ever really wanted in the first place. Time was money. I've been told lawyers suck until you need one. I've also been taught not to believe everything you read, hear or see. Sound advice? Who knows?"

After paying a toll, Cheyenne piped in. "I believe advice is worthless unless it is asked for, and then you should tell'em you might as well take my advice cause I'm not using it."

Popi stopped and smiled, shaking his head in affirmation and renewed his tale. "Lester's mom had a terrible time with the whole divorce thing. She developed a debilitating drinking problem, lost her job as a school teacher and fell in love with a woman, well several women, at separate times. I met my share of them. The last one was Ms. Jess. I couldn't tell if Jess was a man or woman at a glance; you had to study her closely and still it was nearly impossible to determine her gender. Nevertheless, I did my best to respect Jess, and I stayed clear of her as much as possible.

Apparently they had a rough time together, since Lester's mom and Jess were frequently fighting. The house became a wreck; it was run-down, filthy and jam-packed with dozens of cats. Lester and Albury took to hiding baseball bats under their beds for protection because the violence was escalating.

Then one morning Lester told me over our government-subsidized school breakfast 'Mom killed Ms. Jess last night.' He turned his head, fighting back any emotional display, and added 'She stabbed her nearly fifty times in our kitchen.' Today, some forty years later, Lester still lives in that same house; some things are too strange to imagine." These words refused to settle his mind; murder had lasting results.

For Popi, the old familiar route across the St. John's River was not as familiar as it used to be. From Cheyenne's car, they could see a scattering of developments, full of opulent new houses. The developers had taken on the formidable challenge of constructing a system of piers, weirs, docks and boardwalks all throughout the rising marshland. It had once been a freshwater environment, but the rising sea level had forced its way in here many miles west of the ocean. It was a place where every homeowner commuted by boat.

The old roadside fish camp had been transformed into a mishmash of restaurants and specialty stores, surrounded by a vast parking lot that spread across a berm made with the soil dredged from the gut of the river. The water flow of the St. John's was redirected through an intricate system of dikes, and it flowed under elevated causeways. The old two-lane country road had gone through a metamorphosis; it had become a super suburban causeway. Popi looked on in consternation. "They turned us into an Orlando suburb!"

Cheyenne saw him peering out over the river with a pained expression. He had grown quiet again, and she wondered when he would finally unleash the inevitable commentary on the destructive nature of the unwelcome progress. She wanted to hear it, because she felt the same way herself, a little.

A slight smile spread over his leathery face. When I'd get upset, Virginia would say 'Don't you worry about Mother Nature. She can take care of herself.' I say she needs all the help she can get, but I'm of no help anymore. I must go to Matapalo."

After a short break, his autobiography returned. I never met a stranger, and that fruit didn't fall far from the tree. My Daddy, your great-grandpa, could talk to anyone, at anytime, and any place. Virginia called him the impresario of small talk. We'd be stopped at a traffic light with the windows down, and Dad would turn down the radio and start talking to the guy next to us. 'Hey neighbor!' was my old man's patented opening.

Sometimes people would wave back or return the greeting, other times they ignored or snubbed him. It didn't matter to Paps; he always had a followup like 'How about this weather? Does it get any better than this? Thank God for blessing us here in Florida!' I can still hear him mutter one of his favorite lines 'So help me God.'

Daddy gave God all the credit. He had his routine, and it didn't matter to him how the person reacted. Afterwards, he'd look at me and say 'Sure was a nice person.' He'd make you think he was Jim Nabors playing Gomer Pyle. Mom claimed Pap's duty on the front lines in Korea made him a bit sketchy. He had caught malaria there, and had held his best buddy in his arms as he died a graphic death. This all happened while he was at the battle of the Frozen Chosin during the worst part of winter.

The Marines, who were surrounded, had ordered ammunition and mortar rounds by the code name Tootsie Rolls. When the supplies were airdropped in their location, they had to be recovered in an open field, which resulted in a grievous loss of life. When his outfit brought the crates back to their position, they were full of Tootsie Rolls, a chewy chocolate candy. At least they were able to keep their energy up by chewing on Tootsie Rolls as they beat a hasty retreat under enemy fire across the icy, open terrain. Paps was only eighteen. No one would comprehend the depth or profound darkness his war experience seared into his soul until his mind began to slip away. It's the type of crap that can drive a man mad.

When Paps finally shared his pain with us for the first time, he started railing at God while he was carving the Thanksgiving turkey, and then methodically shared his most intimate war story. It was a horrific tale of how his best buddies got killed next to him in combat."

Popi shook his head slowly, and a sad little smile crept to his lips.

"We wouldn't know for sure the depth of his post-battle stress until his hair turned silver and gray, and his mind began slipping away. Then he opened up, sharing his pain for the first time in more than sixty years. Part of the family believed Dad had dementia, but he never seemed to change all that much since I was a kid; he was a simple man.

I remember one time we were having lunch together. He was at least eighty, and had been living in a small retirement home called Living Life for a couple of years. The home assisted military vets who had been diagnosed with dementia. I'd noticed when I was a boy, Paps loved looking at women. He never could hide anything from me. Once we were waiting to split a barbecue sandwich when an attractive middle-aged woman walked into the place. Pap's head nearly twisted off his neck trying to get a better look, and before I knew it, he piped up and exclaimed "I need a woman to love!"

By the time you could say grasshopper twice, I grabbed his hand and fussed at him. "Paps, you shouldn't say that out loud! It's embarrassing!"

He looked at me with sad eyes, like those of a scolded dog. I felt sorry for him, but then a boyish grin popped onto his face. "It's all right, son. I'd be good to her!" Several heads turned to see who was cutting up, but no one was surprised. They all got a kick out of it, but not as much as the attractive woman. In some ways, Dad was always a little lost in space."

Cheyenne let out a slight giggle but kept her eyes on the road. The traffic had grown more intense as they approached Orlando.

"Paps never took me fishing or to a ball game. He didn't have much time for me. He spent most of it working; striving for the American dream can take everything you've got.

Later in life, he agreed to go snook fishing with me, and I took him to Tampa's Gandy Bridge. He showed up empty-handed, so we talked for a spell. I asked him if he'd like to try his luck with some of my gear, and he said no. He had shown up, but he didn't have both oars in the water. He wasn't quite right, you know, like some of the rooms were vacant, but there was still someone home. His mind and body had run down, but his soul was still kicking on all eight cylinders, and I knew he loved me. That was my Dad."

Cheyenne jumped on the break in the story to ask him a question. "Where does your soul go from here, Popi?" He acknowledged her with a sympathetic glance from his baby blue eyes, but he was on a roll, and he couldn't stop himself.

"I didn't get help with homework or even accompanied to church. My parents barely participated in my life. For the longest time I took it personally; it hobbled me until I learned the most basic rules of life, from the infinite wisdom of the Toltec Indians. First, the impeccable word; only speak the truth. Keep every promise, and speak only good, not bad.

Second, don't take things personally. The Bible says 'Be ye not offended.' No one but God can fathom human motive or behavior. We are at war with our spirit, and sometimes there is collateral damage. Never assume or expect anything; until you can do this, you cannot relax. God will provide.

And last do your best. Realize that your best fluctuates from day to day, or even moment to moment. You can never be perfect or do anything perfectly. If a Toltec was near finishing a project without making a mistake, he or she would leave an intentional flaw. They did not want to compete with God. Only a fool would compete with God. I don't want to die a fool."

She kept her comments to herself; she could see Popi was lost in a flood of thoughts. Wise beyond her young age, Cheyenne knew the Toltec folklore; studying North American Indian culture was one of her gigs. For a quick moment, she shared her widest smile with him, exposing her flawless white teeth and strong spirit. Her energy encouraged him to go on and gave him hope.

"Thankfully, I ended up spending some good time with Paps towards the end, so all was not lost. A guy has got to love his Dad, even if he doesn't like to fish! It changes your perception when the Lord lets you see someone through his eyes. You hear talk about all kinds of miracles, but how you see others through God's eyes is the one you should be looking for."

Cheyenne didn't say a word; she felt no need. She'd witnessed a miracle of her own by seeing Popi through the Lord's eyes. She was glad to be accompanying him as he processed his life experience. It had become increasingly difficult and irrelevant for him to discern what was happening, but his consciousness had become capable of projecting him into his strongest, if not fondest, memories as if they were actually the present. Was he telling the story, acting it out, or really living it? He was simply going with the flow, and didn't have the energy to catalogue it. Without Cheyenne, he had no chance of reaching Matapalo. His resurrection called.

"I've been told the master's dog has the personality of its master. My persona has been one of a Labrador retriever; Labs are fearless and love people and water. After getting to know them up close and personal, I figure some of their fearlessness comes from being a combination of hardheaded and slightly foolish; it's usually connected with one or more of these attributes.

Today fear comes in many sizes and shapes, and it is baseless. Fear is an empty, timeless worrisome thought, and often an idea locked into the future. We fear the unknown, so it may be something you never encounter. We wrap our fear around us like a blanket. A good defense against fear is the presence of mind. Staying or living in the moment will fend off fear.

Look around us; people are scared they might not be able to hold out because of the economy, and they'll say 'Someday we may not be able to hang on.' But someday is impossible; there is only today, this present moment. Peace is in the present. The ego wants to talk about the past, or the future, but both are far removed from the present, where peace overcomes ego. When things were simpler, there was less fear of the past and future; only the present moment mattered. Hunters and gatherers didn't worry about anything more than the present; their lives depended on it."

Cheyenne told Popi they'd be getting to the airport within a few minutes. He looked out the car's window, and then turned towards her, raising his eyebrows and tilting his head up and down. She knew this meant he knew where they were. Then he continued, this time in a more uplifting tone.

"Let's discuss a subject much closer and dearer to me; learning to fish with a cane pole. It wasn't very difficult once you got the hang of it. Back then, the part I liked the most about fishing with a cane pole was there were no moving parts. My grandfather tried to teach me how to use one of those bait casters; it was a red Ambassador 5000, spooled with grayish, green Dacron line on a six-foot clear fiberglass rod he got me for my eleventh birthday. Darn thing had too many moving parts!

Later on I started using Lester and Albury's tackle. Their lawyer dad made sure they had the best stuff, even if he didn't have any time to fish with them. I learned to fish with a French-made Mitchell 300; it was a sweet reel.

Probably the only reason I took French in 8th grade was because of that reel being made in France. I had no idea where or what France was, but it interested me. My incapacity for French must've driven our extremely young and demure teacher, a French-Canadian, insane. My attempt to learn the insidious language met with gnarly success, but it was an emotional drain for the both of us. Fifty years later, that teacher probably still remembered me!

My first and only date in high school was with a French foreign exchange student. She had dark hair that hung down past a thin and curvy waistline, wore strictly blue jeans and had hair growing from under her arms. We went to see the J. Geils Band. She giggled each time I fumbled my French trying to impress her, but she did let me kiss her. I fell in love with her lips immediately, but we never saw much of each other afterwards. My heart wasn't broken, but my lips were lonely for a while!"

Cheyenne tried to hide her giggles, but again a bit of them escaped, and Popi's eyes brightened up as he continued.

"Spanish was my language. Tu hablas Espanol, señorita? Yo hablo Espanol muy bien!"

She shook her head in both positive and negative directions at once as she started preparing for their exit from the main highway.

"Growing up near Tampa, you couldn't help but become aware of the area's Hispanic influence. Once they started transporting us to Hillsborough High School the world opened up immensely. Before busing, our schools were lily-white, but afterward, we went to classes with an increasingly diverse mixture of Spanish-speaking and African-American kids.

Our drive to Hillsborough High from outside the city limits could take an hour on a bad traffic day. Could've been part of the reason I changed high schools five times before taking my General Educational Development test, but that's a story for later on.

After high school, Lester lured me to Puerto Rico with a simple postcard he mailed us from Rincon. He diagrammed Puerto Rico's entire northwest coast, mapping out each surf break and adding specific details of when and how each particular wave broke.

Of course, he went first and I followed. We lived in a tiny two-room beach house located directly across from pools and a sandy beach. It was only a short walk to a couple of spectacular surf breaks, places called Marias, Domes and Tres Palmas. Back then the American transplants, labeled Gringos by the locals, called it Little Hawaii. The island had a population of just under a million back in the early Seventies. The last I checked there were nearly four million people living there, and Florida has twenty million!"

Cheyenne continued the thread. "There are seven billion people on this planet, Popi. We have a very serious people problem. How can our planet holdout with such an expanding population?"

The ominous pretext of Cheyenne's remark stopped him, and they continued in silence for a moment. Traffic swept by them like raging water swept down a rain-swollen river. Together they sadly shook their heads. They were almost at the Orlando International Airport when Popi decided to change topics so they could move forward and upward.

"Fishing's great; the catching is what varies."

"I'm surprised there are any fish left to be caught the way tackle, technology, and techniques have improved. The demand on our natural resources increases each generation exponentially" she added. She shared his attachment to fishing, but also understood the bleak reality of supply and demand.

"Darling, compared to today, Florida yesteryear was the Wild West. It was every man for himself; a kill and keep killing until you filled your cooler, freezer or ice box mentality ruled. There were ridiculously few rules protecting our fish or their habitat.

Any angler could keep unlimited mahi and tuna from the blue water. And inshore, the limit was fifty spotted seatrout and fifty redfish a day as long as they were twelve inches or more. No fishing license was required either, and the chance of getting checked by a marine patrol officer was extremely remote.

Gill nets were legal until the mid-Nineties, but then we fought and won the battle to outlaw those monofilament death traps in state waters by getting voters to approve the Save Our Sealife, Ban the Nets Amendment. The state's voters bought into the idea of taking away the commercial fishermen's gill nets, passing the amendment by a landslide seventy-two percent to twenty-eight percent.

As a full-time fishing guide, I helped organize volunteers who fished and cared about the Indian River for the Save Our Sealife, Ban the Nets initiative. In the end, volunteers around the state collected more signatures for Amendment Four than had ever before or ever since been accumulated in one day.

Back then I did my best to attend every Florida Marine Fisheries

Commission meeting within a hundred miles of our community. I also did my best to take full advantage of every opportunity I had to declare my mind on fisheries issues. At that time our Save Our Sealife, Ban the Nets initiative was the state's biggest fisheries issue ever debated.

One of the quarterly Fisheries Commission meetings came to Cocoa Beach that year, just a few weeks before the final vote on Amendment Four was to be taken; I believe it was 1994, maybe around the start of the Clinton Era. Anyway, there was this big fellow from Cortez, an eighth-generation fishing community snuggled onto Sarasota Bay's west-facing shore. This commercial fisherman's hands were twice the size of a gorilla's, and his neck was as thick as a telephone pole. This netter had deep family ties to commercial fishing.

I stood up in front of the commissioners and told them how important the net ban was to our state. Then I told each and every one of the commissioners, plus everyone in the audience, to vote yes for the net ban. My bold suggestions got a severe negative response from the audience. Since most of the attendees were net fishermen from around the state who were there to voice their opposing opinions, they let me know how they felt about it. Afterward, the fellow from Cortez followed me to the back of the room."

"I bet he wasn't so happy with you, Popi."

"No maybes about it. The man walked right up to me and stuck out his hand to shake mine. Being one to be never discourteous, I grabbed his, and he looked me in the eyes as he nearly crushed my fingers and said, 'I'd just as soon slit your throat as listen to ya.' I was lucky to get my hand back from him and thankful he didn't have his knife with him.

A month later, while out fishing Sebastian Inlet with a doctor and his wife from South Florida, I had my truck's lug nuts loosened. At the time there was a four-foot sign hanging in the back window of my Black Cherokee boldly proclaiming Ban The Nets, Save Our Seafood. It was parked alone. The only other vehicle within sight had belonged to a commercial fisherman, but he was gone when we hastily returned from fishing because of an approaching storm.

I didn't realize what had happened until it was almost too late. I can't imagine what it would have been like losing those tires in a deluge pulling a boat and trailer.

There were immediate positive results from the passing of Amendment Four. First and foremost, very destructive fishing gear was removed from Florida's waters. Personally, I'd seen the damage done by discarded or lost gill nets. They're often referred to as Ghost Nets because they keep killing until they're pulled from the water. For this reason alone, the nets had to be removed from our waters.

Unfortunately, this displaced a number of those fishermen who depended heavily on this gear. Commercial fishing has a very long history here in Florida; generations of people have come to enjoy our fresh seafood. Much of this food was taken from our local waters by local fishermen back then, but more often than not our seafood comes from other countries now."

"What about the future, Popi? Getting rid of those nets was a good thing, but what about water quality and restoring the habitat we once had here? Is there a chance to return the Lagoon to its past greatness?"

Popi stumbled a bit with his thoughts, and his uneasiness was apparent in his stiff demeanor. "You're correct, child, the net ban's major effects have long been maximized. Yes, the fish, birds, marine mammals and everything connected to them benefitted, and no, we won't ever invite the nets back. But over time we realized it was water quality and the continuous destruction of shoreline habitat and sea grass beds that would ultimately be the Lagoon's demise."

She shook her head in agreement as she slowed her car down. "Enough of this now, Popi, we're here!"

Surprised, he replied, "Darn, I was just getting started!" She caught herself before tossing him a sly comeback.

Cheyenne parked her car in the long-term parking lot; they caught a shuttle bus and within a few minutes they were standing at the curb under the Departing Flights sign. Soon afterward a steward was there to greet them with a wheelchair. Cheyenne handed the man their credentials, which he reviewed in a snap. As Popi's rear hit the wheelchair's leather seat, the steward said, "Good afternoon, Mr. Manly!"

She smiled to herself as she watched Popi being rolled away, expressively talking with his hands up in the air and his eyes connecting with the steward. She knew in her heart it was going to be a very interesting journey.

Reaching their gate was a breeze. The red carpet was rolled out for them, and a skycap pushed Popi along in his wheelchair; everyone made sure to clear the way for him. This was new for Cheyenne. From her experience with air trips she'd made with Sidney to and from the northeast, and the mayhem she'd encountered before at Orlando's airport, she had never dreamed this would go as smoothly as it had. So far everything was going better than could be expected, but she kept her fingers crossed just in case.

As they made their way through a perpetual maze of travelers, her comfortable illusion was shattered when she heard Popi yelling out, his hands waving even more demonstrative than earlier. "Dream killer ... period! Damn stuff's made by the Devil himself!"

Cheyenne picked up her pace and couldn't imagine what he was saying, but then out of nowhere Popi began to sing a thin, bluesy rant aloud.

Use'ta live my life for surfing
Use'ta live for just one girl
Now I live each day by dyin.'
Ain't found no other way to face this world
With the Blue Devil hanging around this town
Ain't found no other way to face this world.
Gotta' get my Hy-Dro-Co-Done

Yeah, my Hy-Dro-Co-Done Blues, again.

She caught up to them, and while exchanging their backpacks with the steward for Popi's wheelchair, she managed to calm him in one graceful swoop. "Popi, I don't mind hearing the song, but please don't share it with the world." She lifted her arms up towards the sky, and pushed the chair with her thin but powerful legs.

Turning to see Cheyenne behind him, a surprised Popi winked at her and said, "Pardon me my dear, my enthusiasm overcame my sanity." He quietly continued his song, picking up where he had left off.

Use'ta feel so dang superior
Use'ta walk through any door
Now I'm licking from the pavement
After begging to be kicked to da floor.
Ain't found no other way to face this world
Face this World,
Face this World.
Ain't found no other way to face this world
With the Blue Devil hanging around this town
Ain't found no other way to face this world.
Gotta get my Hy-Dro-Co-Done
Yeah, my Hy-Dro-Co-Done Blues, again.
Use'ta be a promise for my future
Use'ta live with my lovely wife
Satan took me to the pill mill
Abused 'em both and gave up on my life.
Gotta get my Hy-Dro-Co-Done
Yeah, my Hy-Dro-Co-Done Blues.

Cheyenne stopped wheeling him as he crooned each word mournfully, like a dirge. When he finished, there was a dead silence for a moment, and then Popi spoke up. "Cheyenne, have you ever thought about it? The Devil and God, that is. They're always portrayed as men, no questions asked; Our Father, the first thing that comes to mind off the lips of the preacher. Like God's some dominant man sitting above us making his final decision on us, based on whether or not we obeyed him. Come on!"

Cheyenne, feeling a little uneasy, glanced towards the ceiling, and in her best Mary Poppin's voice she began to sing "God talk can be personal and abstract, making humans feel uncomfortably uncomfortable."

He shook his head firmly, ignored her tune, and rumbled on. "If God loves us so much and he's all love, how could he ever commit us to Hell? The God I know wouldn't do that!" He had flung his arms out away from his body, and his fingers wiggled in an 180-degree pattern; his eyes had lit up like planets in a clear dark sky.

"Me and the Missus had four children. There was no way we'd ever, ever, ever commit one of them to an eternity of pain and suffering. Think about it. You don't purposely hurt someone you love, especially someone you brought into this world involuntarily, just because they're too stupid or hardheaded to follow your rules. The problem with parenting is you gotta love your children no matter how fucked up they are."

He sat back in his wheelchair, dropping his head and eyes for a moment, like he was catching his thoughts with a tiny net. Suddenly, he sprang up, fully erect and out of his seat once again proclaiming "A real, true dream killer, I tell you!"

"What?" She asked, placing a firm and loving hand on his shoulder, guiding him back into the chair's seat. This time he heeded her request and they started on their way again.

"I wrote that song, Hy-Dro-Co-Done Blues, 'cause I had no circle of influence, only a circle of concern. Stupid, dumb, worthless pills! They make so many lose so much for the gain of so few. In the end it's the pharmaceutical companies who obtain the most. I once coached this kid in his first year of soccer, right alongside of his dad. The kid surfed and played soulful music; he was a real joy to be around. Then his dad disappeared and his family took it real hard. The kid grew up too darn fast; his Mom was a mess and couldn't handle a thing. We all stood back, scratching our heads in disbelief. Everyone who knew the family wanted to help, but no one knew how to stop their pain.

Death can be a serious setback to the living. We take it way too personally and let it drag us down into the grave along with the one we lost. Two years later, our family, along with half the neighborhood, watched Toby and his longtime girlfriend tie the knot on the beach. It was a perfect wedding; they were a beautiful couple. He had plans to join the Marines. We were all giving each other high fives, hugs and kisses, and things were looking up.

Then, just a few months later ... the bad news! He was hooked on Oxies! He and his wife start fighting and lands in jail, and they kicked him out of the service."

"That's terrible, Popi!"

"Next, we found out his mom and her new live-in boyfriend were strung out on the same stuff; synthetic heroin. They defaulted on the mortgage of the family's home we watched them build and grow in for the past thirty years. Oxycodone ... synthetic heroin ... the dream killer. Others we have known didn't make it on their own without some help from the Dream Killer; the Blues controlled their lives instead of them.

No wonder! There are doctors out there who give drugs to kids who show the slightest sign of the latest trendy diagnosis. The power of the medical and pharmaceutical industry scares me. Agony and death for profit!"

Cheyenne's eyes sparkled, and her voice rose a notch as she responded to his outburst. "Popi, did you know fishing can heal emotional distress? It's become a real game changer in helping battle veterans recover from horrific experiences and injuries; better than store-bought drugs at lessening their PTSD."

"Better to use fishing in some beautiful place to heal them than some stupid bluepills" he replied.

"Cheyenne, you think my converting to Catholicism could improve my chance to speak with the Pope?" Cheyenne laughed out loud before she could see Popi was serious, and then said, "It probably wouldn't hurt your chances."

His shoulders dropped a bit before responding. "It's past the time where a Pope needs to sit down and have a serious discussion with an angler. Fishing and fishermen played a role in building the foundation of Christianity; Jesus sought them out. This would be a new approach for the Pope, and I figure I'd be the man for such a task. I can see it in the headlines; Fisherman Seeks Out Pope Francis For A Chat.

Of course, the Pontiff and I would bridge subjects like the church's views on birth control, gay marriage, and the domination of the Catholic Church by European males, but these topics wouldn't be at the top of my list. First we'd talk about fishing, if the Holy One knew anything about it, and then we'd move on from fishing to those less pressing topics."

"I don't buy it for a minute. Tell me the truth, why did you convert?"

He wiggled in his chair, looked up towards the heavens and made a face like someone very important may be listening. "Okay, the truth. Here are the primary reasons why I was baptized, and became and practiced being a Catholic after living fifty years as an independent pagan.

Jesus' teachings were centered on compassion, acceptance, love and service; he helped transform the world and my life. His message, and its spiritual support, helped enrich my spirit; obeying church rules and scripture strengthened my discipline. It didn't mean I stopped meditating or quit yoga; it enhanced these things.

I once visited our pastor, Father Gage, looking for clarity after having a serious physical complication. Going into surgery, I placed my recovery and myself in the collective hands of the doctors, nurses and hospital staff at God's request. See, we discussed it, God and me, in depth, as they wheeled me into the operating room. Somewhere in between when the drugs took effect and the next white room our talk went something like this. 'God, thanks for getting me this far; it's been pretty good, considering I got no health insurance!'

See, there's usually a bucket load of silence when I'm listening to God, but He surprises me and pipes right in instantly.

'Place it in their hands, Stan.'

'Right, gotcha, God.'

'Anticipate a fast recovery.'

'Very cool!'

'Go see Father Gage after it's done Manly, but go surfing first.'

'Say what?'

At this point in our conversation I'm slipping into the next sterile hallway. Rock and roll, Skynyrd's *Oh That Smell*, is being piped into my headphones, and I'm slipping away. The guy who took over for the nurse who wheeled me in recognized me as a fellow angler, lifted my headset, and started talking about fishing in Panama.

'It's awesome to meet you again, man. I was here the last time they wheeled you in.' He only retained a slight hint of his Spanish accent, but his smile was all Latin American.

'Let me tell you how wonderful Panama's fishing and surfing is compared to the rest of Central America. Costa Rica's going to be a thing of the past; Panama's the bomb. Less trash, cheaper prices, better fishing and surfing; tell me when to stop, I get carried away.'

That's the last of it I can remember, except for the part about having a deal with God. Place it in their hands, trust their hands, and go see Father Gage down the road a bit.

Well, after a successful operation, I was surfing and living life the way I wanted, and I nearly forgot about visiting Father Gage. Cheyenne, never forget the promises you make, they can always come back to haunt ya. The day came when Father Gage and I had that heart to heart."

She peered at him. There was more to all of this than she could assimilate and comprehend in this time frame, so she took it and stored it away to figure out at some other time. Watching her eyes, Popi then closed the subject. "Did I mention Lester was a Catholic?"

They sat together, side-by-side, facing a clear thick Plexiglas window. They looked out over a maze of moving planes, industrial gadgetry and humans maneuvering over a giant field of dull concrete dressed with painted lines and coordinated numbers and letters. Her mind and his voice were not completely in tune; while he was busy telling his old stories she was equally occupied by his past.

She tried to string together the pieces of the Popi stories she could remember from her childhood. Being an only grandchild, she had no one in the family near her own age to compare notes with when it came to her collective family folklore. But from the fragments of past stories she'd heard, or could gather from her uncles and aunts, Popi may have been a bitter and lonely man in his later years.

"It was once said if there is magic on this planet, it is contained in water." Popi had tapped her on the arm to regain her attention.

Cheyenne agreed and added "Water is why most magical places are special." Somehow she understood him and his concerns.

"The changes started coming quickly to Florida during the early Sixties; Florida at that time was in a state of flux. We got our eggs from the chicken farm and our milk by driving up to the Turner's Dairy. Life was simple. The roads were empty, and everywhere you looked there were either little lakes surrounded by cypress trees, cattails and bulrushes or thick woods supported by giant old oaks dressed in Spanish moss, with parcels of citrus groves and pastures. There was a lot more cattle than people.

"Across the gravel road from our little house on Garden Lake Circle was a ten-thousand acre ranch run by a Spanish family. I could not tell you what nation they originally came from, but they all spoke fluent English and Spanish. The ranch was an exciting place, with cowboys busy riding horses, fixing fences or rounding up stray or sick cattle. There was a load of work to do with no shortage of chores, even for the children. I loved the place, and never could spend enough time with the fun-loving and kind folks working the ranch. They were the first people I ever saw put ketchup on their eggs. Their lifestyle was certainly a lot more open and free than what I had experienced at home.

"The four strands of barbed-wire pulled tightly between fence posts paralleling the gravel road in front of our house were the only thing standing between me and five thousand head of cattle. My favorite spot was the salt lick. It was a small wooden structure, half the size of our car, with a tin roof and a metal bar covered with a solid, smooth slab of pinkish salt. Cows and bulls would come there in masses. Watching them groom the salt lick puzzled me; they certainly seemed dedicated to it. I tried to lick it several times ... didn't do a darn thing for me."

Cheyenne tried to visualize this image, but thankfully it didn't take hold.

"Our closest neighbors to the south, Mr. and Mrs. Lewis, had a wonderful Cracker house, shaded by a giant oak tree. The house was all wood, with big, tall windows and a sitting porch covered with a huge overhang. There was a chicken coop out back and a small barn right next to it. Mr. Lewis had every tool available to man in that barn, but there was one thing he didn't have; a son.

"The Lewis' were blessed with six daughters, and all of them were real beauties; tall, blonde and smart. The only problem was Mr. Lewis loved to hunt, and back in those days women didn't hunt. He took me with him every chance he got. My mom let him do this, and it was the best thing she could have done.

"He was a giant of a man; not so much size-wise, but his wisdom and skills in the woods were unsurpassed. But it was the way he talked with people that impressed me the most; he was a gentleman, kind and courteous to everyone he met. We mainly hunted rabbits; they were fun to stalk and delicious on the table.

"He also took me after deer a couple of times in Gulf Hammock and Inverness. When I saw them the first time in a big herd of females surrounding a couple of bucks, I realized that deer were extraordinary creatures; they were magnificent to see and watch. Their speed, grace, and ability to jump amazed me.

"I started first grade at five-years old at Citrus Park Elementary, a red brick building with a Spanish-tiled roof. No internet, no wireless connections, no CD's, DVD's, ADA's, or A/C. That's correct; no air conditioning. We didn't get it until after I was nearly out of high school.

"Corporal punishment was the norm back then. If you got in trouble, you'd be sent to the Principal's office. From there, the chances were not good. Usually you'd get whacked with a paddle; it wasn't fun. I was on the receiving end of several whackings during my short and undistinguished tenure at Citrus Park Elementary. They started back in first grade when I was five. Looking back now, I doubt they ever deterred me from improper behavior; back then everything I did was purely reactionary.

"Lester was from a very German Catholic family. You could say he was a Catholic boy; he went to St. Mary Magdalene until sixth grade. Back then I had no idea what a Catholic was, never mind a Catholic boy, but if anyone fit the description, it was Lester. He had a rigid routine. He wore his clothes like uniforms, with his stiff-collared shirts buttoned up to the final hole, and his shoes were always polished. Besides being the smartest guy throughout all of school, he was also the best dressed in a geeky sort of way. Knowing him back then, you could have never pictured him the way he is today."

"Popi, you are talking so much. Please rest." Cheyenne protested.

"There's so little time! I'll rest later ... for a long time."

"What do you mean, Popi? There is plenty of time," Cheyenne said cheerfully.

"Child, you are wrong; time is running out. We need to get to Matapalo."

She gave him a mild version of the stink eye, and he stood up, forced out a meager chuckle and said, "Come on; our plane is ready."

Cheyenne's voice stopped him. "Popi! Your wheelchair!"

"I have no need for such contraptions; I only sat there to amuse myself, and you. Let's go!"

Once she was settled down on the plane Cheyenne's thoughts drifted to the future and all of its infinite possibilities. Popi seemed content to look quietly out of the window as if he was staring off at a dim vision on the horizon. She was intrigued by the fact that he appeared much younger in his repose; he had a smooth glow about him.

She reviewed the tales he'd shared with her in their short time back together. She shook her head and laid it back on the complimentary pillow. She slowly, lightly closed her eyes and gave into her dreams.

There were many things she wished for; accomplishment … adventure … to ascend the highest ranges … to advance her surfing skills … to ride the Pipeline … to dive steep canyons in the deepest oceans … what else? She continued dreaming until Popi poked at her with the point of his elbow.

"So you're getting married soon?" he asked.

Cheyenne, a wee bit startled and taken aback by his question, instinctively responded in truth. "Yes, how do you know? Did I tell you?"

Before she could ascertain his source of knowledge, he changed the subject. "Did you read the book I sent you?"

Puzzled, she stared at him like he'd suddenly vanished. "What book?"

Popi went on. "Awareness seeped into my thinking after I read that book."

The "book;" she realized now that she should have known who sent it. It had come in the mail a few months earlier and had no return address. What about the most obvious clue? The juvenile handwriting and its primitive wrappings should have been a dead giveaway. Wasn't it all so indicative of Popi and his approach to life? Definitely, that's his M.O.!

She forgave herself for not figuring it out. She hadn't seen enough of him to keep him foremost in her thoughts. There had been a wall between them, erected by the family a long time ago.

He picked up where he had left off. "A man I greatly admire named Steven Covey wrote that book. It's called The Seven Habits of Effective People, and I have modeled my life after this man's profound teachings. His work turned me around, and made me see life completely different than what it had been before I read his book. It's an amazing compilation of his ideas that everyone should follow; it would simplify their lives like it did for me. I wanted to share this with you; I think it's very important.

But since you haven't read it yet, let me tell you what it's about, since we have quite a bit of time on our hands. There are seven habits you must form; be proactive is rule numero uno!" he insisted in an emphatic rasp. "Take it from me; this can resurrect a negative attitude. There is far too much blame and pain going around in this world. Being proactive is a step away from the suffering these things bring. How can we change the world? Where do we start?"

Cheyenne followed his drift. "I know; how can we change the world? Where do we start?"

"How can we change our lives for the better? By being proactive. What can we do to prevent or solve problems and set a true course? Start with the simplest task. See the trash, pick it up!" Popi said.

Cheyenne wondered aloud. "What does it mean exactly, Popi? Are you talking about a commitment to being positive at all times, no matter what?"

"It's our human ability to choose to be either proactive or reactive that separates us physiologically from the Earth's other living critters. In the end, our greatest asset may be how we respond to life's experiences. The first three habits Covey discusses are personal and independent of the others. Be proactive, begin with the end in mind, and then put first things first. Covey was a genius!"

"I think I understand, Popi; one must first learn to recognize what is truly important in the midst of all of life's urgencies. Important things take priority." Her cheeks tightened as her eyes intensified and her interest accelerated. "What are the others?"

"Let's just say life's based in interdependence far beyond our conception."

"Like us coming together?"

He nodded his head, and he broke into an expanding grin. "Ah yes, Cheyenne, you've done well to reach out. Being able to understand the compounding abundance of human effort has the potential of being the most beneficial of the interdependent habits. Synergy is the active combination of skill, personality, strength, and influence of the group. In combination, all of these things are exponentially more powerful and effective than the same number of individuals working alone can accomplish."

"Trust is the foundation for a strong relationship; true, Popi?"

"Yes, synergy comes with trust, and it comes from learning and practicing all the habits independently and together. This creates confidence and trust. The trust built into relationships makes it easier to combine the talent, assets, organization and energy needed to generate synergy. Working together for a higher purpose comes more naturally for those who practice the seven habits."

"Like you and me, Popi?" She had begun fully to sense their destinies were intertwined beyond what she had imagined.

"Yes, Cheyenne, we are like a wheel and the axle! Separately, they are simple. Together they created one of the world's greatest, most useful inventions, the ox cart."

"Right on, Popi!"

"Yes, like you and me, Cheyenne. We're creating synergy; we are rolling on!"

"But, that's only six habits."

"Cheyenne, read the book."

An air pocket abruptly interrupted their peaceful reflection. The plane bucked and rolled like a braking roller coaster at the end of the run. Cheyenne clutched Popi's hand. He held on with a kind, confident reassurance, and she instantly felt a loving flow of security generated by his gentle strength.

"Popi, tell me, how did you know I was engaged?"

"From a dream."

"But, Popi . . . ?"

"Rest, child, rest. We have a long way to roll."

When she awoke, it was as if she had been in an enchanted slumber for a century. She was groggy, and everything seemed to be too bright. Popi looked straight ahead in silence. She imagined him as an ancient, iconic statue. She knew his intentions were to be in a high state of meditation, or prayer, or whatever it was that he was doing. "No one I've met is as deep and simple as him or as complex," she thought. Her grogginess disappeared, and she took comfort in her thoughts.

Suddenly, like instant wireless connection, he booted up. "Lester taught me to surf. I could swim faster, play baseball better and catch more fish than him, but he always could out-surf me. Back then, Lester and Albury had blond hair as long as any you'd see anywhere back then. The rednecks didn't take well to Hippies in our neck of the woods, so Lester drew stares all around town. He'd shake his head and flip his hair back, just to make'em stare harder."

"You were Hippies, Popi? Cheyenne joshed.

"Not necessarily. We weren't living in the park or protesting the war or anything like that. Yes, we had long hair, wore bell-bottom jeans and respected the Hippie philosophy. For a while, I wanted to be a Hippie in the worst way. I detested the war 'cause of all the killing and dying we'd see on the six o'clock news.

We lost an older friend from our neighborhood, which had a profound effect on me. By the time we were old enough really to understand what it had meant to be Hippies the war was over, the draft was done, and the Hippies were off to be realigned by capitalism and the beckoning of the corporate world.

It was hard to keep up with the rest of the country from Florida. Back then the Sunshine State was light years behind the times when it came to Pop Culture or progressive thinking. It still is in some ways!

Once, we streaked at a football game!" Popi confessed.

"Streaked?" Cheyenne asked.

"Some other time, sweetheart. We were young. It wouldn't be so charming, now" he chuckled.

His gaze quickly shifted back and forth as if to check around for eaves-droppers. He looked at his feet, and with his head still bowed, he looked up sheepishly. "But nothing meant more to me than surfing. I was hooked. Before surfing, besides knowing that I wanted a family, I had no vision of the future. No depth of field. I was adrift in a tumultuous sea of youth."

"You helped raise your sisters, didn't you? That must have taught you the value and responsibility of the family at an early age, Popi."

It was ironic; Cheyenne knew bits and pieces of Popi's past that he could barely remember himself. He realized that she was wise beyond what his patchy perception of her had been. He thought to himself, "Will I ever learn? Never underestimate or judge too harshly. See yourself in other people. Of course, I bet she knows something about what's up. It was all in the family folklore. It was Thanksgiving gossip over dessert, coffee, and cigarettes when the kids were excused."

His memory drifted back to the present, and he answered her question. "Yes, dear, spending so much time catering to the needs of our family at such a ripe young age taught me some extensive, and some expensive lessons. I learned not to ignore a three-year old the hard way. Kids shouldn't be raising other kids. But, that's the way it was back then around our house. Mom and Dad worked. When I wasn't in school, fishing or playing sports, I was watching the house and my sisters.

For me, surfing was another type of ultimate life lesson. It created a path lined with lessons. It contained so much. Learning to surf, making it a lifestyle, and taking it to the next level were all stepping-stones towards my esoteric enlightenment. Surfing proved to be the perfect escape vehicle."

"Escape from what, Popi?"

"Sad situations and the constant dread of dilemmas."

The overhead light dimmed as the Fasten Your Seat Belts indicator lit up. The flight attendant warned the passengers to prepare for landing.

Cheyenne was sure she saw a tear slide down his face and drop into his open, calloused hands. Without looking up, he resumed his monologue. "Drugs, crime, violence and unemployment were all cankers we were exposed to growing up in our neighborhood. Day by day, all those around us struggled to keep a precarious perch in the middle class.

Over time, it got worse for us, but I guess it happened all over the country. Development to some, progress to others, they called it. Rural areas were cleared and converted to suburbs and shopping malls. It was not a good time. For a guy like me, who changed high school five times, dropped out at sixteen, and ended up with a GED, the future didn't feel very comfortable.

Surfing somehow made all of this acceptable, bearable, transcendent and even transformative. There's nothing uncertain about the ocean; it will always be wet and will always be different every day. There is advanced wisdom in such a basic truth; it applies to almost everything.

Besides, it took the mind off of my nagging troubles. Give a person a task that he looks forward to doing with enthusiasm, and you will see the task done."

"I understand you were a great surfer, Popi."

As a large smile spread across his face, he lifted his eyes with a flutter, shifted his shoulders back and stuck his chest out. "Great surfer? Remember, Cheyenne, the best surfer is the one having the most fun!"

A graceful landing in San Jose placed them on the tarmac and off the plane in the blink of an eye. The city view was nothing like

Cheyenne had expected. Instead of the quaint, sleepy, indigenous, antiquated scene she had anticipated, the modern city was buzzing with a bustling crowd that seemed to have followed them from the theme parks of Orlando. "Nice; modern digs. It looks sparkling new! Is this really Costa Rica?" she thought. It was so much more international, cosmopolitan, and upbeat than she had imagined.

There was a wide range of young people scattered amongst middle-aged and older travelers, wearing a wide variety of fashions. A big, boisterous tourist and his blustery wife stood out in their gaudy shirts, outrageous Panama hats, cheap sandals, black nylon socks and expensive jewelry; it was easy to see they weren't from around here.

Nearby, she saw a guy sporting shoulder-length dirty-blonde dreadlocks. He was tall, maybe 6' 5," and the core of his face was hidden behind oversized, mirrored sunglasses. He had ear buds hanging over his neck while he held court with a gaggle of American globo-trash students. Was he a tour guide or a guru? Two businessmen with cell phones walked by, blathering away in separate conversations; she wasn't sure, but she thought they were both speaking Spanish.

It seemed like something surreal had been superimposed on her expectations. Her eyes searched the crowd intently as she led Popi through a series of bilingual signs that marked the way to Customs.

She spied a married couple, probably in their fifties, who reminded her of Sidney's parents. They were dressed straight from the Banana Republic catalogue in their khaki shorts, and long-sleeved, buttoned-down collared cotton shirts. They were both straining under the weight of huge, reinforced backpacks. White tube socks with red trim showed over the top of their matching suede hiking boots. They were like something out of Indiana Jones, minus the hat, danger or excitement. It seemed this was as good a place to watch people as any place she had ever visited, she mused as they waited their turn.

Popi walked with an air of confidence, head up, and wide eyes scanning the surroundings, as they found their way to Costa Rican Customs. They chose from a series of lines labeled either *Turistas* or *Nacionales*. Cheyenne let Popi take the lead, and followed him toward the *Turistas* lane. His passport was ready in his right hand, and his fanny pack was clasped loosely around his waist and tucked under his shirt. He wore a warm smile that matched his confident stroll. He was ready to go.

Two armed guards stood a few feet away. One looked like Telly Savalas (Kojak), and the other was a Latin American version of Hulk Hogan, or perhaps his darker, uglier brother. Their crisp, dark blue uniforms were freshly pressed with a bit too much starch and overstuffed with a little too much arrogance.

Popi spoke in Spanish to the neatly dressed, raven-haired, hazel-eyed beauty poised perfectly on a raised chair behind a bulletproof window. She presented herself with dignity, but the length of her tight skirt and the stretched fit of her bulging blouse revealed a more sultry side.

During their review, Cheyenne heard him twice tell the woman "Stan Manly" when he was asked his name. "Stan Manly?" the woman asked after looking at his passport a second time. He must have said something coy and clever to her before he gave her his most irresistible smile. She hesitated for a moment before locking on to his sparkling, mischievous eyes, and giggled a bit; she covered her mouth and waved them on.

Cheyenne glanced at Popi. "What was the hold up, Stan?"

"She wanted to know why I had no middle name. She said I must be special to have such a name as Stan Manly. She wondered if I could live up to my moniker."

"What did you say? You sure got a heady response."

"Told her that I am special, but so is she, too; a thirty-eight special … a fully-loaded pistol that's half-cocked … enough to kill ol' Stan Manly. I told her that I couldn't think of a better way to go than being shot by her jealous husband! I saw her ring." Cheyenne squeezed her eyes and wagged a pointing finger of disapproval at him.

They were almost walking out through the front doors of the airport when Cheyenne realized that she had no clue where they were headed or how Popi planned to get there. It made her a bit apprehensive. One step out the revolving doors and an eclectic mini-mob of brightly smiling faces tossed out interwoven streams of excited verbal inquiries and suggestions to the arriving travelers. It was business as usual for the vendors, but a bizarre spectacle for her. She had to stop to refocus her energy, or she would lose her wits. She decided not to succumb to sensory overload, anxiety, indecision, or panic, but to take a deep breath and go with the moment instead.

She was again reminded of their situation by the squawking of the transportation mongers. They barked wildly at anyone potentially willing to pay a little attention and enough money. Some held pieces of cardboard with travelers' last names scribbled boldly in black magic marker, while others held signs denoting popular tourist destinations like Arenal, Jaco, Tamarindo, and Quepos.

The majority of this group tackled their task with brisk, point of sale marketing. It could be confusing. Their spiels were in a hybrid language that was referred to as "Spanglish," and the shouts came from everywhere. "Buenos Dias, you all. Number one! Turistas en autobus to Tamarindo. Safe! Por qué debes morir? Get there soon! Arriba! Fast bus. Safe road! Camino seguro! Ten bucks, senor, muy poco. Ten bucks American dinero! Cash on the burro's head."

"Senor y señorita, do you need a ride?" They heard this line over and over, but they just kept moving forward, away from the crowd towards Matapalo. It now seemed like the path to nowhere, since her expectations had proven to be unreliable. As they stepped out away from the terminal, she found the blue sky and sun liberating. A standard Central Valley Chamber of Commerce day greeted them; the wind was light and balmy, and the temperature was a perfect seventy-six degrees. The air carried a subtle hint of smoke or urban smog.

Popi wondered who could ask for a better welcome. He was exhausted, but restless. He knew that continuing their way from here would be interesting, challenging and uncertain.

Cheyenne lagged a few feet behind Popi. Tufts of her naturally curly strawberry-blonde hair fell discreetly through the clasp of a Boston Red Sox cap she had collected on a visit to Fenway Park with Sidney to see the Yankees and Sox play. A loosely fitting one-piece garment covered her natural feminine beauty, with a cinch at the waist, like a moo-moo, or what you might see a Caribbean lady wearing to the market place. It was dyed in flamboyant tropical reds, oranges and yellows. The dress highlighted the contours of her form as it draped gracefully to just above her knees. A cheap pair of surf shop flip-flops adorned her feet. There was no need to accentuate her innate sex appeal; it was impossible to conceal.

They walked through the parking lot and crossed the street in front of the airport, took a hard right and went about two hundred yards until they reached a bus stop where they saw a group of Ticos standing around waiting together. Tico is the endearing name Costa Ricans choose to call themselves.

Cheyenne could feel the stares. She turned towards a young mother and her daughter holding hands nearby. They turned her way to smile and bestow the comforting expressions of a pleasant greeting. Their smiles put her at ease.

Within minutes, a bus came and stopped in front of them. As the door opened, everyone inside poured down the steps. When those waiting clamored up towards the driver with money in hand, the crowd had swept Cheyenne along. Popi caught up with her just in time to gently grab her arm and redirect her. "Not this one, Cheyenne. You and I are heading towards San Jose." Pointing towards a sign in the window, he added, "This bus is going to Heredia."

The next bus pulled forward and slid in behind the one pulling out for Heredia. Cheyenne spied the sign and gave Popi a thumbs up. He smiled and nodded in agreement. Before they could settle in their seat, the bus, five on a scale of ten, jerked its way onto the road. An indigenous woman with a caged chicken added to the ambience, and it pleased Cheyenne. This little touch revived some of the excitement of her expectations that were quashed in the airport.

Without notice, the bus lurched and whipped into an immediate left turn. Just as abruptly, it turned the other way and leaned over to the brink of tipping as it made its way onto an on-ramp. As it flew onto a bustling major highway Popi was pressed hard against Cheyenne and jokingly said, "Good to know you!" She was having a little more fun now.

A steady flow of traffic screeched to a halt in front of the bouncing bus. The athletic driver cranked the wheel of the aging municipal coach to perform a brilliant maneuver around the logjam, across four lanes of traffic, into the far left lane, which was set aside for public transportation. He cut it sharply into the free lane and stomped the accelerator to the floor with a thud. Popi laughed. "The driver thinks it's a Triumph TR4! No wonder this bus is number 3; that's Dale Earnhardt's number!

I started coming to Costa Rica to escape Florida. I love Florida, but I hate the development. Land-scraping! Strip mining for houses! They ruined her. I came down here for the magic. When you get used to living in a developed area, the unspoiled natural world is magical. Here, their motto is Pura Vida, the pure life. There is nothing pure about concrete, steel and glass, unless it's pure madness.

Back then I had a powerfully negative attitude towards those who desecrated Florida with their development; it represented a giant circle of concern for me. It was a burden, like carrying around fifty pounds of potatoes in a wet bag. It was a constant pain in the butt, and I never knew when it might burst and spill all over. When it did, I was on my hands and knees chasing potatoes all over the floor, if you get my drift. I had a plate on the front of my old blue Ford Ranger that boldly proclaimed If you don't live here, GO HOME! I wasn't very nice!"

"Guess that's why you weren't on the Chamber of Commerce, Popi."

"That was when I wrote this song, Developer Blues. It went something like this."

> *I don't know what you been told.*
> *Big shot developer ain't got no soul.*
> *Tear down our trees and dig up the dirt.*
> *Money and property are powerful things*
> *These speculating dudes gonna drive ya insane.*
>
> *Buy up our land, parcel it off*
> *You ain't got a conscience, but you da boss.*

I don't know what you been told.
Big shot developer ain't got no soul.
Tear down our trees and dig up the dirt.
Is it Mother Nature you wanna hurt?
Crime follows money ... law follows crime!

He sang in an acoustic, grunge rock, folksy kind of way, reminiscent of Johnny Cash, while tapping out a rhythm on the back of the seat in front of them. His style reminded her of mountain or bluegrass music. After all, most of the Florida Crackers were of the same Scotch/Irish lineage as the Hillbillies.

"He sure isn't self-conscious. But no one is sitting that close and I enjoy it. I feel the same way, but he lets it all hangout" she thought to herself as he rambled on.

The traffic was in a state of complete chaos. A couple of policemen on motorcycles raced along the passenger side of the bus between the lines of vehicles. All types and shapes of vehicles were packed onto the road; standardization was not a priority around here. They had passed a rusty, bright blue GEO with bald tires. It had a wire cage strapped to its roof, with a plywood floor and two goats munching away inside. It was sitting with its doors open in front of what looked to be a sparkling new Mercedes.

They were hopelessly stuck next to the blocked lane. She looked down from the bus window to see a very young girl sitting quietly with a couple of hens in her lap. Occasionally, the girl fed them a kernel of corn. It dawned on her that modern Americans relationship with their food is not reality based.

In stark contrast, the girl's family was languishing in the extreme heat while the sparkling new Mercedes had the windows rolled up, the motor running and the air conditioner on. Cheyenne envisioned the driver as an armed chauffeur and the passenger a rich developer who had made a fortune selling retirement and investment property in Florida to gullible, trusting retirees.

Everything around them seemed to be green and colorful; every tree, every bush, every branch, each leave and flower was highlighted in vibrant colors. She couldn't imagine a place greener than this. There seemed to be a magnetic attraction at work that could pull you through and into the lush dark foliage all around them. "Popi, is it always so green?"

"Yes, child."

Her simple question reminded him of a song by the Outlaws, High Tides and Green Grass Forever. He loved that song during the short era of Southern Rock in the Seventies. In his opinion, Southern Rock as a genre began with the Allman Brothers and ended with the crash of Lynard Skynard's plane in the late Seventies. Depending on which expert was sober enough to argue, there was always someone who felt Southern Rock began earlier or lasted longer.

Either way, it was less than a generation; you might even call it a trend. He lamented that there are more trends than traditions anymore. Between Disco, Pop, New Wave and Country, Southern Rock had been squeezed out. Most of the Southern players just took their rock licks to Country Music with them. Growing up, he had listened to a mountain of Southern Rock. So much so, that he welcomed the change that Punk Rock frantically shoved in the world's face, and when New Wave finally broke on the shores of Florida, he had taken a deep breath and jumped right in.

"It took years for Lester to open up to New Wave music" Popi moaned as he placed his head back onto the seat's headrest. "Most of my friends in Florida didn't even like Neil Young. His song, Southern Man, was on the radio, and the wild-eyed southern boys of the day took exception, even though they knew Neil Young's take was true. They chased Neil off of the stage at a live concert in Tampa once. Imagine that? Booed Neil Young off before they even gave him a chance to play. That's a redneck thing to do. I don't care how long their hair was. That's redneck, darlin.'"

The bus scratched and clawed its way into town. It sputtered to a stop in the middle of San Jose's Central Plaza behind four other similar buses at the main transfer station. Popi had picked up his level of intensity. "By then Florida was a mess. Excuse the expression, but by the time Disney came, Florida was one big cluster-fudge of a mess.

Carl Hiassen writes all about how Disney took over in Team Rodent. An investigative reporter for the Miami Herald, Carl can give you the lowdown on that hoedown. Disney made their own laws; they have what I call a Doctrine of Development. Mickey Mouse is an insidious icon if you know the whole story."

Cheyenne felt like scolding Popi for his public expression. He was attracting attention from the locals. The Ticos seemed to know each other; they probably rode the same bus every day. She and Popi were strangers here, and it made her a bit cautious. But after thinking about it for a minute, she stopped worrying and let him ramble on. It had alleviated the monotonous pace of the ride, and had a calming effect on her nerves.

"Hiassen could tell you that blaming Disney and making them the scape-goats for the degrading of Florida would take some selective ignoring. Development strategies for Florida have been woefully questionable since Europeans first stumbled onto the place. Florida has had a long sad history of mad dreamers, delusional desperadoes, treasure hunters, and other displaced deviants who have been willing to help drain her swamps; all ready to grab a big piece of the pie and sell you a subdivided piece at an inflated price. There has never been a shortage of suckers eager to push to the front of the line to buy 'em some of that pie, either, girl. What about that narcissist, Henry Flagler, and his railroad Utopia? That old man bought himself a piece; he choked on it, too.

The whole lot of them saw themselves as heroes. They thought it was some of an epic feat to drain the state to make prime real estate out of the swamp, or to dredge up sand and plant coconuts to make a beach and a spot for a Tiki bar. Don't forget, they drained the Everglades and all the other swamps and wetlands in the ancient system. They started growing sugar! They completely diked one of the world's best lakes, changing it from a wild feeder system to a man-made impoundment, and all of that on top of already destroying and dredging countless miles of pristine bodies of water, habitats and shoreline.

Why can't people just recognize the value of the natural world and work with what is there? The Native Americans were happy enough with it just the way they found it. They didn't improve it; they made adjustments in their lifestyles to fit in with what Nature gave them.

In today's Florida, if you don't time the sale of your boom investments well, you will lose them in the bust period, or be stuck with them until the next boom. It's become a pattern as natural and predictable as hurricanes. You know one is sure to come, but you don't know when. Welcome to sunny Florida, y'all.

Don't get me wrong Cheyenne, Disney has added more than their share to Florida's schlocky sprawl, but they were using the weather and natural attributes to draw throngs of tourists, retirees and investors to Florida for at least a hundred years before Disney. I guess Florida was the first place to screen their windows. They had to find a way to keep the complaints down. Now, I guess we could slow complainers down if we could learn how to make good pizza and have it snow for Christmas. I say if you miss snow, go back up North! You can take Mickey Mouse and Pluto with ya!"

"Popi, sounds like you're a huge Disney fan!" teased Cheyenne.

"Right! Believe me, though, I ain't a Disney hater. I'm done listening to the masses blaming someone else for the problems of the world. We all need to take responsibility. It is what it is; recognize the problems and work to fix them. Period."

The highway began to narrow as the bus entered the inner city. San José's gut, like other big cities, was a maze of cement, lights, cars, and people; the buildings had grown taller, and she had watched as the landscaping paled. The lush greenery of the countryside had disappeared, and her false sense of security had slipped away with it again.

Cheyenne wanted to wrap it up, but Popi seemed not to notice that the bus had stopped and was emptying out quickly. "It doesn't seem to matter that Florida is the lowest, flattest state of the fifty in the Union, and is by far the most vulnerable to sea level rise; development and real estate rule the state's economy."

Not wanting to interrupt, she motioned towards the door with a subtle gesture. "Sea level rise? What a nightmare. It comes slow but steady."

He hadn't taken the hint to exit the bus. "Cheyenne, do you realize there's not one major coastal community in our nation that's not experiencing extreme erosion problems in one way, or another?"

"Popi! We'll need to solve these problems later. It looks as if we've arrived at the bus terminal."

"Please stop me! I'll lose my mind before we get there!" he admitted as he got up from his seat, finally ready to take the next step in their journey. In his heart he knew they were heading into a darkness created in his past, but with her help he'd get past it.

They stepped into the flock of people exiting buses from points located south and west of San Jose. Most of them had come here from Alajuela. Alajuela sits on the west side of the Central Valley; Valle Central spreads in all directions from San Jose, encompassing a fifth of Costa Rica's land mass. The Valle Central is richly unique for its scrambled mix of urban, rural and untouched habitat, and has a diverse terrain, as well.

Rivers, weather and terrific soil combine to make it ideal farmland. Because of Costa Rica's location between the Pacific and Caribbean, it is always thick with humidity, which quenches a vast array of lush, prolific flora and fauna. Three-fourths of the country's population lives within the mountainous perimeter of the valley.

The city of Paraíso in Cartago marks the eastern reach. There are four frisky volcanoes north of the valley called Poás, Barva, Irazú and Turrialba. The Talamanca Range of mountains surrounds the plateau to the south, dividing the valley into two sections. To the north, there are four more volcanoes that are semi-active.

A smaller range, the Cerros de la Carpintera, runs north to south along the border of San José and Cartago Provinces. They affect the weather quite differently, so that there are some areas of the valley that remain extremely dry. This sub-climate adds even more to the list of diverse plants and animals that occupy the region.

"Where do we head from here, Popi?" A nervous tension resonated in her voice; she couldn't shake the insecurity of what lay ahead. She hoped it was travel nerves and not intuitive premonition, but this road had been a little scary in places.

As her mind drifted, the bustling crowd seemed to slip softly into a polite silence. Everyone had become peaceful and reserved, except for one man. A large, well-fed, middle-aged Tico had emerged, thumping a huge, well-worn, leather-bound Bible and in a blustery, pious vibrato, he had begun to cry out to the group assembled before him. "Arrepentirse Hoy, La Salvación Es El Camino!"

Cheyenne made sure not to make eye contact as she glided past him.

Popi had not seen the Costa Rican mountains for a long time. Familiar scenes and sensations flooded his mind. They were indistinguishable from ones he had always associated with the ridges along the Pan American Highway that he loved to negotiate when heading south towards the Panama border on the way to the Osa Peninsula. His mind projected him along that very road when suddenly, in his vision, he spotted a patch of dark blue showing through a low-hanging cloud even with the altitude of the mountain highway. He was totally unaware of his actual surroundings when he called out, "Oceano Pacifico! I can see it from here!"

"You know exactly where we are going, Popi, and we're certainly nowhere near the ocean yet. Right now, all we have to do is get there" she said with a smile.

Her tone with him had grown more relaxed, and he was comforted by it; it gave him a happy lift. He confidently declared, "Yeah, you're right. I know where we are going. I know right where we are. We're walking to the next bus here at the transfer station. Vamanos!"

"Great! Where is it; which way?"

"Well, I'm not exactly sure. The last time I was here, I had a car."

"Popi!"

He felt the command in her voice; its resolve caught his attention.

"This is good. She may be a little unsettled, but she isn't in a panic. She is asserting herself; this is very good. Now we are on the Road to Matapalo" he thought as he came back to the present.

He turned and walked a few steps, and then stopped. He looked up and around in every direction and then back at her. "Child, we will find our way. We will complete our quest, wherever it takes us."

But she had a burning ember of sheer determination going. She was resolute and direct. She pointed towards him, wagging her finger again and in a sweet, calculating, cascading voice and said, "You're going to tell me where we are heading right now, or I am not going to take another step with you. I learned a long time ago not to ever make that mistake again. Anyway, I am not in line for a one-way ticket to nowhere. What is it we have, an appointment with destiny, Gramps?"

He turned, took a false step and stopped in a locked position. He swiveled around sharply, teetering a bit as he did. "I am at a loss," he said. "When I saw the ocean in my vision, it was in the mountains down south. It wasn't a dream; I'm sure it was just a memory."

"Why don't you pullout your iPad? You know, the one with the iGo Primo app that you didn't think I saw on the plane. It's not so damn cute to be naïve in the real world. The darn thing can teach you some real Tico Lingo to ask directions with and maybe keep us out of trouble."

"Ah, what's the first habit? That's right. Be proactive! We'll figure it out. I'll bet you will soon be telling me where we are going. Lead the way, Cheyenne; let's get on our way!"

During this time, he had inadvertently led them out of the bus station and onto the streets. She had instinctively followed. She found herself absorbed in a beguiling aroma of exotic spices and green leaf, hardwood-grilled chicken. She slowed down and looked for the source of the wonderful aroma since she hadn't eaten since their meager breakfast so many hours earlier.

Popi had drifted off into a side street; she followed behind him, going down a narrow back alley. It led them to an open street lined with storefronts and brightly painted signs. The sound of Latin rhythms, rich harmonies and blaring horns emanated from several places at once to form a confusing arrangement of various songs.

The Latin songs were so similar blending into a hybrid style all of their own, and competed with the exuberant chatter of the Spanish-speaking Ticos flooding the streets.

"No one is speaking any English around here" she mumbled to herself.

Popi ducked into a small doorway that led into a tiny, semi-dark restaurant. She saw four tables with sunshine yellow tablecloths, each complemented by four wonderfully hand-painted cane chairs.

She sat down and dug out her iPad as Popi sauntered up to the counter. It was manned by a short, but formidable, man wearing a white bandana, full-length-bib apron and a V-neck, cotton t-shirt tucked in tight. It was easy to see there was no product offered except grilled chicken. Judging by the number of birds being smoked over the massive stone grill built into the wall behind the proprietor, business was brisk. Popi chatted it up with the guy until the cook slapped his stomach and let out a guttural laugh.

He sat down with a smile. Cheyenne was curious about the small talk. "What's the joke?"

"Oh, I was just asking him if he eats his own cooking and he said 'Si, este es el cemeterio de pollo.'"

She checked her iGo Primo. "Here it is! This is the chicken graveyard?"

"Yes, it is! I ordered us a whole one; we can share."

"What makes you think I can eat half of a chicken; can you?"

Popi was undeterred. "You can only order a whole one. It's all good; we'll take some with us. Ya never know when ya might get hungry. Chicken cooked up this way will keep for a day, easy." While waiting for the food, he unfolded a map he had pulled from his backpack. "Where do you want to go first?"

She pointed to the map, and her finger drew a line towards the Pacific Ocean. "We're here; Jaco Beach looks like the closest one to San Jose." She placed a hand on one hip and pointed west with the other. "We're going to Jaco! Jaco Beach!"

"Damn, you're right! I knew that; Jaco Beach, that's right Cheyenne."

More chicken was put to rest in el cemeterio de pollo than they had anticipated. Popi wrapped the remainder in some white, coated paper from the counter and slipped the package neatly into a side pocket on his backpack.

Cheyenne was rejuvenated by the meal and was ready to pick up the trail. "Let's hit the bricks! This is fun."

Besides the meal, the proactive decision-making process had invigorated Cheyenne. She was riding her momentum when she shifted all of her attention to iGo Primo. Popi slipped the map back into another pocket on his backpack.

"I know what to do. I'll ask someone where we can catch the bus. Check it out on the iPad; here, they call it an autobus. Jaco Beach is Haco Beach; their J is pronounced more like an H. Ya gotta love modern technology!"

Unfortunately, there is more to communicating in any language than technical words. She cried out to anyone who might be willing to answer, but her clumsy American inflections disguised the meaning. "Autobus to Hacko Beach?" No one around recognized her question.

She tried it with more authority, but her pitch couldn't coax a swing out of any of the batters. Where were the bus hawkers now that she needed them? Finally, she approached a young man strolling his way down the middle of a one-way street. He was dressed very sharply in his bright white, pressed, cotton trousers and a white shirt belted at the waist; with a red cummerbund and matching scarf tied loosely around his neck, held together with a black leather band trimmed in polished silver. He had jet-black hair, brushed straight back; it was as perfect as his fit, muscular body and black leather boots with polished silver trim.

First he spoke to Cheyenne in fast Spanish. When he drew a blank stare, he spoke to her again, this time slowly in fluent English.

"Excuse me, señorita. What do you seek?"

"The young lady is looking for a bus to Jaco Beach," Popi said. He was caught a bit off guard, looking down fumbling with the clasp holding his fanny pack behind his back. But he had recovered; knowing local custom, he had lessened any apprehension with as formal of an introduction as he could muster up on short notice. "Meet my granddaughter, Cheyenne. She's taking me on a path to nowhere, or somewhere, or wherever else we are led."

"Popi, you don't need to tell the whole world."

Popi continued. "Cheyenne, meet ... excuse me, amigo, I don't know your name."

The young man looked at the two of them with his clear and steady eyes. "No problem; I fully understand. We are all strangers until we meet. I am Jose' Artz, and it is a pleasure to meet you both. That bus stop is not close to here. May I be so bold as to offer to take you there myself?"

"On a path to nowhere? We've got two tickets to paradise, no refunds" Popi joked.

Jose answered with a wide grin and a twinkle in his eye. "No; to the bus for Hacko Beach! We should go right now to be on time. I was going home to change, but there isn't time. I am coming from my niece's wedding. It was a traditional ceremony and celebration; a beautiful day!

As the three new friends walked away, Jose' whistled and waved his right hand in a tactful twist at two men who were standing across the cobblestoned street. Popi watched closely as the men waved back; he figured that they could trust Jose' if they had to. He would be a good guy to know.

They followed Jose' closely through congested crowds of pedestrians and streets clogged with traffic. They walked three blocks west and then a couple south from the Central Plaza until they came to a pair of tall wooden doors. The doors led to a shortcut into and out of a massive indoor market place. They waded their way through a colorful mixture of Ticos and tourists perusing the wares of row after row of various vendors, the types that were more than willing to haggle for the best bargain.

She watched the confidence exuded by their new acquaintance as they strolled through the market. Jose' kept a strong, even pace as he did his best to listen to Popi tell him of how San Jose was once a sleepy city twenty years ago. She was drawn to the attractive kindness in his eyes and his soft, but manly facial expressions; her fear of the city had melted away since they had met him.

The passage finally led out into a completely different world. They were in the plaza, and there were identical buses to everywhere; it was as if they had materialized out of nowhere. The buses were headed to Dominical, Uvita, Quepos, Jaco Beach and a host of other Costa Rican destinations. The three of them came together as they entered the terminal, and before their helpful guide left them, he turned to face Cheyenne. He lifted her hand gingerly, kissed it, and gazed directly into her eyes as if to say "We will meet, again, I assure you."

Then he placed his hands gently on Cheyenne's shoulders and smoothly turned her around, directing her to the ticket booth. He said one last thing before he turned and walked away. Popi strained to hear what he was saying to her, but it was indistinguishable from the combination of the crowd's chatter and the diesel noises coming from the buses. When she returned, Popi impatiently asked to see the tickets. He examined them halfheartedly, but his real interest was elsewhere. His overriding concern for his granddaughter was slipping its chains. He searched for words but couldn't find any.

Cheyenne knew what the problem was. "He asked me to call him Joe, and he told me I was beautiful! He said the sweetest thing." Mimicking Jose's voice and aristocratic Spanish accent, she repeated the young man's parting words. "Our lovely visit has been much too short. It is my hope that we will meet again. I am sure we will."

"Do yourself a favor, darlin', don't pay any mind to those Costa Rican men and whatever they say. He was looking at you like you were a pork chop. Now, please, show me the tickets!"

"They're in your hand, Popi." Cheyenne reminded him as her smile flopped into a disappointed frown.

His words had cast a dark shadow on Cheyenne's delightful mood.

He immediately felt ashamed, as he remembered the very words his mother had said about men from New Jersey. The day he told her he was going to meet his future father and mother-in-law for the first time she had vehemently exclaimed "All men from New Jersey are assholes." His mother's words had brought him down from the heights back then, and now he had done the same thing with his own granddaughter.

"Cheyenne, I am sorry for what I said about your young man; I exaggerated his intentions. You are beautiful; I only meant you need to watch out because of the way things can sometimes be. You are so precious to me, and I know what troubles can befall unsuspecting young ladies. Forgive me; you are smart, and you will do well. Old men often worry about the young because of the sins of their own youth."

He was a wise man, and she knew he was right. She raised her head, and her eyes lit up as her smile returned from its temporary setback. He waved her on. "Come on. Our bus is loading."

As soon as they sat down they dropped their backpacks at their feet, settled into their seats and started to assess their surroundings. This bus was almost identical to the first, and the driver even shared similar attributes. He took their tickets, smiled and encouraged each patron to enjoy their trip. Cheyenne absorbed the excitement of the moment in an entirely different way than Popi, watching everything with keen interest as the bus pulled away from the station. Popi, however, sat motionless. He was unusually pensive, but she suspected the quiet wouldn't last long.

The traffic out of San Jose on Highway 34 was surprisingly light. A thin smoky fog lingered low in the valley, but the high blue sky remained opulent. Further away, on the horizon, the fog in the valley blossomed into puffy white clouds with dark purple underbellies. As the trip went on, the clouds rose in the faraway sky until they towered high in the upper atmosphere above the valley floor from where they had formed. She soon felt a drop of sweat on the tip of her nose, and it seemed to her that the rising temperature and clouds were in concert.

The people in their homes and communities along the bus path kept her riveted to the window. She relished the view and the experience. Valle Central was indeed an interesting, eclectic mixture of inhabitants and cultures. Its population was a rich mixture of many sub-ethnic groups, including the Mestizos, indigenous tribesmen, Europeans, and people of African descent all woven into a calico landscape of busy people walking along the roadside.

The bus began a grueling, non-stop climb that snaked up a mountainside, back and forth, almost forever. The driver constantly struggled for more torque and speed, torturing the engine with no mercy. Near the peak, he imposed his will on the transmission by shifting wildly with the gear lever until he found a sweet spot. He searched for a little more juice and shoved the stick shift home with a resentful shudder from the driveshaft.

Faster traffic backed up behind him. Drivers not content with the pace insisted on weaving around and looking for an opening to pass as if it were even feasible. It was a neck to neck, or perhaps a nose to rear, race to the top with no room for error. The road was narrow, pocked with potholes and busy with people moving about their daily routines.

The endless, carbon-spewing caravan angled up the hill for a solid hour or more until, without warning, the road flattened out temporarily. The bus pulled off the road next to a Mercado, which is the Costa Rican version of a convenience store, where the passengers could enjoy a soda and a snack. Most were ready for a break, and they slowly exited the bus to stretch their legs.

But not Popi and Cheyenne; they soaked in the exceptional view from their seats. Their elevation was over ten thousand feet, and the air had cooled considerably; dew began to settle on the top of the seats. Neither of them spoke.

After everyone had made their way back to their seats, the bus started away and down the mountain road into low clouds and patchy showers that were up ahead of the caravan. Popi nodded his head and blurted "Good!"

"Good?" Cheyenne asked before she could stop herself. She almost regretted her instinctive inquiry, since it might lead into an endless abyss of soliloquy. She resigned herself to the outcome as she thought to herself "Oh well, here we go."

"Costa Rica can be one of the rainiest places on the Earth. This rainforest atop this mountain ridge, the one we are now traveling on, is one of Costa Rica's wettest spots. It should be raining. It averages nearly three-hundred inches a year. Remember; where there are rain clouds, there are also rainbows."

Cheyenne, pleasantly surprised by his sweet brevity, replied "Good! It should be raining. All is well."

She saw taller mountain peaks farther to the southwest out in front of them and more appeared around a bend further ahead. "Look Popi, mountains beyond mountains."

She had learned this expression while working a few years earlier as a teenaged volunteer with Partners for Health in the mountains above Port au Prince, Haiti. Popi looked at her with a quizzical expression.

"Popi, it means there will always be more mountains to climb. It is the way Haitians view their lives; it's their philosophy. They climb their mountains and do it with a cheerful heart. They embrace the climb to the peak and are content with the view of the next. They don't get overly elated at their triumph during the walk downhill because they know there is another challenge ahead. Face one challenge to get to the next; mountains beyond mountains."

"That's rich, darling." Popi approved, appreciating the simplicity.

She nodded in acknowledgement, but her focus was elsewhere. She looked down into a narrow gorge cut by a steep and fast river; the slicing river leaped up and over a car-sized boulder, sending the raging white water blasting away at the steep, craggy banks at the base of the ravine. It was churning like a Norse whirlpool directly below her on the outside edge of the road.

She peered down at a single kayaker, who paddled up and over the steep wedge of the enormous standing wave, hesitated, and launched into a graceful arch. When he landed squarely, he turned into a wave, took two strokes, careened into the swiftest part of the current and whisked on downstream in one easy motion. "I think I can get used to this place!" she said to herself.

The bus began its descent, and the driver frantically changed gears to save the brakes as they coasted down towards the coast. Popi planted a seed, telling her, "Pacific Ocean should soon be within view on our left side."

She looked to their left. A sliver of the dark blue Pacific Ocean filled a gap between the distant mountain peaks. Wonder filled her face as she shifted back and forth in her seat; her excitement could not be matched by any other passengers on the bus. Breathtaking vistas, one after another, unfolded before her eyes. As the land flattened out a bit, he told her the bus would be crossing Rio Crocodile, one of Costa Rica's mainstay tourist attractions, and then from there, down to Jaco Beach.

"You couldn't imagine my first trip down this road, back in the day."

"Yes, you're right, Popi. It is beautiful; I can't imagine it any better."

"Rugged!" he emphasized. "Roads? What roads? It was only dirt and rock, and landslides were common during the rainy season. Four-wheel drive was a must, and you needed to be on your toes all the time. Even the best, most cautious drivers could find themselves in a tight situation; you just couldn't relax for a second."

A minute later, he gave her a little wake up call with his elbow and pointed below. "Timing is everything."

She glimpsed down at a burned-out van sitting upside down and wedged preposterously into a crevice five-hundred feet below.

He continued. "Our trip from San Jose to Jaco may take us only two or three hours today, depending on the stops the driver makes. Back then, it took six or more hours to reach the coast, and that's if you were lucky."

Cheyenne was curious. "Why did you keep returning to Costa Rica? Was it surfing, Popi?"

"It was more than the waves. Yeah, surfing took our family around the world and back. We traveled to Bali, Australia and Puerto Escondido, and to Long Island, New York and to Long Island, Bahamas. But my love affair with Costa Rica was deeper than any ocean.

It also reminded me of old Florida, but truly tropical, not semi-tropical. Tropical Florida is a look, not reality. Still, there was so much that seemed familiar about Costa Rica; the warm weather, the rural lands, the laid-back life, dirt roads, cattle, the snook, and most of all, the kind-hearted and friendly people. It all kept me coming back until I was too old and set in my ways to want to travel anywhere else."

She settled back into her seat; he was rolling again.

"Yeah, there were hardly any autos, and no stop signs or traffic lights. I treasured Costa's great, open, undeveloped spaces. I'm a dreamer, Cheyenne, more or less like you. I thought the family could emigrate here. We could start a new life, one that would be more in tune, sustainable, and balanced with nature.

It got to the point where I was actually looking for property; had a serious eye on a piece of land above Nosara, up on the Nicoya Peninsula. Years ago your uncles and I befriended an ex-patriot living in Playa Guiones. Captain Ed had a boat moored at Playa Garza; we fished with him whenever we went to Guiones to surf. We had the time of our lives, and Ed was a big part of it.

"Ed's property was on the Rio Montana, directly above Nosara, looking out over the Pacific Ocean. He raised trees there. He would also salvage fallen trees from the Rio Montana. Captain Ed always promised to take me shrimping in the river's shallow waters some day, but I guess it's too late now. That's just how it worked out."

She noticed him turn melancholy, then brighten up, and go back to being forlorn within the span of his explanation. She determined that he had some serious emotion invested in this trip to Matapalo, and his investment was compounding daily.

"Cheyenne, like you said before; take my advice. I'm not using it! Don't wait; some tomorrows never come. I haven't spoken with

Captain Ed since the day we walked along the Rio Montana together. Once the bridge from San Jose to Nosara was completed, things started to change rapidly for the worse around here, especially people-wise. The Nicoya's population grew exponentially; crime increased, litter piled up, roadside schlock destroyed the view, developers built those damn condos, and on it goes.

Regardless, the majority of the Nicoya Peninsula remained a wondrous place. But we decided to head south to Osa, to Matapalo, to avoid the Nicoya's ugly urban expansion. The Coastal Highway hadn't been built yet, and most people didn't want to have anything to do with the lousy roads south of Hermosa.

Cheyenne, your grandmother once taught me 'If you're not standing on the edge, you're probably taking up too much space.'"

As the peaks leveled off, glimpses of the ocean became more frequent and longer. This rhythm matched that of the stops that the bus was now making as Ticos were getting on and off every couple of kilometers, and the stops were getting longer.

He suggested that they eat the rest of the chicken; there was enough to hold them both. Their renewed energy transformed their conversation; she began whispering in a giddy schoolgirl's voice, saying silly things that only her grandfather would find amusing. They laughed as she performed her routine again, and then they laughed some more.

This play-acting, as if they were children, made him feel young again. Cheyenne saw it in his eyes. His heart was alive and well; any lingering melancholy had vanished.

The bus turned off of the Costanera Highway at the upper reaches of the Sonesta Jaco Resort and headed down to the coast. A sloppy, well-fed American, previously unnoticed, was slouching behind them. He shot his head forward and stuck it between them. His repulsive breath smelled of stale cigar smoke, strong coffee and cheap wine, but despite being unkempt and beet red, his round and cheerful face was likable. "Did you know we get Howard Stern down here 24/7? It's unreal, isn't it?"

Popi and Cheyenne threw up a hasty wall of stiff body language as they politely shook their heads to his unsolicited insertion into their conversation. The amiable American's head bounced between them like an over-inflated basketball. "Oh yeah! Howard's bad to the bone, don't ya think?"

He tilted and rocked his head a bit in each of their directions several times in an attempt to gain approval. When he was met with their cool response, he lowered the volume and pitch of his voice and continued. "What do you think, friends?"

Apparently, the man couldn't take a hint. Looking straight ahead, Popi announced in a clear, calm voice "Always thought Howard Stern was living proof that an idiot and a genius can occupy the same body. Lost all respect for the man when he divorced his wife, not that he deserved much to begin with."

Cheyenne offered the round-faced man a mint, which he declined.

The obtrusive Stern fan sucked in a noisy breath of air and released it in a slow, deliberate exhale as he contemplated Popi's retort. He struck a low-rent version of the pose of "The Thinker" by Rodin and leaned all the way back into his seat, muttering contritely "You got a point there, mister."

No one heard another peep out of him, even as he exited the bus at the edge of town. A dark flush of red on his cheeks kept him from saying goodbye and wishing them well as he made his way through the crowd.

Jaco was alive with traffic and people, and from the condition of the main drag, it looked like it had been raining for days. In spite of the conditions, the people were nonchalant as they went about their business as usual, dodging the rain-filled potholes and muddy mess with unflinching skills.

It looked like a hardscrabble town to Cheyenne; her expectations had failed her again. In one part of the town, she was surprised by some of the shadowy, menacing characters hanging around in small groups, or leaning alone against a wall. They were almost too much of an exaggeration to be real.

There were more puddles than road, but fortunately the bus halted on the edge of town where the last stop was on a higher, dry stretch of road. Popi said, "We have a reservation at the Beds at Bohio; it is nice and inexpensive compared to a Florida beachfront stay." Cheyenne was as surprised as she was glad to be so close to the shower and a hot meal.

Before she could tell Popi how she felt, he turned and took off at a fairly brisk pace, avoiding the mud as best as possible. He guided her from the bus stop, past the business district, and down a rough, semi-steep sidewalk towards the water. They slipped in and out through a thick hibiscus hedge awash in vibrant red, orange or pink flowers. The hibiscus was joined by other lush foliage, forming a natural foyer that lead into a serpentine passageway. The walkway wound through a marvelous masterpiece of landscaping that had obviously been meticulously kept up by a fastidious landscaper for years.

Had they gone from purgatory to paradise through this portal? She was dumbfounded by the magnitude of the sudden change. She blended into the foliage as it engulfed her. "Wow, Popi! I am very impressed."

"I did my best to keep us away from the main drag and as far away as possible from the riffraff of Jaco. We can get to the hostel from here. It's a pleasant walk, too."

"Do they surf here?"

"Yes, why of course, they surf here."

He knew the break all too well. Many years back, he and three other Floridacentric surfers that he had traveled with got stuck in Jaco for a week when an earthquake caused a landslide that took out a section of Highway 34. It was the only route that connected Playa Jaco to Playa Hermosa. As luck would have it, a powerful south swell reached the area the day they arrived. Normally, Jaco was a beach break that rarely got big; it tended to close out whenever it reached five or six feet, but the big swell had made it almost unrideable. Around the volcanic headland, north of Playa Jaco, there were better, more secluded breaks that they were eager to explore.

The foursome had blazed back and forth in their four-wheel rental, exploring every inch of the coast between Jaco and Boca Barranca. In the early days of surf exploration, the Coastal Highway wasn't much more than a dirt road interrupted by merciless, back-busting potholes, one-lane bridges, dicey ferries and washouts. The driving was hell back then, but it had only served to kindle their thirst for adventure. The rudimentary roads often dished out plenty of pain and suffering and some seriously close calls with vehicles, pedestrians and animals.

Playa Barranca was littered with gargantuan volcanic rock formations that jutted out of the land or thrust up from the sea around a beautiful black sand beach with aqua-blue water and perfect surf. One of the world's longest left point breaks, notorious for its lengthy rides, was located there. They had found it firing off beyond the north shore of the mouth of the Barranca River, famous for its opaque, debris-laden runoff that is reminiscent of the Zambezi. It was also infamous for petty thefts by a rogue element of seedy, predatory locals.

After the swell had subsided, the intrepid group convalesced in a cheap Jaco Beach hostel while they waited for the road to be repaired. They utilized their time by licking the surf wounds inflicted by the Southern Hemisphere typhoon that had pounded the coast with the whopping swell. They had logged hammock time, goofed off, ate and surfed on the smaller, well-formed hot dog waves at the optimal tides each morning and evening.

Jaco's beach is located directly across from the Golfo Nicoya and faces the peninsula of the Cabo Blanco Nature Reserve. It is almost blocked from westerly swells and entirely protected from any swell that pulses from the north. Considering the waves around the area, Playa Jaco is an exceptional place for a newbie to learn. This beach was far less exposed to swells than Hermosa Beach, located just a few kilometers south.

The consistency of fun, shapely surf, accessibility from San Jose, cheap land and breathtaking vistas guaranteed that Jaco would race towards rapid development. The attention that Costa Rica received from word of mouth, and the internet opened a floodgate of international investment and regional ambition. In time, the surrounding area became a prime example of the separation of classes in Costa Rica.

The disparity in the quality of life on the back streets of Jaco and the ritzy mountainside and beachfront villas was as broad as the ocean that they overlooked. Nearby Herradera's lifestyle became a lofty perch for modern day nouveaux riche who looked down and figuratively on grittier boomtowns like Los Suenos. Costa Rica once was a country carried on the backs of the middle class, but it had been bizarrely transformed into an unrecognizable hybrid by the influence of greed.

Cheyenne kept pace with Popi as they descended into the garden of hanging orchids and vermilion-colored vines. The winding path was lined with countless varieties of seashells and paved with white beach sand. Suddenly, they emerged into an open-air lobby, where they encountered an overweight man questioning the woman behind the counter. Everything about him reminded her of the Stern fan they had involuntarily met on the bus, except for one thing; his red face wasn't easy or inviting.

A younger woman, with brassy, peroxide-blonde hair stood watching impatiently a few feet away. She was plenty of woman, but not as hefty as her partner, nor as hard to put an eye on. She stood with folded arms draped just below her enormous bosom, the kind that don't come free. Without saying a word, her posture proclaimed her dominance.

In a pompous tone, the blustery American asked "Don't you have any rooms close to the office? Cable? American TV? It's for the lady."

He gave a nod in his companion's direction, imploring the woman behind the counter to help him out. He did this without looking directly at his companion; she was barking orders with her eyes while holding her arms tightly locked across her ample chest. Her look was intimidating him, but nobody else.

The clerk, unruffled, maintained a pleasant, unassuming smile and replied calmly "Senor, your cabana is the closest we have available at the time. We will reserve the very closest for you. The present occupants will be checking out tomorrow; as soon as we have it in order, we will notify you. We certainly do have American TV, and it is included in the price for your enjoyment."

"Movie channel?" He pointed again in his companion's direction with his head to assure the desk clerk that he was not the source of the problem. "It's for the little lady." He could not keep his feet still, and his eyes shifted incessantly. He seemed to be in a rush, and they both wondered why he was so antsy.

Popi suspected the man had snorted up some cocaine; he knew it was readily available around town. It was a cakewalk to smuggle it up the Pan American Highway from Colombia, Peru and Bolivia. The word was that Jaco had become the stomping grounds for serious foreign connoisseurs of the product. The steady supply was always dependable, and compared to the prices and attitudes in the States, it was an ideal place to cop a cheap stash and use it up. In the wake of the trend, Jaco now had sprouted its very own little Crack Town, replete with all of the trappings.

Before the clerk could answer him, the American reached into his back pocket to pull out a soiled, white handkerchief to wipe and clear his red nose, and added "What's it going to cost us? We're done being gouged down here!"

Cheyenne had worked a short-term, part-time job in retail before. She knew the tone well. What the big fellow was crowing was "Look at us. We're important! Roll out the red carpet and give us the key to the city, peon."

She fully empathized with the desk clerk. The moment transported her back to a sour incident she had with a customer who nearly got her fired. As luck would have it, the manager entered the scene just as she began asserting herself in opposition to the customer's degrading comments and verbal abuse. The manager, without question, instantly supported the customer and openly disciplined Cheyenne. It left her with a nasty, but useful memory. She'd never forget the frustrating humiliation. Since then, whenever she found herself in this type of situation, she did her best to tune it out. Thankfully, the man's voice quickly trailed off and finally evaporated.

Popi threw out an emphatic whisper in Cheyenne's ear. "Americans are needy."

The clerk was unfazed. The charming, attractive lady was obviously experienced with difficult customers. Her radiant smile and demeanor was a permanent fixture.

Deaun (pronounced Day-own) was older and much wiser than she first appeared. She had dealt with these types of episodes on a daily basis for quite some time, and it was an integral part of making her livelihood. She was savvy about people and comprehended their body language. She listened closely to their tone and choice of words to identify their needs, and always did her utmost to meet them. Deaun understood there would always be needy people, and she strived to comfort them. She handled the customer with ease. She had vowed to stay proactive a long time ago.

After piling on a half-dozen new requests, along with one or two that were redundant, the big guy's attitude was tamed by Deaun's composed courtesy. Smiles appeared on the couple's taut faces; they were pleased to be accommodated. The bellhop gathered their belongings as he strained to decipher the large man's misfiring "Spanglish." The man was so elated by Deaun's actions that he even turned back around to bid the obliging clerk a good night in a stumbling attempt at Spanish. He barked out "Muchas gracias notes, señorita!" thinking he was speaking fluent Spanish.

This elevated his confidence a few notches. He was getting in the groove. As the couple left the lobby, Deaun gave her full attention to Popi. "Mr. Manly, we have been expecting you, sir."

Deaun caught Cheyenne's puzzled look by the way she flinched her eyebrows and tensed her lips. The expression only lasted a second or two.

Registering only took a minute. Deaun dropped the keys into Popi's hand, and he responded with a congenial "Gracias, dulce corazón, tienen un maravillosos noche."

She replied in English. "You have had a long day of travel. We'll find time to talk when you are rested and refreshed."

They needed no help finding their rooms. Cheyenne was pleased Popi had selected the inexpensive hostel option. They walked straight through a vine-covered arbor that opened up into another garden. It was bordered by a handful of single cabanas.

Their separate cabanas were simple, with no more than a paddle fan hanging from the ceiling and a tightly made single bed with two pillows. The four cabanas in this section shared community showers; they were clean, and there was plenty of hot water if you timed it right. Conveniently, the price of their cabanas also included the use of surfboards.

As boards go, neither of them were throwaways; they would both do. They had light, even coats of wax. One of the ankle leashes was marginal, with frayed Velcro and deteriorated stitching, but the other looked just fine. She found a half bar of wax that had washed up on the high tide. Popi scraped off the sand with his straight razor. He told her the razor gave him a close shave, and might deter an aggressor. She mentioned that after dinner she wanted to learn properly how to wax her board.

The two hungry sojourners cleaned up and met to dine on the open patio in the center of the compound. There were several tables in a raised, walled patio outside under a canopy of tropical foliage and palms. It all had such a hypnotic ambiance that she wondered if the setting had come from one of her jungle dreams. The dreams seemed real sometimes.

Their typical Tico meal of rice, beans, salad and chicken was served on a single plate and lightly dowsed with Lizano salsa. It was incredibly delicious in its simplicity, having a surprising sophistication of flavor, texture and color. After their meal, they savored a strong, smooth, rich café con leche and ruminated on the evening.

She was familiar with the exotic almond trees, bananas, papaya, coconut palms and flowering bougainvillea that surrounded her, but there were many more unrecognizable plants, trees and flowers than she could count. She wanted to learn the names and everything about every single one of them.

They lingered outside for a while, enjoying the setting sun dropping below the horizon of Pacific. They sat quietly and listened to the waves, watching them peel across the glassy surface of the water where they cast purple shadows below their peeling lips.

Sundown had enticed several Tico families to the beach, as well. Many of them, especially the youngsters, played in the knee-high surf. Others were content to stay dry on the beach while happily pointing and laughing at their younger family members who were enjoying the day's end. By nightfall, everyone had disappeared, along with the shadows, into the landscape.

"Popi, I've been told that Costa Rica has the highest percentage of diversity than any other place on the planet. Is this true?"

"It depends, child; what type of diversity are you referring to?"

"You know; wildlife, habitat, geography, population ... those things."

"You are correct; Costa has great bio-diversity. The Osa Peninsula by itself may be one of the most diverse places per acre on earth."

"What about the Indian River Lagoon; it's diverse. How special is it compared to this?" She anticipated that he would know if anyone at all did.

"Costa Rica's estuaries can't match the abundance of species supported by the Indian River Lagoon. In fact, it has been widely accepted that there may not be another coastal estuary system in the world as rich in diverse habitat and occupancy than our river. It's a nursery for almost every critter that lives in or near the water, whether it's shellfish, fish, birds or mammals.

When it comes to natural springs, Florida has more than any

place in the northern hemisphere. Ponce De Leon blundered when the natives told him of the rejuvenating value and health benefits of the pure springs. The fool thought it would enable you to live forever, when all they really said is it would help you live longer. That's why competent translators are at a premium.

Costa Rica has got Florida beat when it comes to waterfalls and volcanoes, though. As much as I wish we had more cataratas in Florida, I'm happy we ain't got volcanoes ... yet. Bad enough being the flattest place on Earth, adding volcanoes might not be such a bonus."

They both laughed. He slapped his right hand along the side of his leg, threw his head back and let a guffaw escape through his gaping mouth. Cheyenne held one hand flat on her stomach and the other over her chest as she laughed almost to the point of crying. It was wonderful.

He settled down, sighed deeply, and said, "Thank you. I haven't felt this alive in years."

The two of them went back and forth talking about Costa Rica and Florida; Cheyenne was like a sponge. She needed to soak up every single piece of information she could download on Costa Rica or anywhere else he had explored.

The conversation continued to flow down this stream until she remembered the piece of scavenged surfboard wax. Then their talk turned to her questions about early surfing history, and the special places he had surfed. She picked his brain for his techniques and strategies of paddling out, sitting in the lineup, catching a wave, standing up and riding the board. She listened well and asked pertinent questions.

He set one of the boards on the ground and demonstrated the proper strokes and pressure used to cover the deck with an even coat for plenty of traction to avoid slips. She tried the second one by herself while he worked to tighten up the bad ankle leash on the other board by replacing a frayed nylon cord that secured it to the board. He cleaned and fluffed the Velcro, and determined that it would probably hold tight in any surf he would be likely to go out in.

He then quoted Ben Franklin's famous line. "Early to bed, early to rise, keeps a man healthy, wealthy and wise. That's a creed that I live by." They decided it was time they retired, so they headed off to their cabanas. He quickly dozed off into a deep, dreamless sleep.

But Cheyenne tossed and turned restlessly for a long while, excited by the challenges of the next day. When she finally began drifting off towards sleep, she floated away on this thought. "Tomorrow I will attempt to ride the waves of Playa Jaco on the Pacific Ocean for the very first time. I hope I can learn to dance with the ocean." Then her thoughts turned to Joe, and not to Sidney. At first she felt guilty placing him ahead of Sidney, but she realized that she found solace in Jose'. For some reason, he had forged a fast, but firm niche in her heart. She fell asleep contemplating the strengths and fears of this reality.

The steady rumble of waves crashing the beach woke them early. They grabbed their boards and were on their way well before breakfast was served. Of course, Popi had a story to tell even if Cheyenne was listening more to the ocean's serenade than his folklore. "After I got out of bogus drug rehab, around July Fourth, 1975, Lester taught me to surf. Yes, you heard it right. As a teen, I put myself in a drug rehab, but that's a story better told some other time."

Bogus drug rehab caught her ear; she'd heard it used before by a much younger person than Popi. She thought if the rehab worked, it couldn't be bogus.

"How could I ever forget when Lester handed me his surfboard? He figured I wanted to try it 'cause I'd been out swimming in the waves next to him for hours, body surfing. He was correct; I wanted to learn to ride those waves on a board more than anything. The other reason it was so memorable was because it was the only time I ever rode a board that was missing its nose; not only the nose, but the entire top fourth of the board was missing. Lester had nose-dived the board into the sand too many times, but it didn't matter to me a bit.

We were at Shark Pit; the surf was a glassy four-to-six foot, generated by a stationary tropical storm between Florida's northeast coast and Bermuda. By mid-afternoon, Lester was worn out, so he handed me his surfboard and pointed me toward the ocean. Not much of a lesson was it?

I caught a break and paddled out between a set of waves in no time. Each time I paddled for a wave I'd chickened out before hopping up on the board. Thirty minutes went by and then an hour and I hadn't caught a wave. As it got later in the day, the majority of surfers had exited the water. Sitting out there all alone, I saw what I thought was a dolphin fin coming my way. By the time I realized it was not a dolphin, the large fin only ten-to-fifteen yards from me, slipped under the surface. I started paddling towards shore, and caught the next wave on my belly to the sand."

Her eyes popped wide open, and her mouth dropped at the horrifying prospect of him becoming shark bait.

He instantly regretted his tale, so he tried to reassure her. "No worries, child. I've never even seen a shark in these waters, or even heard of a shark attack on this whole coast. A little fear is okay; it gets the adrenaline going. Just show the ocean respect and your fear will subside; at least a little bit at a time, if not all at once. It should never go away completely. You may get a big surprise; I'm sure you'll do just fine, you'll see."

She shook her head and raised her eyes upwards; thankfully, she didn't take Popi too seriously. "The word fear isn't in my vocabulary!"

As they made their way through the coconut trees, she saw white water rolling into the beach. It reminded her of the legend of the unicorn, and how the sea captured them. You could see them stampeding in the windswept advance of the crashing waves the story went. Her excitement lifted her high up on her tiptoes; this was a lifetime habit she had developed as a toddler, according to her mother.

The sun was nearly breaking over the palm-lined beach by the time they got there. Popi, shirtless, with baggies draped low from his disappearing hipline, was carrying his board under one arm and two

Banlon rash-guard t-shirts (one for each of them) in the other. The low, soft morning light illuminated his face in such a way as to defy his age. Without a word, they set their boards down parallel to each other with decks up in the cool dark sand. She had saved a scrap of wax for a final, fresh coat on her board before the paddle out. She did not want to slip.

Popi went through a regimen of warm-up and stretching exercises that reminded her of the yoga classes she had attended since her early teen years. "Yoga?" she wondered aloud.

"Yoga helps me get centered, and helps with the surfing, also. Keeps this old man limber and more balanced" as he patted his belly and faked a full body wobble. "Through the years, I have added some of my own wrinkles, excuse the pun, especially for my pre-surf ritual. I added in some Tai Chi and high school gym class stuff. Sometimes, in surfing, you have to dish it out to keep from getting dished in a figurative way. You can punch the wave with the tail of your board. If you don't land it right, the wave will pound you, and the unicorns will trample you but good. I think everyone should use a pre-surf ritual to get primed. Sometimes it is the best of the day, and you don't want to blow it. When each one gets better, praise the Lord! It is a special day."

She was intrigued. "Unicorns?"

"Unicorns." huffed Popi, as he kept up his routine. "They only run free when a wave breaks, anymore."

"Unicorns? How did you kn ..."

Before she could complete her wondrous question, Popi chimed in, "I dreamed of unicorns last night, or was it while I was walking here to the beach? Didn't we talk of this before? It doesn't matter; I will run free with the unicorns today. I will be ready to paddle out soon, but first things first."

He began assuming a series of yoga positions; the tree, downward dog, half locust and so forth. He flowed freely into each one as he purposely engaged in deep breathing. He continued to speak in a low, steady, measured voice. "All that I teach you today you already know. I have shown you this before, when you were very young. Do you recall?"

He looked at her with a sincere face and inquiring eyes.

"Yes, I believe so, Popi." A chain of memories, back to the days when she first learned to paddle a surfboard, started returning to her.

"Good! You believe. I believe, also. You can see yourself surfing in your mind's eye, and I can see you. You'll do it; it will occur here soon. Never forget, the greatest surfer is the one having the most fun! It is like this with everything in life, but you already know this is true. "

She started her own ritual; a mixture of deep knee bends, push-ups, and crunches. It only took one time for her to realize rolling in the sand wasn't her idea of fun; no wonder they make sandpaper out of beach sand. She was anxious to get out in the surf to rinse off and go for it.

Popi's ritual went on. One moment he was doing a full locust, and the next he was flat on his back on the ground, placing his hands and feet under his sandy body to arch his back, and lifting up to do backward pushups.

Cheyenne watched so intently that she was unaware someone else had joined them, and she was startled by the kudos ringing out from behind her. "Monster pose, old dude!"

Two pre-pubescent boys walked past them with boards in hand. They went fifty feet further down the beach and without hesitation started to paddle out. To Popi, they appeared to be upside down as they popped over the first wave and paddled confidently out through the chest-high surf breaking near the beach.

He was finally ready to go. Thankfully, she was not only patient, but she had been a competitive swimmer in high school. The muscles in her lanky arms were fit and firm. She could swim a mile with ease, a trait she shared with her grandfather, who had been a swimmer all his life. However, she must have gotten her patience from the other side of the family. He was always working on it, though, even at his advanced age when many an old codger just resigned himself to being a jerk. She admired him for his attitude.

She was a natural, and not only had she absorbed Popi's long list of directions, she had paid attention to her surroundings, as well. As soon as she hit the water she ran down the mental checklist that Popi had laid out; chest up, head up, fingers together, hands cupped, dig deep on every stroke, duck dive under the wave; the bigger the wave, the deeper the dive. Keep your body balanced on the board, front to back, too. Once you commit, don't turnback; go for it! As she applied her lesson, she realized that it could take some time to do it.

She found staying centered on the board wasn't so easy at first, but it became less of a challenge with each stroke she made. Together, they gleefully made it over the smaller inside waves and out past the breakers without incident. Popi nodded ahead and said, "Cheyenne, watch those boys. The little Groms rip!"

But her eyes were following a squadron of brown pelicans coasting along the crest of a single incoming wave; they glided in precise single-file formation, undulating in unison with the shape and movement of the wave. It was synergy in nature.

One-by-one, the pelicans dove on scattering schools of mullet, or lisas, as the locals called them, migrating along the shoreline. The graceful, pouched predators had found their gravy train. The leader banked and dove straight down. The others followed, bursting into and smashing up the schools of lisas from above. They sat up to drain their beaks of water, enjoying an easy meal.

Some game fish joined in the fray. The haggard lisas were now being chased from above and below. In a panicked frenzy to escape a savage death, the terrified bait leaped out of the shredded water in every direction. It was very exciting to be so close to the action. Her attention then turned back to Popi.

"What's a Grom? A kid?" asked Cheyenne.

"You got it. A Grommet is a kid who has learned to surf, and caught the bug. You can't keep them out of the water. A Gremmie, or Gremlin, is a kid who is a pure beginner. You can't keep them out of the water, either. Those kids are no gremmies. They shred!"

She kept one eye on the boys as she paddled like heck to catch every ripple the Pacific Ocean sent her way. She caught, or almost caught, more waves than she didn't catch. For a while, she was content to ride them to the beach on her belly. Popi said this was a good way to enjoy the ride and get a feel for how to utilize the energy of the wave.

She loved it! It was fast and fun, and she soon realized how to turn into the face of a breaking wave for longer, faster, smoother ride. Popi even got into the act, and soon they were both riding a long wave together. With her new-found skills taking hold, she dug in on her inside rail, and skimmed along, balanced on her perch while Popi turned and roller-coastered right under her nose. The boys were now watching her!

As they started paddling back out Popi yelled "How about that one! We two-timed it!" After a while, he mostly paddled back and forth, tagging behind Cheyenne, tossing her words of encouragement and coaching her non-stop.

The boys surfing nearby were having their own fun. For grommets, they caught their fair share of waves and knew a few nifty tricks to do on them. They overheard Popi barking orders; "Paddle, paddle now!" and "Stand up, stand up now!" seemed to be his two favorites. Soon they were laughing and playfully mocking Popi's shrill commands when he overdid it. He took the hint and smiled apologetically to the boys. "She's my granddaughter. What do you want? She's doing pretty good for her first time out, don't you think?"

"Sure, whatever. She's catching some waves." Despite their tune, the grommets felt an affinity for the old surfer. He could still hold his own, and they liked the attention when he whistled or whooped for their best tricks. Cheyenne was starting to become acclimated to the activity, and was having no problems catching the waves. She scrambled up to her feet a couple of times, and was ready to make one all the way in a standing position; she just needed to apply the right technique.

All of a sudden, a rogue, overhead set wave came barreling out of nowhere, directly to where Cheyenne was waiting alertly. She eyed the wave and set her sights on catching it, regardless of the fact that it was the biggest one to come in all day, by far. Instinctively, her brand new confidence kicked in, and she wheeled her board around and committed to the challenge. She dug in and paddled deep and hard.

Meanwhile, Popi and the boys could clearly see that the wave would closeout all at once and douse Cheyenne with a wall of turbulent white water. "No! No! Not that one! No!" they all hollered at once.

This wave did not behave as its smaller cousins. It jacked up, grabbed Cheyenne and her board on the way, and launched them both into midair before flipping her into the trough. The lip blew up right on top of her. It drilled her upside down and backwards through the surface just in time to bury her under a significant wall of tumultuous whitewater with a thunderous blast. She tumbled head over heels like a rag doll in a washing machine.

She instinctively held her breath as the spinning current pinned her and the board to the bottom. She remembered Popi's strict orders. "If you know you are going to get drilled, always get a good gulp of air before going under. You'll need the oxygen, and it will make you more buoyant. Do not panic! Just relax peacefully until it lets you go. I open my eyes; it helps. It always lets you go, sooner or later; sometimes you just have to wait it out."

At first there was a loud groan from her all-male audience, but when she came popping up in knee-deep white water and pumped her fist to the sky, they broke into yelps and cheers. She pulled her board under her as she launched it backout to the break to shouts of, "Yeah! Gnarly! What a drop! Yeah!" The enthusiasm on her face was contagious.

As she began to paddle, she noticed her rash guard had nearly been pulled over her head by the wave's tremendous surge. She blurted out "Oops! Better watch out for the ladies!" as she pulled on her top down for a better snug. As she did, she noticed another woman paddling out from the beach.

Deaun was knee paddling out on a solid black surfboard. It looked to be a 9', or maybe a 9' 6". It was certainly not new.

Popi observed as Deaun made her way out and over to Cheyenne. When Deaun reached the spot where she was, she waved the boys over. It was easy to understand their body language; they were eager to be introduced to Cheyenne. The group talked and nodded for a minute before turning in unison to wave at Popi, who was sitting fifty yards to their north, resting on his board. His hand went up as he cheerfully returned their salutations. The sun's light was now glaring brightly, and it limited the finer details of their reflections.

As the morning progressed, those four stayed together while they frolicked in the surf. Popi kept his distance; he knew there was much for her to learn. He had helped her enough for one day; let her learn to apply it on her own. It took him back to the time and place when he was a beginner. He studied the way others surfed, mimicking moves, and improving on techniques. He avoided their flaws and mistakes. He often admired and respected the skills of other surfers, and he had a lot of fun sharing the waves and wholeheartedly encouraging their success. She would do likewise.

Deaun's surfing skills were quite obvious as she caught the best of the waist to chest-high sets at will on her blackboard. She rode effortlessly, riding one right after another of the small glassy faces to the beach, and she gracefully kicked out to leave the petering wave behind as it was spent on the empty shore.

Cheyenne belly-boarded a second wave until she was planing along the face at a good angle. Suddenly, she pushed up with her arms, and swung her feet under her shoulders, with a twist of her torso like Popi had made her practice several times. She stayed upright and maintained her balance. She was flying! She leaned hard on her back foot while pointing the board up and over the back with the other just as the thick lip was lifting to come over. Her momentum took her airborne from the ramp effect of the wave. She floated effortlessly over the thunderous wall of white water as is rushed away from under her. She did a curtsy as she descended into a slapping splash in the clear, smooth water behind the mayhem.

The boys and their mom watched her and then celebrated her success! The four were surfing and getting along together like they'd been friends for a lifetime. Popi had slipped out of the water and was sitting comfortably with his legs crossed under the shade of a tropical almond. He had seen Cheyenne's first-epic drop and the consequent escape, and he was happy for now to watch them surf, smoke his pipe and hide from the sun under the almond's canopy.

"Ah, Paradise, again" Popi cooed as some pelicans sailed by to hone their hunting skills under his wary eye. He narrated their flight. "Faithfully prowling the surf line for their next chance to fill their pouch with a pescado treat; a fine flock of feathery friends for sure. Bon appétit!"

"Hiding?" Cheyenne questioned as she placed her board down next to his and ran up to greet him.

"Only from the sun," he said as he smiled up at her.

"It was incredible! Did you see that Popi? I surfed; I really surfed!"

She plopped onto the dark sand and laid back with her head propped against a chunk of drying driftwood. After holding her pose for a few seconds, she sat straight up, spread her hands out on the sand and braced herself with her arms. She leaned her head forward and let her red curls drip rivulets of seawater down her face. "Ah, Paradise, again," he thought.

Before he could comment on her epic accomplishment, Deaun trotted up to them with her board under her arm. "You were awesome Cheyenne! What a kick-out! You went flying! How long have you been surfing?"

A smile spread across Cheyenne's face. "Thank you, but I just started today! Deaun, you ride the crest as effortlessly and graceful as those pelicans fly — so beautiful!"

Popi's curiosity was peaking and his patience was waning. He could see the bottom of Deaun's blackboard, but he wanted to get a good look at the top to ascertain something. "Please, may I see the top of your board, Deaun?"

She handed it over. His face lit up as he flipped the board over. It was true; it had a step deck. "This is a very special board, one of a kind; magical."

"Yes, it was a gift from my Papa. He gave it to me many years ago."

He reverently lifted the board. "This board is a one of a kind, the Black Cat model. Miki Dora modeled it, and Greg Noll produced the step deck and nose rider. The Black Cat became the symbol for malcontent surf expatriates like my friends and me who travelled to new places looking for uncrowned breaks with no hype. The first board I ever owned was a Black Cat. I learned to nose-ride and get tubed at Sebastian Inlet on it. I loved to shoot the curl from the nose; what a rush!" His voice quivered with excitement as he handed it back.

Deaun shook her head and smiled. "Yes, I also learned on this Black Cat, here on this beach. It is the only board I have ever owned. My father brought it here where he was from, California. He was close, very close, to the men who shaped it. He often surfed and traveled with that crew. They came here; they were perhaps the first men ever to surf Costa Rica's waves." Her voice trailed away as she added "He met my mother at that time."

Deaun's surfing prowess might just prove that the fruit doesn't fall far from the tree. He hopped to his feet, and Cheyenne followed suit. Deaun set her board next to theirs, and they walked towards the swash as he began to explain how he got his first board from a neighbor kid who had carried it from California to Florida. "The kid's dad had been transferred to MacDill Air Force Base in the 1960's. He was disappointed with the Gulf Coast surf and was glad to sell it cheap."

He looked longingly at Deaun's prized possession. "I suspect you appreciate the value of your board. You understand that it is perhaps the most sought-after board ever made."

Deaun listened intently and nodded her head in affirmation.

"Deaun, your board is worth thousands of dollars," he told her.

She lifted her chin and threw her shoulders back with outright confidence. She declared right back "Ah, no; not my Black Cat. My Papa gave it to me, and he taught me how to ride it. It is the only board I'll ever ride; to me, it is priceless."

Standing shoulder to shoulder with Deaun, Cheyenne added supportively "Some things are more valuable than money, like riding a black beauty on white unicorns."

Popi nodded slowly, and the two ladies joined him with nods of agreement as they watched the two boys catch their last waves and perform their frenetic maneuvers all the way into the beach. Before they could run off, their mother said, "Miki and Grady! If you want to surf later, come see me after you get cleaned up and eat your breakfast. I have a few chores for you boys to do."

Always in chorus, they yelled back "Yeah, sure, mom!" as they raced off playing a game of grab fanny. Deaun shook her head. "Boys! I pay them when they do extra chores, but all they ever want to do is surf. Grommets!"

Popi chuckled in their defense. "Thank God, some things are more valuable than money." His words echoed back at him carrying a cryptic message. He realized what he had with Cheyenne was priceless; he wouldn't sell it, nor could he buy it.

A delightful selection of fresh slices of chilled pineapple, papaya, mango and banana, kicked off their morning feast. One of the groms had placed everything on a finely varnished rosewood table, enhanced by a centerpiece of fragrant flowers. The spread was positioned in an Eden-like alcove across from their cabanas.

They savored the fruit as it cleansed their salty pallets. Cheyenne devoured the Tico house special of rice and beans topped with two fried eggs, bacon and toasted, homemade banana-nut bread to boot. Popi stuck with his traditional bowl of boiled oats, garnished with more fruit and homemade granola. He claimed it kept him regular. "Oats don't clog your heart and arteries."

Cheyenne, red-faced from the intense tropical sun, finished the first pitcher of water with very little help. Then she let out a man-like belch and a hearty laugh to match! As Popi squeezed a fresh lime into the second pitcher, he teased "You must've swallowed too much saltwater and air when you got pounded."

Later in the day they combed the beach, searching for sea beans. The high tide had left a broken line of flotsam, seaweed and debris in its wake earlier, and thankfully, the greatest concentration of the ocean's litter was high on the beach under the shade of a grove of tropical almonds. It was the perfect location to search for the seeds that Popi loved to collect. He could do without being scorched, and he was pleased not to be baking his feet in the hot, dark sand. The two of them walked slowly and studied the ground with anticipation.

Within a hundred feet, they had collected a handful of sea beans. He found an old plastic milk jug amongst the seaweed and driftwood, and he cut its top third off with his Swiss army knife, leaving the handle on it for convenience. He stashed their collection of sea beans in the jug one at a time. Lifting his first find up to tell her about it, he said, "First one is a Carao, or Stinking Toe. This tree's fruit can straighten out your blood!" He held it up for her; she gave it a sniff and wrinkled her nose. "The majority of the world's medicines originate in the fauna and flora of tropical rain forests. Sad to know only one percent of the world's plants have been assessed for their medicinal values."

Without warning, he tossed the seed to Cheyenne; she swiftly grabbed it from midair without a bit of hesitation. Then, he went on. "Next is a Monkeys Comb that looks more like a club, then a star nut, and this one is a walnut. I don't know what that one is doing here. This nice one is a West Indian locust, and here's a bloodwood seed, a Mexican oleander and a sea heart; you found this one, so you may have luck in love soon. That's what they say, anyway.

Here is a hog plum; I hope your new lover isn't a plum hog! And here's a palm nut; the locals call it a monkey face ... can you see it? Better your man has a monkey face than be a plum hog! Let's find some more sea beans; maybe we'll find a Prince Charming Pod. You can always kiss a frog if we don't; ha, ha, ha!"

Cheyenne feigned embarrassment. She gave him a little wave of the hand to brush him off and focused on the tide line again. There were many shapes and sizes of multicolored objects; they were parts of objects and containers made of plastic strewn all along the high-water mark. "Look at all of this junk, Popi. Where does it all come from?"

He grew serious. "Plastic is one of the biggest problems for the ocean. It makes up ninety percent of all the trash floating on the surface. Why is there so much plastic in the ocean? It is hardly biodegradable at all, and sunlight breaks it down into smaller and smaller pieces that never really go away. Tons of plastic items get caught in ocean currents and form swirling vortexes of plastic debris called ocean gyres. The Great Pacific Garbage Patch off the coast of California is the largest ocean-going garbage dump in the world; it's twice the size of Texas. It will be impossible to clean it up completely."

Cheyenne fired back. "All marine life is at risk, great and small. It's estimated over 100,000-marine mammals, and a million seabirds die each year from ingesting it or getting tangled up in it. Plastic is toxic once it hits the ocean. The particles are magnets for all types of chemicals, toxins, and insecticides like DDT. That stuff just keeps traveling up the food chain until your seafood dinner is not fit to eat. It is a crying shame; we don't need it."

"Well, nevertheless, this jug came in handy for these sea beans!"

She looked up again from her search. Trying to be cheerful as she readjusted her eyes, she said, "We can only do what we can do."

He shook his head in agreement.

Walking slowly, combing the wrack, they made their way along quietly for a while. They both spotted the same small black seed perched on top of a pile of bleached out driftwood twigs. It stood out like a black pearl on an ivory-colored incense altar. She bent down to pick it up and inquired, "What's this one, Popi? Is it my Prince Charming Pod?"

"No, child, but it is still good luck. It's a Mary's bean! It is also called the Crucifix Bean. Do you see the cross? A Mary's bean holds the record for the longest recorded drift; fifteen thousand miles. People around here use them as good luck charms and to ward off evil spirits, and women in labor hold one tight to make for an easier delivery. Some seeds have been handed down for generations as treasured keepsakes. They use them as an antidote for snake bites in

Nicaragua, and I hear they use them to cure hemorrhoids in Mexico, but I have no idea how, nor do I care to know how!"

After they'd scoured the beach, her attention was drawn to a lone surfer riding the waves with command and grace. His turns were long and ended high on the wave, and he careened off the top of the wave to reverse direction. He worked down the face, cutting at its surface incredibly fast. He paddled out with equal power, just barely making it out to a set wave.

Without breaking his stroke, he whipped his board around mid-face and cupped his hands as he dug deep to catch it. She watched and thought the wave would surely close out, but the ocean lifted him way up as he launched into the wave. Within a second, he was up on his feet, and in a flash he was sliding straight for the bottom on the chunkiest wave of the day.

Turning off of the wave's bottom so hard, he easily dragged one hand in the water by barely reaching out. Up he flew, almost straight back past the face, thrashing the breaking curl; he rebounded quickly back into the wave. Then he charged down to the bottom again, where he leaned hard into a fish-hook turn and sprung like a slingshot down the face.

He did a 270-degree turn back towards the curl, pointed his board's nose straight up and was upside-down and backside, before he blew through the lip and snapped himself back into position on the face. Barely escaping the crashing lip, he leveled out and stood up straight in a casual pose that he maintained all the way to the beach. Cheyenne picked up her pace and hustled his way as he picked up his board and stripped off the leash from his right ankle. They were soon face-to-face.

Popi saw that it was Jose'. Popi knew he would find her, or she'd find him, when she found the sea heart, even though he wasn't superstitious that way. These things have a way of working out even without the bean.

It took him back to the time when he met Virginia. Everything happens for a reason, doesn't it? These two had a natural attraction, a powerful chemistry, a passion held in reserve for each other. It was clear to Popi, but Cheyenne and Jose' were only approaching the realization for themselves.

She immediately asked him "Why didn't you go for air, like I always do in the closeout?"

"Like you always do? I thought you had never surfed before" Jose' retorted.

"I catch on fast."

"Not too fast I hope" Jose' bantered.

"Whatcha' worried about, Joe? 'Fraid I'll catch ya?" she taunted him in a playful singsong.

Jose' ended the spirited volley. "That's the very least of my worries, my dear senorita."

Popi kept a discreet distance until Cheyenne called him over.

"Popi, do you remember Jose' Artz? From San Jose?"

Their hands connected as they made cordial eye contact. Popi looked to Cheyenne, and assured her that he did. "Of course! This is the fine young gentleman who guided us safely to the bus terminal. Good to see you again, Jose'. You and I were never properly introduced. I'm Stan Manly, Cheyenne's grandfather. Most young folks just call me Popi; you might as well join them."

"Alright, Popi. It is my pleasure to know you."

Standing ankle deep in the swash, the three of them stood there talking. "Do you surf here often Jose'?" Popi asked.

"Not really ... sometimes. I came here to find Cheyenne and you. I had a feeling you'd be somewhere nearby if I didn't wait too long." Popi's eyes casually watched Cheyenne as the corners of her mouth rose. Below them, the swash washed up their legs, spitting sand and salt. They all turned up the beach together as Jose' continued speaking.

It turned out that Jose' was related to Jorge Rossi Chavarría, who fought with José Figueres in the Civil War against the hardcore Communists. Figueres and Jorge Chavarría both had family back in Catalonia, Spain; their lineage went back to the days of El Cid.

Don Pepe, as Figueres was known by the people, was a champion of the middle class, usually. Jorge Chavarría, since he was honest and astute, had a falling out with Don Pepe over financial policies. Sometimes it was not always an advantage to be a Chavarría; there was still ill will in San Jose amongst some of the old hardliners. Usually though, it was a blessing.

His grandfather was well-liked and made many friends at every level of society. He helped to orchestrate the growth of private banks to allow competition with the state-owned banks of the old Junta, and he also helped to establish credit unions for the rural Indians and Mestizo farmers. Some owed their property and livelihood to his efforts.

However, Jose' was only interested in being a modern, progressive, independent Costa Rican lawyer, working to protect his country and its resources. He had no political aspirations at all.

Popi turned the conversation back to surfing as his pace led the group on a walk along the shoreline. "How about Hermosa? I love that break!"

"Yo amo Hermosa; the tree," said Jose'. "It's a wave magnet. It catches the swell as well as most anywhere in Costa Rica, even perhaps as much as Dominical.

Popi recalled the first time he saw Hermosa's iconic tree. "Back in the day, Jaco and Hermosa didn't exist, other than being names on an Old Spanish map."

Popi raised his hands and arms up, motioning to the surrounding lands. "It was all undeveloped; not a bit like now. We had to drive on the beach because there were hardly any roads at all. Buildings near the beach were few and far between. The first time we came, we had to drive through a pig farm to reach the Rio Tulin. The only passable trail was right through this farmer's pig gate.

It was a pretty big area he had cleared off by hand; he had just left the big stuff and gnarliest underbrush. The locals used the path through there for donkey carts, bicycles and foot traffic, but sometimes he didn't see anyone come through for days. Funny how those four-hundred pounders would lay right there in front of you. You could honk all you wanted, but I can't say I ever saw one getup to move out of our way; not once.

Later, when word got around about the good waves, clean drinking water and pristine conditions, surfers started trickling down here on a regular basis. The farmer's kids would run out to open the gates for them. They'd have huge smiles, and were always shoeless, and usually shirtless, happy, and just looking for a handout.

I can hear them in my head. 'Pura Vida! Mi! Mi!' They'd extend their grubby little hands for the money. I considered it an urchin toll; I always gave the cute little crumb snatchers an American dollar bill each. My buddies would get bent and say I set a bad precedent; they would expect a dollar every time from now on. They might get mad if they don't get one."

Eventually, the old guy got a tractor and graded a decent dirt road, and he never charged a toll. The kids probably collected more without a set rate.

I imagine that eighty percent of the surfers who have ever come to Costa Rica have been to the Hermosa tree, even if they got there just to chicken out on the biggest day."

Jose' and Cheyenne respectfully agreed, nodding their heads, as Popi rolled on. "That tree is the undesignated symbol of Costa Rican surfing. Today there are condos lining the section just south of that tree, back off the beach, where the pig farm used to be, and that dirt road is a paved two-laner now. You can only reach Rio Tulin by foot or boat. Those crumb snatchers probably made out alright. Why beg money when you can pave the road and build a resort?"

With downcast eyes, Jose' shook his head affirmatively and added "One day soon they're probably going to take the tree down."

They all chatted as they made their way up the beach to the shade. Jose' utilized his allotted time for communication well, explaining how he was working his way through graduate school in San Jose.

He shared the story of how his mother's family migrated to Costa Rica from Ponce, Puerto Rico, when she was a teenager. "The island was becoming over-populated and the culture of their ancient neighborhood was digressing into a rough, barrio mentality. Her family feared for her future and that of her brothers and sister. If they were to move, it would be to a place that was not spoiled by too much American growth. They sought a fresh start in Costa Rica where they could maintain dual citizenship.

My parents' insight was extraordinary. They are both college professors. My mother's transition from Puerto Rico was difficult at first, but manageable. She was surprised by the cultural differences. After all, they are both Latin American countries. Once she finished school, she got a job teaching at one of the city colleges in San Jose. There, she met my father, who was teaching economics and mathematics. They married, settled down in their careers and decided to raise a family. It has all worked out well. They teach at the university, now. The education here is top notch and well-balanced. That's why we are almost all conservationists."

He told the story exactly the way he had always heard it; it was obligatory. Cheyenne listened attentively while she unconsciously fiddled around with an odd-looking sea pod that she had picked up. She secretly deemed it her Prince Charming pod. It was the size of a squash ball and oddly similar to a sea urchin, minus the painful needles.

"Senor Manly, I would like the honor of taking you and your granddaughter out on the town in Jaco tomorrow evening. Indeed, things have changed since you were here last. Please, be my guest, and I will show you some modern-day fun."

Cheyenne's contracting fingers cracked through the stiff outer shell of the strange sea pod at that very instant. The brittle ball shattered in her hand, exposing a small army of tiny crabs. "Oh, my gosh!" She lightly screamed and threw her hands up. The mini crustaceans were broadcast everywhere; they scampered in all directions as soon as they bounced in the sand. She looked to escape, sending dust up in a rooster tail behind her as she wheeled around to cut a quick circle in four hasty steps backward.

That gave the men a quick chance to chuckle before she killed the comedy with a shot across Jose's bow. "Where I come from the man asks the lady before he speaks to her family! We make our own decisions in this day and age!" Cheyenne's eyes locked on to Jose' as she slipped him a wink. She wanted to be firm, but by no means did she want to scare him away.

"Pardon, senorita Cheyenne! I meant no disrespect to you. Where I come from, showing respect for your grandfather comes first." He took her willing hands, crossed them into his, looked affectionately into her eyes and said in a low, sober tone "Even if our hearts were to become one, our cultures might not always meld."

She was caught completely off guard, but not Popi. As he started back- stepping away, he thought "Here we go; I knew it. Sea bean or no sea bean, it's on. The poor girl's heart ain't got a chance, and his chances don't look so good, either. Life is great, but love can hurt." Popi tickled himself, again, and he laughed out loud.

He lounged in an old hammock while he enjoyed a smoke and watched the sun sinking toward the sea. In the distance, Cheyenne and Jose' walked on the beach, hand in hand. From his view, they seemed to be looking at each other much more than talking. "Ah, go on. What are you waiting for?"

He recalled his and Virginia's first kiss; it was electric. It seemed like yesterday, not more than fifty years ago. The sight of Jose' with Cheyenne flooded him with precious memories. From his hammock, he twisted his head to stare a little harder at Jose' and said aloud "Go on, bonehead. Kiss her!"

Popi was pleased with himself. Jose' followed his psychic directions and gave Cheyenne a tentative kiss on the lips. She drew back slightly, but only to give Jose' a sweet look of approval. Then, they embraced to savor a prolonged rendering of the original, while framed and backlit by the setting sun.

Settling back into his hemp refuge, Popi whispered to himself. "If you painted a picture, or put it in a story, they would call you a liar."

They soon returned hand-in-hand. Jose' had to head back to San

Jose for his early morning classes. He promised to be back in time for their date in Jaco the next evening, and reminded Popi that he was more than welcome to be his guest for the entire night.

"Guest?" Popi jested. "You two might just need a chaperone."

As Jose' parted, he spoke in Spanish to Popi. "Por lo que oigo, es posible que necesitemos para encontrarle un chaperon."

"From what you hear, I need a chaperone? That's funny! I wish! I truly wish."

The hues of the evening began to change in the ambient glow of twilight. Popi started to the hotel ahead of Cheyenne as she watched Jose' recede into the dying embers of the day. She had no trouble catching up to him, and she placed her hand on his shoulder. "Popi. Eat and then to bed; that's the plan."

"Sounds like a plan to Stan!" As he drifted asleep again he sorted through the fragmented segments of Alina's halting tale, revisiting them as if they were pieces to an impossible puzzle. Then the sheer force of his incubus shook him awake in the pitch black night.

The next morning Popi arose before the sun when the Pacific Ocean mysteriously called him from his slumber. He had been listening closely to the sounds of the sea since early in the predawn hours, and now the melodic rhythms of waves breaking were joined by a chorus of birds chirping, chattering and cawing to compose the morning's song. "Nature's music," he thought to himself as he was climbing out of bed.

The deep, enduring rhythm and shrill melodies beckoned like a psalm, and he began an impromptu chant.

You are but a simple man, The Lord, he hears your prayers.
He does the same for any man or anyone who dares.

I say that you are rich in him; no matter you are poor.
He sent these gifts for you; rolling thunder as they roar.
There is no time for sleepy heads; I'm knocking at your door.
I beckon you from dreaming; come out deep beyond my shore.
Come on, come on and dance with me, the day is yet begun.
Dance you with the unicorns, and dance with the rising sun!

A Buddhist monk he was not! "Who needs Haiku when you can sing the morning's song with the ocean and the birds?" he said to nobody in particular.

He lay motionless, counting the number of waves coming in each set. "Six to eight waves to a set, and a set coming every five or six minutes. A big set every twenty-five minutes or so, with three-medium waves followed by two huge ones, and one undulating 'tweener wave. All three are closeouts! Take the third wave of the thirty-minute set, it's the best."

He listened so closely that he swore to himself that he could hear the steady, low whoosh of the wave flow underneath the relatively higher din of the crashing waves on the surface. The tide was on its way in from low tide; it had been slack when he first listened. That's why he didn't hear it at first, but now it was making some ominous noise. He found the pulse of the flow and began another ditty in a mock bass voice.

I Hear the tide a' coming, it's chugging like a train.
If it gets much higher now, I know I'll lose my brain!

He stopped and mumbled. "That's dumb. My mind might be playing tricks on me again. Auditory hallucination? It happens this time of the morning; before the darkness fades, I always think the aquarium pump sounds like people talking, and I find myself straining to eavesdrop. I couldn't find the groove, so I might be wrong about the tide. I guess that wasn't the morning's song; I already got that. Why be greedy? I'll just leave that one for Johnny Cash."

He was sure he had separated the sound, but how could he prove it to himself? Oh well, it didn't matter. He would be in the ocean with Cheyenne soon, and it would all sound so good.

Sometime earlier, when he first awoke, he was consumed by powerful thoughts generated by powerful feelings. He couldn't seem to identify where they were coming from. He was tired, but he couldn't shrug them off to get back to sleep. After a while, it was almost overwhelming. There was an unidentifiable apprehension, like a specter lurking in the shadows. He didn't know how to feel; frustrated and anxious? The break of dawn was so far away. He was inexplicably lonely. Was it guilt? For what? There were so many things.

Facing the dilemma with prayer, he started with gratitude and ended in intimate meditation. Feeding his spirit, applied a healing balm to his heart. "Re-creation can come through deprivation or indulgence in recreation. Get it? Re-creation/recreation. Take your pick; I've had enough deprivation for one day, thank you. I'll take recreation, please! Dang! I tickle myself sometimes!"

His exit from bed, accompanied by a low, painful groan, was slowed down by a deep soreness that had embraced each and every one of his aged muscles. He did the sign of the cross as he stood up, thankful for another day, another chance. Soon he sidled up to Cheyenne's door, took a deep breath and broke out in a loud song that strained the limits of his range.

Good morning to yoou! Good morning to yooooo-ooh-ooou!
Here we are in our places with bright shining faces ...
Waiting to see what the new day will bringgg!
Good morning to yoou! Good morning to yooooo-ooh-ooou!

"Let's hit it hot dog! Woof, woof, woof! He could mimic a border collie's bark perfectly; a couple of dogs from nearby yards responded. "Get's em' every time. When they catch on, I swear they get mad at you for being a wiseass."

Cheyenne's sleeping experience was quite the opposite. She was out before her head hit the pillow. The whole night's sleep seemed like an instant, and she was rejuvenated by pleasant dreams that she couldn't remember. But there was no time for remembering dreams; she heard Popi's morning song warbling in through the door. She woke up giggling, stretching her arms out and high above her head. The sweetness of her rebuttal serenade rivaled Popi's in a different kind of way.

"We find ourselves here today facing the sea; we're here to play. We follow the sun it leads our way down to the ocean; we're here to play! Listen to the sounds that start the day; the ones that beckon, reminding us we're here to play!"

Her singing reply surprised her as much as it pleased Popi.

The early start was auspicious in itself and boosted her mood even more. She was almost drunk with enthusiasm. The morning light was the only thing that wasn't bright, yet. It was still looming lazily behind the mountains, casting a bright orange glow that reflected from the bottoms of the luminescent clouds and ringed them with halos. Yes, it was early, but she was ready to go.

As she freshened up and got ready, Popi made two-mixed-fruit smoothies with a blender. Each cabana was self-sustaining, with a combination of wind and solar-generated electricity. She loved the fact that they could enjoy the use of the blender without obtrusive overhead power lines. "Everything is so right!" she thought.

While looking into a mirror at her slightly sun-baked nose and semi-crisp face, she applied a thick coat of sunscreen. Two names came to her lips as she quietly said, "Jose'. Sidney." She took a deep breath, and smiled at her reflection as she wiped away the remaining lotion on her thighs. "Oh boy! What am I getting into?" she said to herself as she went out to greet Popi.

Within minutes, they were standing shoulder-to-shoulder at the beach looking out in awe over the Pacific. To them it seemed there was more of everything today. More waves, more offshore wind, more tide, more pelicans, more fish and much more energy.

Without saying anything, Popi started his pre-surf yoga ceremony and prayer on the damp, dark sand. Nearby Cheyenne waxed her board with a new bar of wax that Jose' had given her and eyed the surf intensely. She saw that Michael and Grady were already out in the water.

"No beating those boys to the beach. I guess that's what makes them grommets."

She walked thigh-deep into the water, tossed her board out ahead, dove in right behind it, caught up and pulled herself on board. Without slowing down at all, she stroked for the horizon. She thought she had made it out when bigger waves than she'd yet seen began breaking well outside. She muttered under her breath. "Special delivery! Reality check for Cheyenne!"

She remembered Popi's advice and paddled as hard and as fast as she could right at them. She duck-dived deep, avoiding the full force of the first mass of white water. She did it again on the second, and third, but the white water from the fourth, fifth and sixth waves would have nothing of it. They rolled her backward in succession. They pounded her all the way back to the beach, where she lay on her board, semi-exhausted in the lapping leftovers. Popi had watched as the ocean expelled her, but he was willing to teach her, if she was ready to learn.

Her youth and confidence from yesterday's success pushed her back out towards the horizon. It was to no avail; she experienced the same result. This time she got out of the water and walked over to Popi. "I can't do it! The Oceano Pacifico is too powerful today! I'm too weak!"

He rolled his eyes, shifted his shoulders down a bit and tilted his head sideways. "You are correct. The Oceano Pacifico is powerful, and you are weak! Why should today be any different?"

Cheyenne dropped her board into the sand and sat down on the deck, dejected. She looked up to see what appeared to be a much calmer and kinder ocean. She knew it looked different from the outside. Popi sat next to her, cupped his hand, and in a low voice, forced her to listen closely. "Child, you can't win every battle with brass. Depend on your strengths, and overcome your weaknesses."

"Popi, I'm just a puny girl; how can I overcome such power?"

"Make an inventory. What do you have that the ocean doesn't have? Listen closely; you have heart and brains, and soul."

The taste of defeat was too fresh. She watched the boys riding the waves as she struggled to get focused. She wanted to ride those waves. Her frustration was apparent. "Popi! Heart and brains and soul? They can't overcome the whole ocean!" She shook her finger towards the water as if the ocean were a misbehaving child.

He instructed her in a calm, steady voice. "Common sense and presence of mind will go a long way. You know the waves; they come in sets, correct?"

She looked at him and nodded.

"The sets come in intervals, correct?"

She nodded again.

"There is a pattern, and timing of the pattern is the key. Strength, courage, and brute force are a waste. Timing! You must learn to watch and study, look and feel. It will lead you to the answers. Remember, Cheyenne, I just remind you of things you already know. You know the motion of the ocean is deep in your heart."

She looked to Popi, and nodded one last time as she turned to look out to sea. Of course! Count the waves, find the day's pattern, measure the time between sets, and use energy wisely. There are times to run, and times to gun.

"Wait for a lull to paddle out. Wait it out; it will come sooner or later." He insisted.

He pointed to a set of five-to-seven foot liquid mounds of stretching, lifting, shifting ocean surface steadily approaching. She was anxious to warn Miki and Grady, but as she cupped her hands to her mouth, Popi settled her with a light touch. "Child, they can't hear you. Remember; do not waste energy."

The set loomed closer. The boys scrambled for the outside for all they were worth. Miki saw possibilities, and he looked right past the very first wave. This might not have been smart. The smallest wave in the big set might have been the only one that wasn't a big close out.

Instead of an exhausting battle with mountains of powerful foam, he could get a good ride on a smooth face, and wait for the chaos to subside before paddling back out. Instead, Popi watched him scratch away from shore and over the safe bet wave.

Meanwhile, Grady spun around, stroked twice, let the wave lift him and hopped up. He dropped in and carved his way down the left. The top of the hurling face feathered from the wind as it hung motionless, right over his head.

The two spectators suddenly forgot about Grady. Somehow, Miki managed to paddle diagonally up, and barely over the next four cresting, vertical mounds, before seeing his chance for what he thought might be a good ride. He paddled and turned in one easy, arching motion across the face of the heaving wave. He kicked like a tapir in a crocodile's jaws. He rose steadily to a crouch, held on dearly to the board's outside rail and raced at breakneck speed under the lip of the wave. With the heel of his foot he pushed down to bury the tail, and dug his fins in deep, leaving a wretched gash in the curve of the wave.

He made a quick, precise turn, stalled, and disappeared behind the thin curtain of the pitching lip. Somehow, he materialized from behind the veil and came flying back out onto the face of the speeding wave. Miki had repeated two more variations of the sequence before he launched a spinning "360" over the back of the powerful beast. He used his forward momentum to head back towards the horizon for another go.

After the last and largest wave broke, Popi, who had just finished his rituals, made the sign of the cross, picked up his board, and stepped into the ocean. In a couple minutes, he was sitting on the outside with dry hair. He paddled up and engaged the boys in conversation.

Cheyenne waited. She counted the waves and the time between sets as she got a bit sandy stretching and warming up. After the last wave of the third set dissipated, she walked her board out calmly past the first sandbar. She paused for several waves to break before pushing up and jumping over an insider. She sprint-paddled out, and she was easily through the impact zone in a minute flat. By pure luck, or divine Providence, she made it out to Popi with dry hair, too.

She sat up, slapped herself on the leg and said, "Timing! It's all about timing." She contented herself with watching the others find their way into the forceful waves. "For real, Popi, the swell is bigger today! I really don't want to get slammed again! I can't figure out where to take off. They all seem to closeout."

"Just sit by me for a while, and feel it out" he reassured her.

Popi cheered for Grady and Miki, sharing a wave with each of them. The boys initiated their new comrade by taunting him mercilessly as they passed by him on the waves. Of course, they knew he was giving them plenty of room to pass back and forth like fighter planes around a lumbering bomber. "Look out old dude! New school is in session. You're tardy, Popi!"

An hour into it, Cheyenne saw Popi catch the first wave of an oversized set. It took him a full count of two seconds before he got to his feet, and then glided to the right and turned to the inside. Walking back to the tail, he whipped his 8' longboard around like it was nothing; then quick stepped forward to trim it through the boiling white water and into a newly forming left. He cross-stepped all the way to the nose and hung five toes all the way over as he elevated the board like an airplane wing near the top of the curl. He held the position until the wave collapsed inside, where he centered himself on the board and rode the chalk-white soup all the way to the beach. He let it stick in the sand onshore, and took a couple of wobbly steps forward before catching his balance. He dragged the board up from the edge of the water and sat on the deck.

Cheyenne tried to keep her excitement at an even keel. She was ready to try again. She didn't need a coach; she needed a wave.

From the beach, Popi was staring blankly out to sea when he saw feeding roosterfish and pelicans having a field day with the thick schools of migrating lisas that were swarming the scene. This kind of frenzy was not an everyday occurrence. The pelicans and roosterfish combined efficiently to feed on every possible vantage point. Aerial attacks, maniacal assaults from below, mop up operations by both brutal factions served to keep the bait in an utter panic. The strategies of the predators worked to great advantage; they had every angle of escape under control.

After Popi had come in, it was at least an hour before Grady was able to catch a ride on the encore wave of the morning. Like Popi, Grady took the first wave of the set. He blazed left down the shoulder, dipped to the bottom, turned hard, shot to the top, hit the lip, and used his pumping adrenalin to roller coaster his way back to the beach. He pulled a round-house cutback in the shore break, caught his board as it shot straight up at the end of the spiral, wheeled around, gave his back to the ocean, waved over his shoulder and said, "See ya!"

Popi ecstatically bellowed "Aahhh-Whooooo!

Cheyenne kept waiting in her spot. Miki was ten or so meters inside of her when he lined up to catch the reasonably-sized, last wave of the set home. She made sure she was sitting far enough out to avoid disaster by a rogue bomber. "It ain't catching this girl off guard, this time. I'm on it like Calamity Jane."

Abruptly, Cheyenne realized that she was becoming part of an active, dreamlike scene playing out before her eyes. Miki was suddenly escorted by three dark, translucent, silvery fins spreading as they knifed through the water. Sailfish! They broke the surface, in line, at the top of the wave. They made a beeline across the crest, fast on the heels of their terrified prey. Several more were trailing behind them under the surface.

It was difficult to say if they were chasing the mullet or roosterfish. Michael's eyes were fixed down the wave's face, so he hadn't noticed the events taking place right over his head. As he extended his right hand to paddle, it slapped the surface at the very moment that all hell broke loose around him. Mullet exploded like fireworks, shooting through the air, and leaping for their lives to escape the denizens that were in hot pursuit.

Miki was still oblivious to the melee. As he stood up to drop in, a brown pelican was swooping in for an easy meal from the opposite direction. Miki thrust up at the very instant that the pelican tilted his wing to accelerate into a committed dive. The two collided with a loud, wet, smack, and they both landed upside down in the drink.

Cheyenne's jaw dropped as she noted, "Timing is everything."

Before the white water foam could settle, she immediately paddled to the collision site. The pelican flapped furiously to right itself and pulled up high enough to escape before she could get her hands on him. He reacted like it was a fate worse than death. Cheyenne had to stop short and flinch away from the flying spray as the pelican flapped its wings to freedom in a low trajectory right over her. "Well, he's no worse for wear; how about Miki?"

Still miffed by the unlikely spectacle and incomprehensible collision, she desperately searched around for Miki. She was temporarily relieved when she saw Miki's board and paddled over to it, but Miki was nowhere to be seen. Fear did its best to grip her, but she muttered under her breath "Don't panic!"

A moment later Miki surfaced a few feet away. He was choking, and spitting, while holding his hand tight to the left side of his forehead. She paddled his way, pushing his board towards him. Blood was flowing freely between his fingers from a gash above his eye. He struggled to grab his board as he continued coughing and floundering.

She had an idea. She slid off her longer board, released her leash, and then helped Miki onto her board as she undid his ankle strap. She saw his blood mingling with the water on her hand and said, "Oh, my God, what next? Why did I have to say Calamity Jane?"

She decided to leave Miki's board floating and worry about it later. His arms were nearly limp by his sides, and his awareness seemed to fade in and out. Swimming next to him and her board, she pointed him towards the beach, keeping an eye on the horizon as she kicked, paddled and pushed him along in front of her. She exhorted him along the way. "Let's get to the beach. You can do it. Work with me. We can make it."

Luck was with them; in three or four minutes they were halfway home. His bleeding wasn't as bad, but blood still oozed from the gaping cut above his eye. She talked to him, trying to keep his spirits up and settle her nerves. "It looks like it's helping your wound to soak it in the saltwater. It looks clean, and the bleeding has slowed down a lot. You'll look like a tough guy with that nasty scar." He was too groggy clearly to respond.

Between the blunt force of the blow, loss of blood, and his lack of response, she worried she might not be able to get him to the beach fast enough. She kicked even harder when she considered their odds of making it ashore without getting pounded by the next set of waves.

She kept talking to the injured grommet. "No sets yet! We can make it; come on. Lord helps us! We will make it!" She knew their luck might not holdout much longer. She had been counting the minutes between sets all morning. One every five to six minutes, like clockwork, and that was just the average set. She struggled to keep him centered on the board and continued their progress moving forward. His eyes looked as if they were rolling out of sequence in their sockets.

Her fears were soon realized; a series of ocean swells, each stacking higher than the one before it, appeared above the far horizon. Panic nearly spread its dark grip over her, as she cried, "No way this set will wipe us out!" Fighting back, she shook his right arm and hollered "Michael! Michael! Wake up! We can do it if you will only help. Help!"

The first wave of the set was only fifty meters away when a low moan came from deep inside of Miki. Her legs kicked wildly with all her might, pushing the board and Miki desperately ahead. His hands moved; he put one to the cut on his forehead and grasped the rail in a firm grip with the other.

The wave broke way outside and sent a tall wall of whitewater rolling steadily towards them. Cheyenne wasn't sure if Miki was going to be any help. She kicked harder, pushed the board toward the beach, and prayed. The avalanche of thick turbulence ripped the board from her grasp, and her heart sank as she saw that the board and Miki were gone. It was over; she was sure she had failed.

She let the wave have its way with her. She was buried completely by white water, sand and foam. Her broken spirit was ready to accept her watery trap, but her lungs demanded air immediately. She forgot her remorse and fought for the surface, opening her eyes to find the direction of the light. As she lunged and kicked furiously toward the surface, her foot hit something solid; it was the bottom. When she stood up, she found herself in hip-deep water. A little bit ahead of her,

Grady was attending to Miki; Popi was making his way over to her.

A welcome peace and security covered her as Popi lifted her up in his arms. She closed her eyes and drifted off.

Cheyenne feebly called out to Miki as Popi carried her to shore. He soothed her anxiety with not much more than a whisper. "He'll be okay with time. He's in one piece; he'll heal up by the time he is married."

She looked at Popi as he placed her feet down on the beach. "You're lucky you're in one piece. You really got blasted! You pushed him into the wave pretty good for a first-timer. He belly-rode it right to the shore as pretty as you please."

Looking up and down the shore she asked, "Where is he?"

"Deaun has taken him to the hospital to get stitched up. The boy will have a sore head tomorrow. I'll bet the pelican will be feeling it, too."

A mid-morning onshore breeze brushed their faces as they sat for a spell under the almond tree. The wind was fresh and nurturing with its misty, saline breath.

Somehow Popi felt responsible for what had happened. His nerves surfaced as he spoke to Cheyenne. "You need rest. Is this shade good? The wind feels nice; it's thick with oxygen." He avoided touching on the subject of what had happened in the waves.

"Popi, the blood! That was no fun. I was so scared."

"I should have been there with you; it's my fault." Popi's tone paralleled his guilty feelings, and his words were emotional. "I shouldn't have come all the way in; I just didn't feel like paddling back out. I was sure you were doing so well, and the boys were with you. I am sorry. Please, forgive me."

She heard his pain, but she couldn't help herself. She had

experienced similar feelings, but she would have no part of his guilt. She wasn't going to his pity party. She hopped up, took a chin-first pose of dainty defiance and let him know how she felt.

"Wait one-darn minute, Popi! I may have been afraid, but I did fine without you. Anyway, I can see it now; a fine mess that would have been. Me trying to help the boy and watching you at the same time!" She shook her head in mock disbelief and cast him a slim smile.

Her face was lit by a slice of sunlight piercing through the almond branches. He readjusted his eyes, looked from another angle and squinted, but it was still there. He saw a perfect halo framing her face like an angel, or a saint, or something. He thought her grandmother, Virginia, would have been proud of her.

"Fear is dreadful, Cheyenne. Few handle it well, but some handle it better than others. I was afraid you were hurt, or maybe even gone. It shook me. I didn't follow the buddy system, and you must always follow the buddy system."

She regained her composure quickly. She sat back down next to him and offered him an apology straight from her heart. "I apologize, Popi. I shouldn't have said that."

"Said what?" he said as he lifted his chin and shoulders, casting away all his doubt.

"That I didn't need you." She had yet to notice Popi's fast rebound.

"What? You never said that."

"I said something like that."

"Like what?"

"Never mind, Popi, just you never mind!"

"Never mind, what?"

She gave up with a shrug and a smirk. "I don't have any idea, anymore."

"Good; me either."

He smiled and gave her a nod. "Lester once told me anger is a result of fear. He claimed they were directly connected. He would say, 'Fear is one step from being mad.'

Can't say I ever seen a man more scared than Lester was when he told me how his mother murdered Ms. Jess. Fear on his face was all I could see — plenty of fear; no anger, yet. He was right when he told me it took years for his fears to fully manifest themselves into full-blown anger. Then he told me that until he conquered his fear he would never have any rest.

Come on, child, let's get something to drink and put a little food into you. You look exhausted."

After replenishing their fuel they found out that Miki had received thirteen stitches and was being held overnight for observation; the doctor thought he had suffered a mild concussion. Fortunately, he was recovering nicely; his eyes were dilating and contracting, as they should, but the doctor still kept him there as a precaution.

It was time to go back to their cabanas for a long siesta. Cheyenne applauded the custom, sleeping until late afternoon. Popi was restless, and left her to rest while he paced the beach, deep in contemplative prayer. The cool, dense shade of the shore's lush vegetation, combined with the hypnotic rumble of waves, exotic birds, and the hushed tones of the luffing breeze as it sashayed through the foliage all composed an ancient love song in his mind. Their siren voices sang of radiant beauty too convincing to resist. He felt the intoxicating rush of youth, strength, endless possibility, desire and the delusion of being in command of his own destiny. He had often felt this way after overcoming fear and guilt.

He savored the rush but only for a moment. He knew all too well that it was a flawed emotion, and he wouldn't be able to continue for long in its spell. Reality betrayed the illusion long ago. This self-indulgent, self-delusion of command, of control, of forging your own destiny can give a person an incredible ego boost and a sensation of power. It's almost as if the Devil is allowed to give it out by the spoonful so that weak-minded men will sell their soul for more.

"The only thing that is not an illusion is our responsibility. Life runs its course, and sooner or later it humbles all men." He stopped to look out over the vast expanse beyond the curve of the horizon, but again, this too had failed. He exhaled long and low, bringing back equal volumes of air with his mouth and nostrils. He slowly filled his lungs and uttered a humble phrase. "Every knee shall bow."

He continued walking along and breathing steadily. "You can control your breathing. That is one thing you can control, usually. Presence, peace … presence, peace … presence, peace."

He walked on like that for some time, enjoying the presence of peace when Cheyenne interrupted the ether. She came trotting and skipping up, and yelled out to him "Popi! Joe left us a message at the desk! He'll meet us at the chicken place in town! Let's go! It's time to get ready!"

"How many chicken places can there be in Jaco?" asked Cheyenne.

"At least one more" he replied. They had been looking for nearly an hour, but no Jose'. "What's up with that? Meet me at the chicken place in Jaco" he teased. "That's like saying I'll meet you at the clam stand in Ipswich, Massachusetts."

The western sky held the day's final hint of faint light, casting a magenta glow that was slowly sneaking out from behind the dark violet silhouette of a vertical thunderhead. The humidity was thick; one could slice the air with a knife, as the saying goes. The air was saturated; it wasn't raining yet, but it was imminent. As soon as darkness rushed in, lightning flashed in crackling branches along the breadth of the horizon.

"Is this it, Popi?" She turned and pointed to a quaint, early Spanish Colonial café with a broad portico. The bright yellow and red sign flashed "Palacio De Pollo." They could smell the roasting birds a block away. By the time they stepped into the restaurant a light rain had begun to cover the ground behind them.

Jose' was standing right there, chatting it up with a couple of kids standing behind the counter. They were all sporting broad smiles as they turned to see Cheyenne and Popi making their way. "I thought you stood me up!" Jose' admonished in a lighthearted jest.

"You could have told us the name of the place!" Cheyenne volleyed.

Their flirty game was not holding Popi's attention. He scoped the place out; it was Friday night, but it was still early for Jaco. There were only a few customers; he wondered if the rain was slowing the action. Sitting about were two couples and one ex-patriot American, who sat alone skulking over some paperwork, at a small table with his back to the farthest corner from the door.

Popi noted the stranger's ruddy face, greased-back, bottle-dyed, brown hair, ratty flip-flops, baggy khakis, and wrinkled, white cotton Tico shirt. He concluded that the guy had been in Costa Rica for long enough to turn half-local. The American looked like he could handle himself in a dangerous city; he might even make the town a little dangerous. It would be a gamble to trust him for anything, short of murder.

Popi assumed he was the type who is known to travel down to Costa searching for a woman who is twenty or even thirty years his junior. Some displaced country girls are desperate enough to marry or play concubine with any American for the security that they believe he offers. The arrangement could be a tragic mistake for all involved and had often led to miserable conclusions for both sides. The guy looked up, saw Popi's gaze, nodded slightly without changing his attentive expression and went about his business, whatever it was, with a pencil pressed to a yellow legal pad.

The chicken cooking here was purely traditional Tico; roasted, not battered or fried. No pollo frito here; it was delicious, and he savored each morsel. It was served with three or four warm tortillas, but beans and rice were extra. He passed on paying extra for beans and rice. "It never used to be this way. Years ago, every Tico meal was accompanied with corn or flour tortillas, rice and beans, and Lizano salsa; there were no additional charges. Thank you, Club Med!"

A couple minutes later, Emilio, the head cook, came barreling out with a big plate of rice and beans for Popi. A young waitress, a girl of less than fifteen, came scurrying over with a bottle of Lizano. Emilio declared, "In honor of Stan Manly, we will no longer charge extra for rice and beans. This is the Tico tradition, and we will keep it from now on!"

Popi raised his voice. "Bravo! I'm honored, indeed!" as he looked down at his plate, sprinkling Lizano, the go-to Tico condiment, over his arroz y frijoles. Emilio came back with a joke as Popi was digging into his chow. "Thank you, sir. That will be twenty dollars extra for the Lizano! Ha, ha, ha." Everyone but Popi had a good chuckle before he caught on. He would admit at times his self-importance obscured his capacity for laughing at himself.

Cheyenne and Jose' sat close to each other on the bench, across the booth from Popi. It was as if they were a world away from him. After their meal, they stayed to enjoy a guitar duet that came in to provide some ambiance for the late evening crowd. Cheyenne spent much of her time giggling frivolously when not listening intently to Jose's every word.

Popi was glad to see her so carefree and comfortable, and mumbled to himself as the two youngsters enjoyed themselves. "That other dude Cheyenne's dating is too staid and pragmatic. He wants to be sophisticated, but he has a long way to catch up with Jose' in that department."

He didn't care much for what he knew of Sidney. He seemed nice enough, but his inordinate need to manage and control everything around him, especially Cheyenne, made Popi nervous. He had only met him once, and he believed Cheyenne changed her personality to fit within her fiancé's parameters. What would she do with the rest of her personality? Jose' brought out the exuberant side that had been reigned in for her fiancé's comfort. Popi decided he liked Jose' a lot, but what did he really know about him? The reality was; not much.

They stayed until closing. By then, Cheyenne knew a little bit of the life story of everyone employed by or patronizing Palacio De Pollo. Jose' knew them already; he had worked there every summer since he was fifteen. The owner, "Uncle Emilio," was an old associate of his grandfather and was like a second father to Jose'.

Throughout the night, Popi kept a watchful eye on Jose'. He looked tired from his grueling schedule and his day of mountain driving, and Cheyenne was still a bit wiped out from her rescue experience. He thought she should take it easy. Young love would have to wait to express itself; he thought this night was officially over in his mind, but the reality was quite different.

Together the three of them reached the door and peered outside in unison. The rain was still falling softly, but steadily, and lightning strobed in the distant night. Lazy thunder followed much later. The street's potholes were once again becoming mud holes.

They accepted Jose's offer of an escort and off they went, with Jose' leading the way. The rain began to fall harder, so Jose' cut through a small courtyard with a narrow exit under an arbor covered with flowering vines. He entered a poorly lit back street and picked up the pace. Cheyenne and Popi could barely keep up as he turned down an even darker, steeper side street.

The only light in sight was a tiny corner market, or what looked like a small bar. The rain picked up even more, and so did Jose's pace. His hurried steps stomped through the wet ground, splashing mud and puddles up the cuffs of his tailored pants. Cheyenne and Popi did their best to keep up, sloshing along in their flip-flops.

Without warning, three dark figures slipped out from the edge of the street to block Jose's path, and he stopped abruptly to avoid a collision. Trying to keep pace, Popi and Cheyenne came rushing with their heads bowed to the steady rain, and ran right into Jose's backside, almost knocking him into the most formidable looking member of the three.

The bigger kid standing in the middle couldn't have been more than seventeen. "Qué pasa; cuál es su problema?" he asked Jose'. In the confusion of the moment, the smallest of the group stepped in close, bent down low and thrust an extended ax handle behind Jose's leg. The brute of the bunch gave Jose' a hard shove that upended him completely as he tripped over the obstruction placed behind him. He hit shoulders first on the cobblestones with a wet thud.

Jose' started to his feet, but the bigger punk kicked him hard in the liver. The third weasel showed Jose' a cheap, Mexican stiletto, and waved it near his face. Meanwhile, the big thug reached over his shoulder and pulled a machete out of a sheath he had slung over his back. Jose' sat up, and the thug kicked him square in the solar plexus.

The threesome laughed to see Jose' wincing in acute pain and gasping for air. They turned their heads in unison towards Popi and Cheyenne. The sounds of rain hitting the surrounding foliage and Jose' trying to regain his breath were the only sounds as the thugs gazed at the two of them with evil intent. Cheyenne stared back in ready defiance, while Popi shifted his head left to right, seeing if there was a nearby escape. "Ella es muy linda!" he heard one of them say.

As the three boys seemed about to pounce, a husky voice came from deep in the shadows. "What the hell are you doing?"

Recognition of the voice halted the street vermin dead in their tracks faster than a paddy wagon full of cops. The big one lifted his machete and cocked his arm. The deep voice resonated again. "Te cortan tus "albóndigas" y hacerle comer (I'll cut off your "meatballs" and make you eat them)!

The two mangy little hombres bolted, snapping knives closed and dropping the ax handle as they ran. The big matón was left alone, hesitating like a snake in the shadow of a marsh hawk. Without moving, his eyes darted between Jose' and the unseen specter in the shadows. Cheyenne reached down and retrieved the ax handle; she rose up, appearing eager to use it on the bully.

The big, sociopathic scumbag pressed his foot firmly against Jose's stomach and gave a push. In a flash, Jose' grabbed the heel of the assailant's foot with his right hand and yanked as hard as he could. The young criminal fell hard to the ground. Like a cat on a mouse, Jose' reacted, landing on the creep's abdomen, hitting him with a hard elbow to his Adam's apple. Simultaneously, with his free hand, he grabbed the handle of the machete, twisted it out and shoved it under the mugger's nose as the defeated punk gasped for air.

Jose's rage was ablaze in the drenching rain. He pushed the blade up harder and growled "Quién es el loco jodido, ahora? Yo debería Marque te para toda la vida con su propia espada para mostrar al mundo que eres un cerdo). (Who is the crazy badass, now? I should mark you for life with your own blade to show the world that you are a pig.)

Cheyenne protested. "No! He's just a kid."

The bulky form of the Ex-Pat from Palacio De Pollo materialized from the darkness, clasping Jose's arm to prevent any regrets. Jose' turned and saw his face.

"That's enough! Let him up!" ordered Cheyenne. "I'll just hit him with this and send him on his way with a lesson learned."

Jose's elbow rose just enough from the fledgling crook's windpipe to allow him to suck in a precious breath. He shoved the hooligan's face to the stones, helping himself up to his feet. He stood over the young ruffian and spat on the ground next to his face as the reptilian picaro slithered away into the tropical tempest.

Jose' called after him. "May you spend your life sucking the hind tit of a dry sow! Basura!"

The four of them stood facing each other silently for a long moment in the rain before the stranger finally inquired, "Are you all alright?"

The all nodded yes, and thanked him for his assistance. Jose' had been lucky. Besides having a bruised ego and the tousled look of a kid who had been playing soccer in the mud, he was fine. They all were fine; a little stunned, but okay. Popi asked, "How can we repay you for your help?"

"There is no need. I am Deaun's husband. Miki is my son. Thank you for saving him today."

"I'm Lonnie; Lonnie Picco. Deaun told me you would be out on the town tonight and asked me to keep an eye on y'all. You know, just in case something popped up. I didn't come over to your table earlier 'cause I was unpleasantly occupied with business I couldn't put off. I have to stay on top of things, so they don't get out of hand. I think one of my so-called partners is skimming the till. I'm glad I put it away to follow you; this area can be dangerous sometimes."

The steady raindrops began to slow up as the drenched foursome walked shoulder to shoulder down the gravel and stone road, avoiding potholes and puddles as they made their way back to the hostel. Lonnie shared part of his story with them in a low, but clear voice. Cheyenne, Joe and Popi listened closely and matched his pace step-for-step.

"I know these scrums who tried to mug you; they're trouble and getting worse as they grow older. They're street urchins, with no parents to watch out for them. I'll speak to the police, but they probably won't do much. Someone is going to get killed around here any time now. Drugs, mainly cocaine, fuel their violence. Unfortunately, the village has failed them."

After living in Costa Rica for nearly thirty years, Lonnie understood all too well the downturns that development and tourism had delivered to Jaco over the last generation. He had seen it from every angle, from the top to the bottom. "I got out of the States to get away from this kind of stuff, and it followed me here! I don't know; maybe I brought some with me."

His Costa Rican resume was one of decline. He began as a land developer, but after his unethical business partner had left him in the lurch, taking the profits with him, he had to get a job as a construction foreman. When the project was complete, he became a charter captain for a rich American, who owned several boats. He also managed a resort that the same guy owned, and it was there he found the secret to the rich American's cash flow; cocaine.

He had legal and financial issues hanging over his head from his days as a developer, so he had been easy to recruit as a dealer. He ended up smoking some rock with a couple of Colombians who worked under him and became a full-on crack head in one easy lesson. He added prescription pain pills to the mix, and drank himself into oblivion. He found himself involved with the worst elements of society and did things he never imagined his conscience would allow. Eventually, he became homeless and helpless.

As his story came to its conclusion, his tone rebounded and he turned to face the soggy threesome. "Thankfully, for the past four years I've cleaned up my act. Except for burning a little weed, I've been straight. I don't even drink coffee anymore, or use sugar. Healthy living has changed my life. Now, I just grow some pot to sell to tourists. No more hard drugs for Lonnie. Hell, Deaun has me on a wheat-free diet!" A smile crossed his face for the first time and then they all laughed. By sharing his story, Lonnie had become their friend.

The rain had stopped by the time they reached the cabanas. Lightning flashes out were illuminating tall, shadowy thunderheads over the Pacific Ocean. Above them, the stars were slowly filling the void vacated by the passing clouds, and only the faintest layer of cirrus wisps veiled the bright heavens. It seemed you could almost reach out and stir the Milky Way with your fingertip.

As they parted ways, Lonnie again thanked Cheyenne for saving Miki. She did her best humbly to play down his accolades and reject any glory, but he would have none of it. "You are my hero. You saved my son, and I will never forget."

She gave in a bit as she felt a sense of pride rise in her, and she answered right back at him. "I guess we're both heroes, today!"

Before Joe or Cheyenne could say their farewells, Popi smiled at them, waved his hand, and retired to the comforts of his room in silence. Above them, the clouds continued to thin out long enough for them to witness the moon's arrival over the eastern mountains' crest.

Its mystic silver glare danced across the Pacific's rippled surface, and its light drew them closer together until they stood inches apart, then face-to-face, in each other's arms. Their eyes connected like they had been lost and searching for one another for eternity as they fell victim to the undeniable power of their individual desires. Neither of them spoke for what seemed like a few long minutes; their bodies did all the talking.

But she knew Joe had a long day and a rough night, and now he faced a trying late-night drive through the mountains back to San Jose. She reached deeper into his eyes as she struggled with the thought of his pending departure. She touched his body and then wiped away a clump of mud from his chin as she gently asked if he was all right. "I'm so right with you here with me" he answered.

"I believe Popi and I leave tomorrow, Joe. When will I see you again?" Her tender voice trailed off like that of a kid giving up a puppy or kitten. Joe pulled her closer, and again there was no sound other than their breathing. Finally, he calmly reassured her. "These things will all work out."

His hands dropped lower around her waist as he seductively kissed her. Then he released her and turned to walk away. Unable to resist his allure, she reached out and slipped her hand into his, giving it a slight tug back towards her.

Popi heard Cheyenne's cabana door ease shut. As he listened closely for the sound of Joe's parting steps across the narrow gravel path leading under his cabana's open window, his mind drifted. A vision of Eden slipped between his semi-consciousness and vivid perception of stark reality.

A perfectly matched pair of beautiful great southern white butterflies appeared separately at opposite sides of the lush garden. They had fluttered aimlessly from a manifestation of twisted mangrove roots and swaying limbs into a magnificent maze. They flew through trees and ferns, lilies and orchids, flowers and mosses, mushrooms and endless greenery until they nearly missed each other like passing ships in the dark of the night. Then, as if simultaneously caught in a captivating updraft, their flights intertwined as they reached the center of the Garden.

Oscillating and spinning out of control in wild, passionate circles, they touched and affectionately caressed each other time and time again. For a single moment, time stood still as they fluttered in midair, antenna to antenna, thorax to thorax, throbbing abdomen pressed against throbbing abdomen, wrapped and tangled proboscis coming together, surrendering to each other before they resumed their flight in and around the Garden of All Life. In a single magical moment their fates had been consummated, sealed in procreation to the benefit of all future generations in a sliver of time.

Outside Manly's window a light mist returned, transforming itself into a gentle rain that pattered on the tin roof of his cabana. It blended perfectly with the sounds of the Pacific Ocean's energy bursting on the nearby beach. As the sounds carried into his cabana from the distance, Popi drifted dreamlessly away.

Across the way, a timeless bond had been consummated between the young lovers, and a new seed had been planted. A new Garden of All Life would soon take root.

The sunlight was bright, and the cicadas were blaring as Popi stood on the natural-wood porch connecting the cabanas. He simultaneously swung his arms and crossed his hands up over his head as he inhaled a slow, deep, breath until he had connected his fingers and palms perfectly in place. He concentrated as he wiggled, lifted on his toes, rocked to his heels and settled back down flat on his feet.

He loosened his shoulders and snugged them tightly against his ears. He tipped left as he dropped down and over, like a teapot while keeping his feet firmly planted. Then, he repeated the same motions on the opposite side. After a couple more of these, a series of "Sun-Xu-station," and some prolonged downward dogs, his rigid limbs and joints began to be lubricated, restoring most of his flexibility.

Cheyenne was up at dawn listening to the surrounding sounds all about her. Her mind was full of thoughts and doubts, but mostly, and more importantly, dreams. For the first time, she seriously evaluated her future with Sidney; she realized now that she had other options. She missed him, but more like she would miss a brother or a good friend.

Until now, with Joe, she had never felt her heart take the lead. Now, it wasn't waiting around for permission. She had never been intoxicated like this before, and she couldn't quit smiling. Her mind was just along for the ride, but it didn't seem to be complaining at all.

When she climbed out of her bed and slipped into the sunlight of the terrace, she found Popi sitting cross-legged, meditating on the porch. "Good morning, sweetheart! Ready for our bus ride?" he asked.

They were going to catch the bus heading south to Quepos later, but first they had an early brunch with Deaun, Miki and Grady, exchanging heartfelt goodbyes. Michael had taken off from the medical center as soon as he awoke. The nasty gash above his black eye was not as noticeable as the toothy grin that erupted when he saw Cheyenne striding up. The warm hugs and acknowledgments that were exchanged between them testified to the bond that the ocean had sealed between them. Before their departure, Cheyenne walked with Michael to the beach, reliving their incident to the smallest detail.

Later, as they walked their way towards the bus stop, Cheyenne thought about how Michael had sweetly scolded her when she had said, "Adios!"

"No adios; hasta luego amigos!" he told her.

Cheyenne saw the road conditions hadn't improved much since the previous night's rain. One false move on this sparse gravel over clay path with flip-flops and down you could go. "Probably why they call them flip flops and not sandals," she thought out loud.

Popi didn't quite make out every word, but he replied anyway. "Yes, the roads are trouble, but they will dry quickly if the rain stops for a few days. Then the dust will be our next complaint."

The sky was entirely blue. The wind was not even measurable, and the air was thick and oppressive. It was not even nine o'clock yet, and it was already the type of day where you could cut the humidity with a plastic picnic knife, eat it with a fork and watch it reappear a second later, with a little salt added, as sweat dripping from your brow.

They arrived at the bus stop. Made with four three-inch metal pipes that paralleled the ground in a somewhat secured arrangement, it sat on decaying wooden posts. It was rigged up with a tattered, leaky piece of tin on a sparse frame for a cover. A few Ticos rested there, while others stood about here and there under the branches of a massive mango tree. There were young, unattended children playing, stray dogs sniffing about for a morsel or a hand out and a fragile old man sitting on the lid of a yellow five-gallon bucket selling newspapers. He used the bucket to transport his papers and his few worldly belongings.

Popi's arm reached deep into the foliage of the big tree and pulled out a nearly ripe mango. He handed it to the man selling papers, and they exchanged nods and handshakes. A few feet away, Cheyenne approvingly laughed as she watched her Popi. Then her thoughts turned more to the people milling about the stop. "Costa Rica's mass transit system is more extensive than back home; so many more people seem to depend on it."

Popi shook his head in agreement. "There are only a few places these buses won't take you to in all of Costa Rica. Unfortunately, one of them is Matapalo."

Before they knew it, the bus was pulling up in front of them. The clicking of the cicadas had nearly drowned out its approach. They got in and took a seat, placing their backpacks on the floor in front of them. She noticed her arms, and torso, legs and neck were all equally tight and sore from her surfing experience, but it was a good pain. She would cherish her surfing memories, unlike the evil encounter with the dark side of Jaco the night before; that she would rather forget.

The bus was packed, but once again they had managed to find seats together. The weather stifled all of the normal conversation on the bus, and the noise of the big machine had no competition other than the cicadas. Everyone but Popi stared listlessly ahead, frozen in the grasp of the wet heat. Thankfully, the window by their seats was open. He was looking out and watching things go by them. "This is why it is better to take an early bus through here. Buses are wonderful places to watch people. Notice how quiet everyone is now? This is a very low lunar activity period; when the moon is right, they will become more energized. The same goes for the cattle; watch them and you will see there is a correlation between people and cattle, moon-wise. Lester taught me that one."

"Where has this Lester character gone?"

Popi kept looking out of the window as he spoke. "The funny thing is, it would seem, Lester has gone nowhere. He's at the same place he was when we went to school together. As I told you, he still lives in the same house where his mother killed..." His voice had trailed off as he stumbled to complete his thoughts.

The notion puzzled Cheyenne, so she pried a little deeper. "How can that be, Popi?"

"Looking back, there was a time when Lester had become a practitioner of nihilism, and he acted as if he didn't care about anything. Life lost its real meaning for him, and all its intrinsic value eroded away. He was a moral nihilist, and his days were filled with nothingness. His only ambition was debauchery; he was the champion of the apostate and non-compliant.

But later on, he finished the University of Central Florida with honors and got his degree. He would have been at the top of his class if he hadn't been working at the ABC Liquor Store Bar as a bouncer six nights a week. One could never question his work ethic when he applied himself. He got married right out of college and was hired by one of those highbrow financial accounting firms. You know; the type that handles the accounting for the Academy Awards and big stuff like that.

Within three years, he stepped right up to managing an office in Northeast Florida. By then, they had a daughter and another child on the way, and it looked like everything was going to be as sweet as apple pie. They had the All-American family life ... little pink houses for you and me. Lester was going to escape his past, but as we all know, there's no escaping one's past.

A promotion took Lester and his young family away to Honolulu. It broke Albury's heart, but he would never let his older brother know how much he meant to him. The Honolulu office begged for his attention, and his average workweek was fifty to sixty hours. His unquenchable desire to surf and tendency to spend his free time away from home with coworkers caused problems with his new family.

Lord knows what all he was into, but his family played second fiddle while surfing, skirts and the firm took all of his attention. Home life wasn't very exciting compared to all of that."

Cheyenne eyed Popi closely as his story unfolded. She had the impression all of this had a twisted impact on his life, also.

"Occasionally Lester would call me and when I reminded him of family time, he would refer to his wife and kids as Sadie-Can, or Diana-Can. Like, as in Diana can wait, Sadie can wait. Sadie grew weary of Lester's selfish indulgences. Divorce was clearly on the horizon by the time she was pregnant with their third child, and Lester received transfer orders. They were heading back to good old F-L-A, Florida. Sadie was relieved at first, but nothing changed except the location. All of the despicable things he ended up doing back in Florida sealed and stamped the divorce decree. He unloaded his young family with a pitchfork!

At first, when Lester realized the error of his ways led to the ugly termination, he fought it, but after time he slid backwards. He continued on his quest for conquest. The king of the jungle! If a man ever believed he was an island, it was Lester."

Popi's voice gradually trailed off again; his pain was obvious. "Lester's sanity tests the parameters of extremism, anxiety and alarm." Looking out the bus' window, he added "May we continue this story later? It hurts."

He touched Cheyenne's arm as he pointed out the window towards the mountains. "Follow that dirt road and it will lead you to three-cascading waterfalls called Tres Cataratas!"

She thought a moment, before asking "How many years has it been since you traveled down that road?"

He gave a shrug and acknowledged the many years that had passed since he saw the waterfalls. "Been awhile."

"Hasn't this area changed quite a bit?" she asked after a pause. "How can you remember such a thing? It all looks the same to me!"

"Child, there are some things even an old man can't forget" he replied, shifting his bent body up in his seat. "Besides, in this case it was the big green hedge, shaped like oversized bouncing soccer balls back there by the soccer field that tipped me off that the road was near."

Now thirty kilometers south of Jaco, the bus stopped, and he watched three-teenage boys step aboard. They were similar in age and size to the ones who had attacked them the previous night. However, these young men greeted the bus driver politely and were respectably dressed and good-natured. They both wondered what made them different. Where did the community of Jaco go wrong?

Along the way, the bus driver performed his task with the precision of an Olympic athlete as he hurtled the steep foothills of the mountains. The guy was an ace at passing on double yellow lines while heading up or downhill, where you could only guess if there were oncoming traffic ahead. He knew these roads like sweat knows wet. He knew and used every inch of the highway. He leaned hard on the horn as a tactic to get plenty of attention from other drivers; everyone seemed to know he was coming.

Flowering gallinazo trees created a wild patchwork of color throughout the jungle, forest and fields. When she pointed it out, he expounded on its origins. "Gallinazo is a pioneer species that was planted for reforestation, but the wood is so soft it's only used for pulp, boxes and pallets. Beautiful flowers, though. Scarlet macaws like to nest in them because they can dig out a cavity in the wood without any problem."

About halfway to Quepos, Popi crinkled up his nose when he spotted a high-class billboard outside of the Hacienda Monte Mar gated community. It read "Lots from $18,500 Lot - House Packages from $59,000 - 9 Different Floor Plans Available - 15 Lots Total - 8 Lots Still Available."

He muttered a snarly response to the obtrusive sign. "Sounds cheap, but it will cost you to live here, no matter how much money you have. It starts with the gated community and ends up with bullet-proof glass for your SUV."

Meanwhile, the driver was still performing near superhuman feats at the wheel. With miraculous timing and skill, he artfully dodged obstacles like oxen, cattle, dogs, other buses, motorcycles, bikes, potholes and perilously close steep ravines that ended in dry or shallow creek beds.

However, his marks were not as high for sudden braking, nearly simultaneous acceleration and deceleration, making change while driving with his cell phone to his ear, and almost missing many of the bus stops. To his credit, he'd backed up for the disappointed people who had been waiting patiently for the bus. He was also patient with his customers, and not once did he drive off when someone arrived late and made him wait until they caught up.

The dedicated driver was a fairly young man with a young family in Heredia. He slept on the bus five nights a week to keep his job and save money. It was easy to see why his passengers respected him. His nature demonstrated sympathy and compassion, unless, of course, there was an obnoxious drunk to deal with or something worse. But that would be a rare case; Ticos are easy-going and hard-working people.

The sun was dropping, and the moon was overhead when the passengers began to stir and come to life as they drew nearer to Quepos. The cows in the nearby fields stood quietly, feeding in the deep grass of their pasture. It was just another day in Costa Rica, after all!

Quepos had not changed much at all during the past generation. Coming down the road through the flooded mangrove forest into town past Dumas, Popi and Cheyenne paid close attention as they crossed a short, nondescript bridge that led into midtown. The waterfront sat to the right and the bustling business district to the left. As it had been in the past, it remained a busy, well-worn port town. Locals and tourists mingled on the sidewalks and overflowed into the streets lined with storefronts, stands, bars, and restaurants.

Quepos' had earned a worldwide reputation as a sport fishing hub in the Seventies and Eighties, but it had not endured the stress of time well. Recreational fishing interests had been losing a head to head battle with subsistence and commercial fishing. All the years of locals heading offshore at dark in nothing more than tiller-driven pangas to fish their little rigs and the new, modern fleets of large vessels running miles of lethal long lines had taken a tremendous toll on the fishery. It was not what it used to be anymore.

The bus station — the hub of the area — still looked and smelled just like it did thirty years ago. Dozens of Ticos politely waited for the next bus to somewhere, side-by-side, with a small scattering of Americans and Europeans. Under the minimal cover of the portico, it smelled of sweat, farm produce and mildew. It provided little shelter from the tropical elements.

Beneath the rusted tin overhang, an old disheveled man sat like a petty bureaucrat behind a well-worn wooden desk. He collected five hundred colons in a dirty coffee can from anyone in need of the powder room. The flat, once-white, stained toilet was hidden from view by a grubby sheet hung from a dried bamboo stick; privacy was at a premium.

The ticket booth, enclosed in wired glass, was directly connected to the bathrooms. A young stiff-necked fellow working the cash register was talking on a cell phone and smoking a cigarette as he took passengers' money. Cost comparisons affected their travel decisions. It was forty dollars (eighty thousand colons) to take the luxury ride to Dominical in a cab, or two thousand colons (four dollars) to ride with Costa's working-class Ticos on the public transportation bus. The bus was relatively clean and comfortable, but it would make numerous stops between Quepos and Playa Dominical.

As the "Marco Polo" bus got underway from the station, Popi reminisced about the one and only time he had been to the iconic national park nearby. "It has been over thirty years since I've been to Manuel Antonio Park. I've heard Americans refer to it as a tourist trap. Tourists certainly frequent the park, but Manuel Antonio is extraordinarily beautiful, tourist trap or not.

Back in the days before paved roads and buses had reached Quepos, the road to Dominical and beyond to Provones were the worst of the worst. There were over thirty-river crossings just along this stretch of coast. We crossed them on single-lane steel bridges, hand-pulled ferries or by driving through the river. Each method had its own level of excitement attached to it.

When getting anywhere south of Quepos via truck in those days, you needed to carry all your own provisions (including camping gear) if you were serious about surviving in the wilderness of the Puntarenas and the Zona Sur. Traveling here has changed drastically since those days. The jungle had given way to the expanding date palm plantation, and now there was new pavement and new bridges.

Back in the day, travel was far more tedious and stressful, especially when the weather was foul. The roads were so bad here in this area, so primitive and rough, that we'd find ourselves somewhat discombobulated after only a few hours of bumpy travel. It was usually like a mud bog, but at other times it could be hot, dusty and dry. Occasionally, we'd see a truck filled with date palm nuts or migrant workers plunking along."

"Funny how times have changed," she said.

"Time is relative; relative to the task at hand and your perception of the task. I am no more satisfied riding along today with these modern conveniences, smoothness and speed of the travel than I was before we had them. Do modern conveniences make one any happier for life? I think not. Convenience shouldn't override common sense or quality of life. Sometimes, it can cause more grief!"

She paused, patiently listening to see if it was the proper time to present another perspective. "I certainly don't agree with a portion of your insight, Popi. If you were to ask the locals, they might also disagree."

A big smile creased his face, and he told her to "Go on."

She did. "You came here to escape the world's new modern conveniences, and then went back home to them, embraced them daily benefitting from them. These people here were stuck with the routine inconveniences of living in a third world country. There were only two options; fight change or welcome progress. Costa Rica's leaders understood the importance of infrastructure. They put their money into the roads and the transportation systems and now this is a strong, developing country."

Imagine, back then, living under the constant stress of struggling in a third world country; not like what you faced when you came here with your pockets full of Gringo cash on vacation!" She used her fingers to indicate quotation marks around vacation, driving her point home.

He realized he had tapped a nerve. His convivial body language and tone of voice let Cheyenne know that it was perfectly acceptable for her to voice an alternative opinion. He replied somewhat contritely "I can only imagine the great difficulties the Ticos faced day to day, then and now."

"But?"

"But, perhaps in many ways, those days were more fulfilling and rewarding," said Popi, looking at her and raising his eyebrows.

He seemed to enjoy the exchange more when Cheyenne shot back in rapid fire. "Watching your children grow up without essential health care, transportation and opportunity, knowing there is a better world available for them; that's more fulfilling and rewarding?" She raised her hand, letting him know she wasn't quite done yet. "What did you see happening here? Ticos standing by and watching well-to-do travelers invade their universe?

What about being proactive? It's like Kurt Vonnegut's Cat's Cradle, where the well-healed travelers deliver the glittering treasures of literacy, ambition, curiosity, gall, irreverence, health, humor and considerable information about the outside world to the locals. We invade their land with all of that, and they do everything possible to climb aboard the American Dream. What did you want, your own San Lorenzo?"

"Cheyenne, I don't disagree, but there is no way to gauge if those days were more fulfilling or rewarding. You would agree with me that more is not necessarily better, and sometimes, more is less? Are our lives more intrinsically valuable because of our wealth or the ease of our living?"

"Popi, this isn't about any of your yoga thinking. It is about the Tico's low standard of living!"

As the bus glided past a row of shanty shacks assembled only a few feet from the new road, three shirtless, dark-eyed kids stood in the yard waving as the bus zoomed by their neighborhood. The way his shoulders tightened up and moved back a tad and his eyes opened a little wider, she knew he was about to begin one of his stories.

"Take for instance, the Hadza tribe of Tanzania. Since before the beginning of recorded history, they have been sustaining themselves strictly by hunting and gathering near Kenya's Lake Tanzania. They have very few possessions. The vast majority of Hadza have been getting by with only a bowl, mat, spear, and perhaps a pipe for countless generations. They are generally a happy, carefree people with no knowledge of the outside world. None!

They live a life of monasticism. They keep no records; they don't recognize or celebrate birthdays, holidays, anniversaries, or deaths. They follow the seasons and the moon. Baboons are their prized game, and they live just to hang out, eat and socialize. How can they be any better off than they are? They have no idea that there is anything else to need. Will the progress we represent uplift, or destroy the Hadza and their rich and simplistic culture?"

He went silent as she considered his questions. The bus came to a sudden halt outside of Jack Ewing's Hacienda Baru to pick up three generations of a Tico family. The mother, daughter and granddaughter, in their festive dresses, were probably going up the mountain to San Isidro de General for the day.

In the trees nearby, a dozen or more capuchin monkeys seemed quite impressed by the bus as it ground to a stop. Like restless teenagers, this breed forever seeks playful ways to expend energy. They always dangle their arms and legs from the trees, hop from branch to branch and constantly climb up and down in search of snacks and amusement.

The commotion of the bus captured their collective attention. They moved closer as a committee to judge the value of the bus and its passengers. As the bus roared away, they screamed and scattered in every direction. Popi, Cheyenne and nearly everyone on their side of the bus laughed out loud at the comical gang of juvenile, white-faced monkeys.

Popi smiled and nodded his head toward Cheyenne with a bit more serious look. "We'll be at Playa Dominical very soon."

The idea of finally reaching Dominical had an appealing ring to Cheyenne. The bus came to a crawl as it passed a guard shack, and two young men outfitted in navy blue listlessly waved them on to the molding, gray cement bridge leading into Dominical. The sudden change in scenery piqued her inquisitive nature.

Sitting up, she noticed the Rio Baru come into view. Thankfully, the driver slowed as her eyes followed the river's path to the ocean, expanding their focus along the way. The surf was pounding, and white water blasted house-high into the air each time a wave broke. The thought and sight of it made her dig her hands and fingertips into the top of the plastic cushion of the empty seat in front of her. "Popi! The surf is huge; will we surf here?"

"All in good time. If it is meant to be, it will be."

The driver downshifted to turn the bus down the pitted gravel and dirt road leading into Playa Dominical. When they slowly came to a halt at the top of the hill, the driver reached over and opened the door. A deeply stored vault of memories and incredible encounters that hadn't been accessed in years flooded Popi's semiconscious mind.

How many long years had it been? Was it possible for him to erase the Rio Baru from his memory? No sane man could fail to recall the first sparkle of a rare jewel. Before he calculated how many decades, or put any number on the years, other pressing memories popped to the surface of his now active mind. He was transcended to a time when Dominical was nothing less than a magical paradise for him.

Cheyenne looked at him, seeing his face light up like a kid getting his first bike. He relived the special times and shared portions of his hazy memories etched here along the dusty road into Dominical. He told her about the soccer field, where he had joined the locals as they watched and played games on Sunday afternoons.

The small one door, one window cement block police station was almost exactly the same. Like in many other places, development had finally reached this magical paradise. A bakery, several real estate offices, a yoga studio, abundant cabanas and restaurants all lined the dirt and cobble-stoned road leading through Playa Dominical. A church and surf shop shared the same side of the road only yards apart.

The church was adjacent to an expansive estate once owned by a Californian from San Clemente who had migrated to Dominical before it had been discovered. The man had many strong attributes; among them were an agreeable demeanor, incredible genius, foresight and exceptionally strong business savvy.

He had enjoyed his partying, too, so he had bought himself a sizeable parcel of Dominical real estate in the early 1980's when local owners were selling out for pennies on the dollar. His first business, the San Clemente, was a solid financial success. It had earned a reputation as Dominical's foremost watering hole for locals and tourists alike; a great drinking atmosphere and good music had been the draw.

He whipped his head around in child-like wonder and pointed his finger at a spot in the trees. "I slept in a hammock roped between two trees once; right behind there, back when its name was Ranchero Mimo. It was the only place to stay within walking distance of the surf. I was so in tune with the whole scene back then that my surfing put me in the best position to expand my parameters. You know, like what could I do physically and mentally, in harmony with the wave's energy? Where could I go on the wave? It's all about the waves; you know even light travels in waves, every schoolchild knows that!" She could see a younger, stronger Popi emerging with each word.

It felt as if the bus had stopped a dozen times before reaching its final Playa Dominical stop directly in front of the state-owned Costa

Rican Electricity Institute (ICE) tower. A fence topped with three rows of barbed wire wrapped around the modest, barely landscaped property.

The walk from the bus to the beach took two minutes under a thick canopy of tropical trees. The low rumble of the surf busting on the sandbar greeted them before they could see it prompting her to increase the cadence of her stride. When she finally saw the break, it wasn't completely gratifying. The tide was low, and the waves slammed the sandbar with harsh authority. Solid ten-foot walls of impassable white water rolled and thundered without a let up until they exploded on the gray sand and cobblestone-littered beach. A couple of kids paddling around on boogie boards close to shore were thrilled to catch the swell's concussive climax in the shallows.

"With few exceptions, the surf here at Dominical has always been best on a higher tide," he told her.

They sat together on a worn slab of mahogany driftwood under a cluster of immature coconut trees and almonds as they studied the surf. Her concern over where they would be staying, or any other future details, slipped away as she counted the minutes between sets, and the number of waves in each set. Six to eight waves to a set, ten minutes between sets. From her calculations, she figured she could easily paddle out between the sets if she paid attention.

As the tide rose, a handful of surfers showed up to check for improvements in the surf. Two brown-skinned, dreadlocked surfers ran into the water and paddled full speed ahead into the break. Within minutes, they had each caught a long and powerful wave; their energy and skill were remarkable.

Feeling a little more confident after watching the two men, she decided that maybe this wasn't so bad, after all. "From what I've read and heard about Dominical, it's the world's seventh most consistent beach break. I heard it's a load of fun once you get it wired. Everyone finds their own lines."

The two dreadlocks paddled up and over a big cleanup set, but two other surfers weren't so lucky. One guy nearly made it over the top of the last of the big waves before he was thrown over upside-down and backwards by the wave's thick lip. He flipped head over heels like a rag doll after he wisely pushed his board away. The other guy tried to play it safe by pushing his board away and diving for the bottom, resulting in him and his board getting sucked back up into the next wave's face and over the falls together.

"Wrong place; wrong time" muttered Popi. "These waves demand respect. Most of the time it isn't a good wave for beginners or old men."

Cheyenne agreed with a nod of her head.

After spending so much time watching the water, she looked around and noticed a few of the obvious characteristics of Playa Dominical. Both tourists and locals were attracted here because they could drive right up to the beach, park under the shade of the trees and watch the surf. Lush jungle climbed the steep oceanside mountains behind them, adding greatly to the ambience. Vendors lined the beach road; they sold handmade Tico jewelry, bright, light tropical attire and glass pipes. Others displayed artwork, pottery and fake Indian artifacts. As they say in real estate; "location, location, location."

After a while, Cheyenne's curiosity resurfaced. "Where are we going to stay, Popi?"

"Up the river road at Manga Manor."

They were soon walking back through town up and then along the Rio Baru under the old bridge. There, nailed to a dying limb, was a rudimentary hand-painted sign on a 2'x 2' piece of plywood coated with white paint. In bold black letters it read Fumigación Necesitado? 9155-7176.

"Ever tell ya about the month I spent rooming with bats? Besides their dung, they were pretty darn good roomies. We humans have some amazing relatives" Popi chirped.

"No, but I'm sure I'll hear about it and our relatives very soon!" Cheyenne sighed. It had been a long day.

"We used to have bats by the billions in Florida. They're mammals, you know. They devour their weight in insects each day. They're like Florida's snakes and toads; most of these species have been pushed aside in the name of progress and development."

They reached an opening in the jungle by the river; they removed their backpacks and sat down on a smooth, round boulder. The river's sounds calmed Cheyenne for a while, as Popi reminisced. "I can remember how there would be a gazillion toads everywhere each summer when the heavy rains came. You could hardly get around without avoiding swarms of toads and tadpoles that filled each and every puddle. It was a wonder."

"What about now, Popi?" Cheyenne prompted him, trying to bring him back to the present moment. It seemed her comment had little effect.

"We hunted and collected snakes; dozens of different species. I recall one long and very fat banded water snake we had. One day it was the only one we had, and the next day she had thirty-eight baby snakes! Back then, on almost any clear and moonless Florida night you could see with the naked eye that we were part of the Milky Way; you could nearly reach out and touch it. Today, the city lights get brighter as the light of the stars slowly fades away. We won't be able to see the darkness soon."

"Dark sky legislation is a must" she offered up. "But must we have laws for everything?"

Popi, lost in his thoughts, spoke them out loud. "Yes, I lived under the same roof with a family of bats, while the rest of the world was going batty!" Out of right field, Popi reintroduced a previous thread. "What do you think the Hadza do for entertainment?"

Cheyenne turned, looking directly into Popi's eyes with a look of puzzlement and shrugged. Where was he going with this?

"The single most important thing the Hadza tribe did, other than hunt, kill and eat baboons was to gather around their fire to smoke ganja, strong tobacco, or a mixture of the two."

Cheyenne grinned and said, "Is that it?"

"Well, there is a little more to it. See the men of the Hadza sit around the fire passing a pipe. The first, let's call him the smoky, takes absolutely the biggest puff from the pipe he can draw until he falls back coughing his lungs out while all the rest of the tribe laughs until they have tears rolling down their cheeks. Once the smoky regains his composure, he hands the pipe to the next smoky, and they all repeat the same scenario until each one of them has been the smoky, and they are all in stitches."

"Sounds like half the guys I know back home!" she quipped.

Before they got up to complete their short trek to Manga Manor, Popi shared all he knew of the Rio Baru as they watched its current drift downstream in rhythm with his oration. "The last time I checked there was a grand steward, Jack Ewing, living at the Hacienda Baru Lodge. Jack wrote Monkeys are Made of Chocolate; he's a genius. Sweetheart, you have to meet him!

In the early 1980's Jack was a huge contributor to the beginnings of Costa Rica's ecotourism movement. At the time, the Hacienda Baru was a beachfront cattle ranch and estate. Blessed with brilliance, though, Jack's gift went beyond intelligence. He restored the Hacienda Baru and protected the surrounding area from the more commercial Acapulco or Waikiki-style of tourism found in the more crowded coastal towns to the north. He kept it pure and became a wealthy man in a more significant way!"

As they made their way down the dirt road to the Villa Rio Mar, a red taxi pulled up beside them. The driver, a Tico with a wide happy face and a touch of gray at his temples, climbed out with extended arms. "Is it Stan Manly? Mi amigo! It is Arturo, Brother Stan! I heard you were in town from my cousin who saw you on the bus!"

Surprise swept over Popi's face for it had been many years. How did Arturo remember him? "Arturo!" bellowed Popi, as they came together in a bonding embrace. They both stepped back to analyze their physical changes.

"Arturo, you look the same as you did twenty years ago!"

Arturo relished the complement, and smiled proudly, puffing up his chest. He gave it a brisk thump. "Stan, I wish I could say the same for you!" as he reached out to pat his old friend's midriff, keeping them laughing and speaking in Spanglish for a few minutes.

"Oh, Arturo, I apologize. This is my granddaughter, Cheyenne."

Cheyenne stepped forward. Arturo didn't skip a beat; taking her hand softly in his, he looked her directly in the eyes. "It is my great pleasure and fortune to meet you, Ms. Cheyenne. I am blessed."

Popi shook his right index finger towards Cheyenne. "As I've stated, you must beware of these Tico men. They are muy machismo, and always after the pretty women!" A wide grin appeared on their faces as the two old friends laughed even harder.

"Cheyenne, did your grandfather ever tell you how he lived a month with a family of bats? Stan is an hombre muy loco!"

After many more laughs, handshakes, and hugs, Arturo announced that he was on his way up the mountain to Gringo Gulch near Alfombras to pick up some paying passengers. "If you need a ride, I can take you and your beautiful granddaughter to Manga Manor first."

"No, we haven't got much farther, but gracias, amigo!"

"Stan, I will come visit you soon," Arturo said as he pulled away.

Cheyenne and Popi shuffled past the Villa Rio Mar before getting to the Manga Manor. The place had a brilliant marketing plan; the full name on their business card and web site was Hotel & Conference Center Villa Rio Mar Jungle & Beach Resort.

They reached the Manga Manor just as dark began settling in. It was a lavishly landscaped compound comprised of four two-story houses with a cantina that sat next to the dirt road across from the Rio Baru. They made it to the door of the last building after the sun had slipped well below the towering tops of the hundred-foot tall guanacaste trees, whose binding roots hold together the banks of the Rio Baru.

Instead of going inside, Popi suggested they sit on the front steps and savor the last sunlit moments of their day. The sky was washed with a low blanket of slowly creeping cumulous clouds, and a higher stationary sheet of thin, pink cirrus wisps reflected the day's final breath.

They sat peacefully; watching and sharing the twilight. He knew what would come next, but Cheyenne was clueless. A moment later, without warning, a flash of black fluttering wings flew by before them.

"What was that?" Cheyenne's voice rose in decibels.

"Our relatives" he chuckled.

"Was it a B-A-T?" Cheyenne whimpered as she closed her eyes tightly. "They're disgusting!"

"No big deal; I'm pretty sure it was a fruit bat. Sit still, and be quiet. You'll be amused."

A minute or two passed before a trio of sparrow-sized, black fruit bats zoomed in and out before them, performing unbelievably amazing feats of aerial acrobatics. Some of them came within inches of their faces at times.

At first, she was squeamish, but after a short while her misgivings turned to amusement and giggles. The bats did their work in an area about the size of a small gymnasium, but at times they tightened their formation to show off directly in front of them. After a couple of minutes, Cheyenne said, "They're like butterflies on steroids. I can't believe their abilities. They have mastered the art of flight!"

She sat and evaluated their flying skills, which included stopping on a mosquito (smaller than a dime), instant acceleration, loops and somersaults at lightning speed. Their ability to effortlessly change direction multiple times within a second was their most astounding feat, hands down.

As darkness descended, and the bat's feeding frenzy dropped off, Popi let out a slow, deliberate yawn to indicate the flying mammal show was done, as was he for the evening. Once inside Manga Manor, they found humble but clean accommodations. A note to Popi from the cuidador, Melvin, and his wife, Yearly, outlined the house rules. It also mentioned a Tico dinner of rice and beans were ready, and waiting on the stove with a chilled pair of orange Fantas in the refrigerator.

After they had finished their meal, bed and sleep came fast. Despite Cheyenne having a bat dream, the first night's sleep was sound and uneventful for both of them. Five a.m. came fast. With a little effort, they found a quiver of surfboards of various shapes and sizes stashed in the bodega. She chose to ride a Greg Loher 8' fun shape; it was set up as a thruster, with two smaller outside fins and a larger fin fixed into the middle back box. It was probably thirty years old but looked surprisingly new.

Popi went with a weathered and mature 8' 6" Wooster. It was also a fun shape thruster, but the fins were of equal size. It was a meaty board; a thick floater, easy to paddle, and hell to duck-dive. It had repaired dings (brownies) galore, and was certainly a board that had seen more than its share of action. He laughed, thinking the board was just like him. "I've had my share of action, too, and I'm a little beat up, so let's get it on! I know what to do with this old thing."

Thankfully, the swell had dropped a bit and stayed that way over the next few days. The form remained impeccable; the wind blew offshore morning and evening, and the tides befriended them with fun surf. Arturo drove them up and down the coast searching out surf breaks. They surfed Playa Dominicalito and Hermosa. They even traveled all the way to ride the surf at Playa el Rey. They both grew stronger as they lost count of the days of surfing, eating, resting, and soaking up every nuance of their experience.

She was quickly becoming an accomplished surfer, catching her share of respectable waves, wherever they found themselves surfing. However, they had purposefully avoided Playa Dominical's thumping beach break; it was best to leave it for the experts.

Yearly made breakfast after they surfed each morning and dinner every evening. She also kept the tile-floored house spotless.

She and Melvin worked at both the Mar and Manga Manors. They explained how the Mar was the first resort to be built near the Pacific coast of the Puntarenas Province. However, in the more than thirty years since it was constructed, a number of high-end luxury resorts that were bigger and ritzier than the Rio Mar had infiltrated the area. They had pushed the locals aside to make their profits. Their attitudes towards the locals hurt more than the pride of the loyal people who were not remembered for their service or the humble ambiance they had provided for so many years.

But the Rio Mar had preserved the tradition of being a place for great service, food, and comfort. It was successfully marketed as a luxurious base camp for raw adventures in the middle of a tropical paradise. It was a contemporary oasis in a primordial paradise, having all of the amenities and technological conveniences of home. It was perfect.

The property had an artsy, bohemian appearance. No room was exactly alike; some had thatched roofs, and each was uniquely designed with tropical motifs and colors. However, genuine Hippies, globo-adventure seekers, surfers, and other travel purists felt as if they were being robbed of the full, authentic, Tico experience. Amenities included cable, internet, room service, an Infinity pool, tennis courts, putt-putt golf and a booming real estate office offering cheap lots and timeshares.

Tourists came and went daily in their rental cars and by cab. Then, there was the brand, spanking new Marco Polo bus. It offered wireless internet, AC, TV/DVD, reclining cushioned seats, personal reading lights, and extended seat trays for the tour groups that it shuttled between San Jose Airport and the aristocratic villas. A steady stream of upper class, foreign students, bikers, hikers, naturalists, gurus, meditators, bird watchers and other eco-tourists made Villas Rio Mar their home in Dominical.

On one of their morning walks, Cheyenne and Popi caught a whiff of bleach used by the cleaning staff to clean the showers. Then they heard the mad clunky banging of hammers as workmen repaired a leaky tin roof on one of the villas. These were subtle reminders that it wasn't easy to escape the mundane human activity of modern civilization.

Later in the day, Popi was sitting on the patio having a glass of limeade with Arturo after work when he brought it up. "You know, brother, you just can't escape progress.

Arturo agreed, offering his own opinion. "One of the good things about Costa Rica over the past generation has been our strong resistance to building significant structures near the beach. Yes, there are many more houses dotting the mountainsides, but the big developments are few."

The days went by, and each evening, after eating their meal, they made some strong coffee and sat on the front patio to wait for the bats to entertain them with their aerial circus. Watching this ritual brought Cheyenne and Popi closer each day. Thinking back on their days here, and the enjoyment she had each day, Cheyenne thought "I could do this forever." What she didn't know yet was Popi had made that decision many years before.

The day had come. Arturo was away in San Jose visiting family, and Popi and Cheyenne would be hoofing it to the beach on their own for the remainder of their stay in Dominical.

The sun was hiding behind the high slope of the mainland as they made their way to the beach. It was a sleepy start for most of Dominical's people, but not everyone would miss the sun's first light. Together, with boards under their arms and bare feet, they had equipped themselves with a jug of drinking water and a small tote bag packed with provisions. In a town full of unusual people, there was no better example of an odd couple in all of Dominical.

An abandoned and dilapidated house sat a short way back from the dirt road, perched on a short incline overlooking the Rio Baru. A dingy, mold-covered For Sale sign sat cocked over at an odd angle at the base of the front door, serving as an indication that there had been no recent visitors. The roof sagged noticeably to one side, and the jungle had done an impressive job of reclaiming the property.

The sight was proof that the world's economic downturn of the new millennia had not excluded Costa Rica. The Second Great Depression had affected places like Florida and other areas where land speculation money flowed freely prior to the Crisis. Millions of suffering people had watched helplessly while their life savings tumbled, crumbled, and decayed like this once-prosperous homestead in the hands of unscrupulous investment bankers, real estate mortgage brokers and get-rich-quick land schemers.

They hiked barefoot up and over the rough, rocky dirt road, and down under the bridge until the surf came within sight. The view was incredibly serene; with machine-like precision, swell after swell bumped on the ocean's horizon. As they broke, liquid walls of pluming white water shot up and rolled over, one by one, systematically breaking in their pre-designated spot. The waves here were being delivered by surges of energy caused by a turbulent weather system thousands of miles away that had peaked days before. The result was a surfer's dream, one filled with tremendous speed, power and infinite absoluteness.

In silent unity, grandfather and granddaughter watched, safely catching and riding the waves in their minds. The river's flow outward towards the sea indicated the tide was not yet high. They gathered their boards and provisions, and continued their way toward the beach.

By then the businesses along the town's main thruway were stirring. Storeowners watered the road in front of their venues to keep the dust down. Stray dogs hoping for handouts greeted anyone willing to acknowledge their bleak existence, and close by a tardy rooster called to announce another day had dawned. The sight of half a dozen men with their boards bobbing over a long wedge of whitewater bouncing over the inside sandbar, greeted them as they reached the beach after their thirty-minute walk.

Biding their time, they sat on a piece of familiar driftwood in the morning shade. They studied each wave and more. The tide still had a bit more to come up before it reached its pinnacle. This lower tide made the waves break a little too quickly, so neither of them even considered paddling out yet.

A set of five waves, each bigger than the last, approached the outside bar and Popi calmly said, "The last wave will be the best wave."

Closer to shore, two men paddled quickly for position, looking to escape the wrath of the outside monsters by snatching an early ride on the first waves to come through. Three other guys sat safely and further outside as their two companions made the best of their discreet choice to go on the first wave that they could catch.

All the attention was soon focused on the outside three. The mogul of the group raised his head high and dug deep, stroking for the horizon as a huge wave approached him from behind. This last wave in the set was a monster; it stood vertically, looming dangerously over the seemingly doomed martyr.

He fearlessly faced the moment and didn't hesitate before whipping his board around 180 degrees and launching himself down the face. As he stood up, the wave's thick lip lifted and tossed him and his board for a free fall, but the board's fins miraculously caught the face of the wave as the rider somehow managed to stay low keeping contact with his board.

At the bottom of the long drop, he planted his feet, critically bent his knees and charged forward. His race to the shallows was nip and tuck with the curl. He disappeared and reappeared from behind the green curtain of the spiraling lip several times. The wavesmith finished off, triumphantly escaping danger as the few witnesses whooped their approval.

His two buddies were not as fortunate. They struggled as they each barely missed catching the first two waves of the set, and they both vainly fought with all of their might to catch the third wave. They simultaneously slumped in defeat when they saw the fourth wave, followed by a fifth that was larger than all the rest. The enormous wave bellowed and rose before them like a screaming tsunami destined for destruction.

They had foolishly been lured into the impact zone by the hope of an easy way out. The last wave lifted tens of thousands of gallons of water, pitched, collapsed, and its long-travelled surge exploded onto the two unfortunate souls. The whitewater pounded them so hard that the earth shook in response.

The riders and their boards were separated under the Pacific Ocean's purgatory of foam. They were tossed, ripped, crumbled and defeated, as the spectators wondered momentarily if they were gone, but resurrected as their heads came up out of the foam. As soon as they got a good breath of air, they celebrated their own survival and their friend's breakneck victory with whoops and whistles."

Cheyenne cheered! "Unbelievable. Boy, were they lucky!"

Popi seized his opportunity. "Have you ever heard the definition of luck? Some say it is where skill and opportunity meet, while others believe it is the drudgery of hard labor."

"Perhaps there is truth in both of those adages" she countered.

"In our hearts, we know nothing can replace training and practice. Without proper training, proper practice is impossible. Without practice, one establishes and repeats ineffective habits. Ultimately, one can work towards improving his or her effectiveness, or luck as you call it."

"Popi, I believe I'm prepared to practice my luck with these waves." She pointed out towards the next rising set, seeing that the elated group of surfers was maneuvering to battle another onslaught.

In his estimation, she was more than willing. She was prepared to surf with Dominical's best, but now, more importantly, in her eyes she was ready. Ready to ride this unicorn!

They sat a while longer watching the ocean. As the tide rose, more surfers ventured out. The waves, still violent, were dropping in size a bit and were less frequent. Still, they maintained the same majestic form, as the offshore wind combed and groomed them into razor-sharp perfection. They could both see how fast they were, and they knew they would have to be quick to their feet to have a chance to make it beyond the take-off point.

"Cheyenne, you realize I can't come with you?"

Without making eye contact, she agreed with a slight nod as she picked up her board and made her way to the edge of the swash to wait her turn to test the surf's fierceness.

Before the Pacific's roar drowned out his words, Popi gave her his last bit of advice. "Remember you can't tame an ocean any more than you can a unicorn!"

She hit the water just in time for a helping of humble pie. All at once, everything she had learned flushed through her mind. Only one thought remained as a beacon; timing. Her instincts began to take over when she screamed out loud like a war whoop "Timing!"

A grueling paddle out was not an adequate description of the challenge she faced. The sets were coming fast and frequently. Duck-diving the fun shape nearly sapped all of her strength. Cheyenne, a full, six-feet tall, waited patiently on the inside of the outside sandbar. When she saw a partial opening between sets, she paddled hard and deep with her long muscular arms. When she needed an extra boost to climb the face of an oncoming wave she kicked with both feet, as well. When she finally reached the outside, and saw the vast emptiness greet her, she stopped and turned towards shore, lifting both of her arms over her head with clinched fists as if to say "Look! I've made it to the big leagues!"

The Pacific Ocean would not have anything to do with an early victory celebration, though. The empty horizon filled with rising, mounding swells, taking a direct path towards her. She cleared the tops of the first three waves, then turned and paddled over the edge and down the face of the fourth. She magically rose to her feet momentarily.

To fully escape the wave's fury, her take-off should have been angled across the face, not directly down it. While she did an excellent job of negotiating the turn at the end of her drop, it put her in a perfect position to get hammered by the leading edge of the heaving twelve-foot lip. The impact of a ton or two of water flattened her before pealing down the bar like a gargantuan, windblown zipper.

After what seemed like a long wait she popped up from the deep into the chaotic white jumble of turbulent water surrounding her. She reached out with her hands and immediately found her board. She pulled herself up for a welcome gulp of air and gasped "Timing!"

Popi remained positive, generating inspirational thoughts as he watched her endure the test. Success or failure was fully up to her, and of course, the ocean. He concentrated on projecting his Chi (life force) directly to her through a form of Chi Chat by which he transmitted his message directly to his granddaughter. "Survive the detonation... defer the hesitation ...use your imagination...join the deliberation... experience your resurrection. There is no imitation for the ideal surf sensation. Freedom is only one ride away. You want it, and you'll have it."

The ocean, the Great Disrespecter, is unmerciful to the uninitiated. As soon as she gathered the board under her and caught a lung half-full of air, the next wave's looming lip dropped from the top of a twelve-foot face and pitched out until it exploded twenty-something feet in front of her. It discharged a flume of white water as high as a light pole into the air.

She pushed the board away from her and dove for the bottom. She had repeated this tactic twice before the set went by. Once the coast was clear, she paddled back into the lineup like a predator glaring at the horizon line for her prey. She was ready, as she thought "Timing!"

Pain; he could feel it in his Chi. There must be pain in the process, but she must make up her mind to ignore it he thought to himself as he watched her wait for her next ride. Surely, with strife came liberation.

In a relatively short time that she had been surfing, she had developed a firm foundation; she might even have the potential to be a maestro. Almost a generation earlier with her grandpopi, she had paddled out, caught and rode her first wave; it had been a week after her fifth birthday. She had proven to be a fearless natural, and now, it was all coming to fruition in front of him. These were some serious waves and would require some serious skill and nerves to negotiate. He could hear his heartbeat accelerating in his ears.

She took the next right-hander, a medium-sized hot dog wave, to the beach. With luck, or timing, her paddle back out was a breeze. Once out, she dropped immediately onto a long left-hander. She made a couple of fast backside cutbacks before kicking out halfway through the wave, keeping the hope of catching another monster set alive. It was either a smart move or good timing. She stroked hard and steady to position herself for the next wave.

As if it wanted to host a rider, the double overhead wall of water picked her up and literally shot her down the face of the wave like a cannon. A sheet of spray chased behind her as she toyed with the wave by stalling under the racing lip and finding the slot deep in the hollow tube. The lip nearly caught her. She twisted her body and board to dodge the collapsing ceiling, and bit into a quick succession of full-faced roller-coasters to pump more speed and beat out the stampeding unicorns.

As she flew out of harm's way onto the clean face of the pitching wave, she struck a graceful pose of gratified nonchalance by performing a long, top to bottom, round-house cutback, circling back around and high up onto the approaching whitewater. She then bounced the board in the opposite direction by banking hard and floating over the turbulent ball of suds as it tumbled underneath her.

When she cleared the whitewater, she turned hard off the bottom just in time to get locked into the longest tube of the day. The wave spit her out with a blast of spray as it collapsed in the trough on the other side of the bar.

From the beach, Popi watched and celebrated. He soon lost count of her rides. It seemed, like a perfect sunrise, she could do no wrong. Her time had come, and the time was now.

Later on, with a relentless smile and boundless energy, she gave him a wave-by-wave commentary as they devoured their tote bag snacks. She continued her accounts as they made their way through town, under the bridge and past the river. She was so caught up in recounting her every experience of the morning's surf session that by the time they finally reached Manga Manor she was surprised and a little startled. "We're here already?"

"Yes, child, we are, but not for long. We leave in the morning."

Things didn't always happen according to plans in Costa Rica, especially when the rains arrived. It had begun around midnight, heavy at times, and didn't letup until mid-morning. Standing in the slop, waiting for the bus, didn't make much sense, so they took advantage of the low light and slept in for the first time in more than a week.

The sun was still hiding behind a cauldron of dark clouds, and the sky was emitting a steamy mist when they finished their breakfast. Taking advantage of cloud cover is a wise choice, since the equatorial sun always takes its physical toll on a person, at times as much as the relentless surf can.

They talked and decided to save the trip south for a drier day. They headed out for the beach instead. Their track along the mud-stained Rio Baru was tricky because of the slick, soft clay and numerous rain-filled, rocky potholes. Popi slipped twice and came within a fraction of an inch from kissing the ground before regaining his balance.

Cheyenne thought it was hilarious and loved it, until one of her flip flops slid when it should have flopped and sent her in a tailspin and onto her rear end in a jiffy. Luckily, or perhaps due to timing, she landed as elegantly as possible in the wet mud. Of course, Popi went on about the perils of wearing flip flops, and the value of feeling the Earth with your bare feet.

The rainy night had vanquished the ocean; it was nearly flat. There was no trace of the giant, dangerous surf of the previous morning, and there was hardly any whitewater appearing across the mouth of the river. It seemed like an illusion; the drop-off past the break was sheer blackness, and the surf on the sand bar looked to be quite tame and very manageable. They made their way past two anglers testing their luck from the base of the lichen-encrusted bridge. The water was heavily stained with the blood of reddish-yellow clay.

Watching the surf from the bridge, Popi remarked "This late-rising tide, combined with the surf's diminishing size, will increase my fun! There are lots of old man waves to ride today!"

"Age. It's subjective. You act like a much younger man! It's all in your head and your heart. You're living proof of that, for sure!" Cheyenne said.

The refreshing offshore breeze whispered through the leaves of the trees shading the edges of the Baru. The fresh mountain wind blew life into the palm fronds, scattered the previous day's deadfall, and sauntered up Playa Dominical's main street like it was the boss. Its briskness swept the clouds and early morning moisture away, and a cool breeze followed the two of them down to the ocean's edge.

The waves lacked an immediate appeal, stuck halfway between low and high tide, so the two of them sat and calculated their paddle out from a half-buried stump and the enormous root of a monstrous ceiba tree. The decapitated tree, a keystone species of the surrounding rainforest, had helped sustain a unique and complex habitat that extended miles beyond its colossal two-hundred-foot spread for a hundred years. But like many other matriarchal trees, it had been chain-sawed from the forest along the Baru somewhere up the road from Manga Manor, and had just washed downstream with the overnight deluge. Its base had more girth than one of the massive tires of the semi-trucks that hauled its other, more-valued pieces out of the jungle to a local mill.

"Making toothpicks out of logs; the demise of the jungle, a death of a billion cuts." The thought upset him as he mumbled the words.

While they waited for the tide to change, Cheyenne turned an eye towards the tide line, searching out sea beans and ocean-weathered tidbits of hand-sized driftwood. Popi alleviated his stiff body and dull mind with some vigorous yoga, followed by long, peaceful periods of motionless, meditative silence.

In time the high tide prevailed, and the offshore wind backed off, strengthening the surf. The waves peaked and peeled off in both directions, and the sun once again won its ageless battle with the clouds by exposing the timeless blue sky, creating a post card setting if there ever was one.

Popi slipped into the water with his blistered old Wooster. As he paddled off, his age and minor dings disappeared. His worries and concerns vanished, too, as he was transformed by the cosmic energy of the waves.

It was a magical session. He rode wave after wave, catching them outside and riding them all the way into the very inside. On the biggest wave of his session, he gouged a huge slab of wave meat as he carved a wicked bottom turn at full tilt. He went straight back up and held himself motionless; he seemed stuck there. But after hanging at the top of the wave for what seemed like forever, he side-slipped the board back down into the sweet spot, doing a long soul arch under the fast folding lip.

As the wave became steeper and more critical, he walked to the nose of his board and struck a pose. The wave rolled up into a deep spot and slowed down, and he cross-stepped back to do a drop knee turn from the tail. When he had the board all the way back around, he cat-stepped forward and trimmed it out with a cheater five. He then shot the curl in total harmony with the ocean from a perfect Quasimodo squat. He continued his passionate dancing with Mother Ocean until the high tide finally maxed out.

Now and again, from a distance, Cheyenne could hear Popi laughing out loud to himself. By the time he rode his last wave to the beach, his level of exhilaration was only matched by the level of his exhaustion. He stepped from the water, hearing the old, nearly forgotten, cry of the collective humming of cicadas above the reverberation of the ocean. It was a sound that could make a man lazy.

"This is not the Old Man's Club! All kooks must get out of the water immediately!" The slur sounded more like a Wal-Mart super sale announcement than a jovial greeting. It came from a tall, thin, weathered man standing shirtless and shoeless on the shady side of the lifeguard stand. The intruder directed a semi-grouchy "K pasta, mi amigo!" in Popi's direction.

His play on words tipped Popi off; he recognized who it was in an instant. It was Burt, an old time friend of his from Florida. They had their fair share of stories to tell, but they were all from long ago. They hadn't stayed in touch, and he had all but forgotten their days of misadventure.

"I heard you were here in town, so I took me a drive down the mountain just to see my odd friend, oooold Stan Manly."

Burt's voice and mannerisms had not changed a bit in the many years since they had last seen each other. He still talked with his hands almost like he was using sign language. The sun and hard living had obviously taken a mighty toll on his body, but he seemed to be as sharp as ever. Popi walked right up to him with open arms and delivered a strong, sincere embrace. He could feel Burt's lack of enthusiasm and body strength. Was the end near for his old friend?

Burt didn't miss a beat, and loudly began questioning his longstanding companion. "Still living in the good ole' United States of Lies, are ya? The land of freedom? Standing by the old 'Give me liberty or give me death' bullshit, are ya?" Burt hushed his tone a bit and crackled his tune with a wee hint of too much drama. "You one of those Sheeple, yet?"

Popi didn't respond to the question, but instead held Burt's shoulders lightly, and looked directly into his bloodshot eyes. "Thank, God! Oh man! It's wonderful to see you. You look great; sort of!"

Burt gently pulled away. He was disgruntled, but not angry. His eyes shifted away, and back again to Popi's gaze. "Bullshit. You've always been full of fluff, man. I am a dying soul, like the rest of the freaking world. And keep God out of it, if you don't mind."

Popi took note of the concern in Burt's voice but didn't address it. They'd known each other since childhood. He had been there when Burt moved from the west shore of the St. Johns River near Deland to the mountains above Dominical with his wife to create a life and family in their newly-found paradise. Burt's extremely analytical, critical thinking had been both his lifetime ally and nemesis. He was truly a Free Bird, but he was often tormented by debilitating fears that had clipped his wings.

The two friends stood in the shade in silence, but after a moment or two Burt looked squarely into Popi's eyes and began to rant. "So many sheeple living the path of least resistance back at home in the United States of Fear. The sheeple's fatal flaw is their quest for the most amount of amusement for the least amount of outlay. Shit floats downstream, and there is an awful lot of shit nowadays; here, there, and everywhere. Them sheeple are a spoiled flock; a useless generation."

Popi listened to his long-lost friend until the offshore breeze began to die. He empathized with him and shared some of his feelings. Speaking from his heart, he agreed. "Yes, there are many people following this path of least resistance you speak of."

As if in a trance, Burt blathered on about subjects that were on his mind. He went on about bullets, gold, the collapse of the middle class, politics, and the media. He kept referring to God and the country he claimed he still loved. "Your friend, Lester; did he ever escape the United States of Injustice?"

"No; family disrupted Lester's quest to become an Ex-Pat."

Before he could get a chance to completely explain, Burt interjected with his own version of star-spangled bravado. "I'm no Ex-Pat. I love our country! I just don't trust the people running it!"

Popi remained silent as he watched Cheyenne making her way up the beach with her board. Burt's red, steely eyes stayed glued to Popi's face.

"If you are ready to fend for yourself you are welcome on our finca anytime. It's a place where you can see the stars clearly every night. Tell Lester he is welcome, too. Our goat would enjoy a new pair of hands on her udders.

Be sure to tell him about the people in Gringo Gulch; none of us trust the government. We all have guns, food and plenty of ammunition." He pointed up to the mountains. "Most of us been living and fending for ourselves up there for a long while. Neighbors got a different meaning here; it ain't like back in the Steaks. We don't depend on the government for nothing." Burt finally ran out of energy, and his hands dropped to his sides.

Before Popi could comment on what had just been said, tears began to flood Burt's eyes, rolling down his leathery cheeks. He got a wild look in his eye, as if he was frustrated beyond words, and he abruptly turned to leave. He yelled a warning from over his shoulder as he walked off. "Remember! The lost sheep have been called. One day soon they will awaken to who they really are, and cry out to their God, and He will save them yet again."

As Burt melted into the fading shadows, Popi mumbled "So much for leaving God out."

"Who was that man, Popi?" Cheyenne inquired as she stood

beside him watching the fumbling man fade away into the shadows.

"He's an old friend, child; an old friend."

His mind percolated. It's ironic how memories brew when prompted by events, people and feelings. Burt had dislodged some old forgotten experiences. Black and white bits and pieces of distant memories were now floating to the top of his mind like nymphs that hurried to metamorphose into fresh gyroscopic masterpieces. Images of Lester and Albury's mother, Grace, reemerged from his childhood. Popi was in a lonely place, lost for a time.

Cheyenne took the lead, walking away from the beach. He automatically fell into line next to her and started talking. "She took the three of us to the drive-in movie theater to see Clint Eastwood in "The Good, The Bad, and The Ugly." She demanded complete and total silence so she could hear Clint nail his lines. There weren't many in that movie, either. It was one of the first times I ever truly paid attention to every bit of a movie."

"Popi, who are you talking about?"

"Oh, I'm sorry, Cheyenne! Seeing Burt brought me back to a different time. I started remembering Lester and his mother, Grace. She's who I'm talking about."

"Oh, okay; go on."

"Grace drove a cool 1970 two-door blue Pontiac with a decent stereo. Whenever she took us somewhere, a Pall Mall non-filtered cigarette dangled from the corner of her lips. You could bet classical music, like Wagner or Bach, would be blaring from the Bonneville's dashboard speaker, too.

She was super intelligent, but she was also a tough woman. She was naturally dark-skinned for a German; she might have been part Jewish. She was as quick as a whip and as sharp as a tack. She loved them boys; everything she did was for her boys.

Once, she took us on the backside of the Melbourne Causeway after blue crabs. It was right before midnight, and the tide was right. With flashlights and dip nets, we netted a half bushel of big ones, 'jimmies' we called them, in no time. Then we drove home under a full moon listening to Ludwig Von Beethoven's Fifth Symphony full blast. Grace boiled up them crabs in the wee hours of dawn with a Pall Mall dangling from her taut lips, and a can of ice-cold Schlitz Malt Liquor clutched in her hand. In some ways, she was ahead of her day; she recycled aluminum cans way back in the early Seventies.

Grace and her boys always kept late hours, but their strangeness only started there. They were infatuated with animals. Dozens of cats lived with them, and it was rare for the house to ever be clean. They always had a couple of dogs, too. Their favorite was a Chihuahua that they knighted with an old sword; Sir Grover Cleveland. The little lump of dirt ruled the house. Lester was wild about raising gerbils, too; he usually had cages lined up in his bedroom with lots of gerbils and their babies. Those darn cages smelled foul. I don't remember his room ever being clean!

Eventually, things spiraled into darkness. What I didn't understand then, I do now. Grace lost her mind in alcohol after the boys' dad divorced her, and she lost her teaching job; something had broken in her. For a period, there were often strange men and women who would come and go freely from the house.

Then one evening Grace introduced Ms. Jess. The sun was setting, and the light was growing very dim. I could only remember thinking 'Is Ms. Jess a man or a woman?"

A blaring auto horn snapped him back from his visit to the past. Usually no one paid any mind to the stop sign at the foot of the hill leading into Playa Dominical. Anyone with local knowledge would be prepared to yield to drivers running the stop sign to allow them to coast down the hill without braking. Whoever might be intent on following the rules was usually paid back with choice expletives and a honk of the horn. This time, however, the horn was coming from behind a vehicle that had stopped at the stop sign. " A two car traffic jam? Only in Dominical." The ensuing discourse of the drivers left them both smiling; the bats weren't the only entertainment around!

Halfway home on their long walk he burst into song. He turned to his only audience, Cheyenne, and strummed his old Wooster like a Stratocaster guitar to the tune of Lynyrd Skynrd's *Gimme Back My Bullet*.

Surfing my Wooster,
Been giving me quite a booster,
Catching waves like a rooster, crowing all morning long.
Gimme back, gimme back my Wooster
Gimme back to me.
Turned it so hard, fell on my cooster
This revealed that I am an aging kookster.
Gimme back, gimme back my Wooster
Gimme back to me.

Cheyenne laughed so hard that she almost peed her shorts. "Apparently, the bats and crazy drivers aren't the only entertainment around!" she proclaimed.

Tomorrow, they would be creeping deeper into the Osa, but for now, they paused to relish the simple pleasures of this moment, in this place. Before they made it back to Mango Mar, they walked down the Baru's bank to take a dip. The waters were clear again, and they were rejuvenating. It was true; the best things in life were free.

She had a hard time dropping off to sleep later. She had the same dream over and over. She kept reliving her tube ride, and each time the thought put her in a new place, covered by the wave's lip; a sweet place she had never been before. Every time she would almost wake up, but then she'd slip back into the dream that was so realistic she could taste the salty water. She was glad to be stuck in such a loop, and was delighted that her subconscious mind was still processing the experience. It was pleasantly intense!

The next day found them waiting for the five a.m. coastal bus south with a dozen minutes to spare. They had come prepared for rain;

Popi said he could feel it in his bones. But he reconsidered, and added "Perhaps it's only my water-logged body talking and not the rain. Who knows? Play it safe and keep the gear handy."

An American couple in their mid-twenties had joined them with their surfboards and backpacks. The fellow was shirtless with only a pair of baggies, worn beatnik sandals, and a huge smile for a wardrobe. Except for a pink bikini top, his girlfriend was dressed the same. Her smile was just a little smaller. They were both deeply bronzed from time in the sun. The guy looked over at Popi and said, "Jodi and I are surfing our way through Centro. Panama is where I've heard it's the best, so that's where we'll end up!"

While they waited for the bus to depart, Cheyenne and Popi heard the full rundown on the young couples' long trip, which had started in Puerto Escondido, Mexico. Their fresh, youthful exuberance and wide-eyed sense of adventure was contagious. The young surfer swore that he had almost just decided to stay in Escondido for a steady dose of the Mexican Pipeline, but the fabled consistency and variety of Panama's surf was still a draw. "Puerto Escondido gets too crowded on the better days. When it gets big, it isn't safe with all of the California Cornflakes taking off on everything. They even ride skimboards all over the place!" he said, smiling broadly as he spoke.

As the bus driver helped them stow their boards under the bus, Jodi summarized their journey so far. "Costa Rica has been a dream. The people, the surfing, the jungle and mountains, all of it is so magical; nothing like back home in the States!" She punctuated the statement with an annoyed roll of her eyes.

Popi and Cheyenne sat directly behind the driver, where there was more room at their feet for their packs. It was still dark when the bus rolled out of Playa Dominical and turned right onto the paved highway to Playa Hermosa, Playa Uvita and points south.

The sun's light began to slice through the mountains above the Coastal Highway as the bus made its daily rounds. The Pacific Ocean played peek-a-boo with them, poking through the hills as they rambled along. Once again, they were amazed and amused by the driver's deft skill, curious idiosyncrasies and aggressive driving tactics.

Rain arrived, along with the bus, when they stopped near Playa Pinuelas, and it grew more intense as they neared Playa Ballena, the Whale Tail. By the time they were beyond Playa Ventanas, dubbed the Window Arch, for the natural arches carved into the volcanic rock by the elements, they could see little more than low clouds and rain.

Despite the inclement weather, the farther they went down the Coastal Highway, the more comfortable they became. In no time they hit Palmar Norte, where there was a longer transfer stop in town. A vendor cut them some fresh pineapple for a welcome treat. They weren't bothered at all by the rain that seemed to taper off to a steady mist, giving them just enough time to enjoy the juicy fruit. As soon as they got going again, the rain picked back up. The friendly vendor stayed dry under the awning on his old farm cart, waving to them as the bus drove off.

The bus crossed the brown and swollen Rio Sierpe not far from town. The Sierpe is the region's kingpin river; it feeds one of the largest mangrove forests in the world. When they reached Chacarita at eight o'clock, the rain had gotten pretty heavy, and their rain gear was now a necessity.

They made their way off of the bus to board another one that would give them a ninety-kilometer ride to Puerto Jimenez. It was due at 8:30, so they waited under a grand manga tree for some shelter from the rain. There was no lightning, so Popi deemed it safe. Thankfully, the bus pulled up right on schedule, and they were lucky enough once more to find a seat right behind the driver.

No one on the bus appeared to be wet, but the two of them were drenched. He leaned over to Cheyenne and spoke to her in a discreetly low voice. "Ticos deal with Costa Rican weather like they were born for it. Rarely do they seem disheveled, or sweaty, or wet, or even stressed out, for that matter. They take it all in stride. Like magic, they know exactly when to step out of a dry place or pullup in front of the bus in a car just in time to avoid the puddles and the muddy mess. Look at us; we look like a couple of drowned rats. I guess Americans don't cope as well."

The rain came and went in sheets for so long it was easy to forget when it started in the first place. If it were snow, the drifts would have piled high above the road, and roofs would have collapsed under the load. Popi overheard an old man climbing aboard tell the driver how this was the wettest dry season in fifty years. Looking out the bus window, he lamented "To love the Osa, one must love the rain."

Cheyenne responded to his crazy statement. "Is that right?" She pointed out the window and added "Love this?"

Popi reached into his backpack and removed a couple of wrinkled pieces of paper from a worn zip lock bag and handed it to her. The first was a weathered postcard, and from the looks of it, it had been around for a long time. There was a picture of a mountain on the front with a wisp of smoke lifting from the vent of a volcanic peak. There was a brilliant blue sky in the background, and what looked to be a small Tico town in the foreground. A bold caption read "VISIT ARENAL!"

It was addressed to her grandmother, Virginia Manly, at 265 South Schrader Drive, Satellite Beach, Florida. The inscription read:

Virginia, I'm now visiting the far tip of the Osa Peninsula in Matapalo. I'm staying at a friend's place called Tres Palmas. The view looking out and over the confluence of the Oceano Pacifico and Golfo Dulce is reverent and peaceful.

Miss the family, miss you and miss our routine. Actually, there are many things and people I miss, but I am enjoying the moment. This place is Heaven on Earth!

Stan

P.S.: Did ya know there were more than 200 volcanoes in Costa Rica? Most are under the sea.

The second piece of paper was a letter. She opened it and began reading it to herself.

April 4, 1984, 5:55 AM
Tres Palmas
Matapalo, Osa Peninsula
Clearing skies, with a bewilderingly dense fog spilling over the mountains of NW Panama across the Golfo Dulce. Light southeast wind, mild temps and thick humidity (the wet stuff you disdain).
 Surf: 5-to-8 feet (depending on the tide) ultra-clean and rideable at Cabo Matapalo. Seas 9 feet at 17 seconds.
 Howler monkeys are howling and shaking the trees above me. A foursome of scarlet macaws is loudly announcing their passage, and a pair of hummingbirds has gravitated to a red hibiscus a few feet away. It's just an average Matapalo morning.
 Cheyenne read the words silently, without raising her eyes. For her, the letter explained a bit of Popi's pain.
 Dearest Virginia,
 Love is distant without you. I'm not trying to break your heart. What was I thinking when I let you go? As much as it hurts to miss you, I live here.
 What was I thinking when we said 'Good-Bye?' What was I thinking when we walked away? What was I thinking allowing us to part? What was I thinking . . . ?
 My love for this place turns to despair without you. It is like I am torn between two lovers, Matapalo and you.
 Loneliness tears at my heart and it may soon stop without you. As much as every day without you is painful, death awaits me back in the States. I'm no fool, I want you, no one else, but the idea of leaving Matapalo is painful. I am afraid that we are drifting worlds apart. Why am I being pulled apart by love and paradise?
 Stan

 After she finished the letter she looked at him with caring eyes. She placed the letter into the baggie, handed it to him, and touched his hands, covering them softly with her hands. They both noticed that the rain had stopped. As the bus clambered and crept its way over the devilish road deeper into the Osa, the sun quickly washed away all of the gray gloom.

"Your Aunt Irene hated parts of her first trip to the Osa."

She gave Popi an inquisitive look as he went on. "It was the roads she hated the most. She came along with her brothers and me the first time we drove this road to Puerto Jimenez."

For the fifth time in as many minutes, the bus came to an abrupt halt, moving forward carefully to maneuver over a stretch of potholes and broken pavement.

"These roads beat her back up pretty bad. I didn't know the definition of slow back then. I was full speed ahead!

I can remember it like it was happening right now. It was a late Sunday afternoon, and we were jamming the stereo full blast, listening to the Clash or B-52's, and singing along out loud. The road had been all but unmanageable for hours. It featured steep inclines, dangerous potholes, deep mud bogs, sharp pavement drops and a couple of white-knuckle river crossings. Somewhere very near here, in the middle of nowhere, was where she finally demanded to get out of the truck. She refused to go another inch.

We had to sit through a tongue lashing and listen emphatically for a long time before she relented and came back aboard. Somehow, we still managed to make it to Puerto before dark."

"Did she come back?"

He smiled and nodded his head yes. "By the time we made it up to El Mirador Osa and stopped, she saw it in a completely different light. It will improve anyone's outlook to behold the view of the Golfo Dulce and the Osa valley from up in those mountains; you'll see."

The bus twisted and turned its way up a critical segment of shattered pavement. The edge of the road, which dropped vertically to the jungle floor far below them, was too close for comfort. They shifted their attention to the driver. He winced and grimaced as he fought in vain to save his tires from being harshly punished in the minefield-like road full of gaping potholes. For most of the trip he played a game of pothole cat and mouse like a world champ. After successfully negotiating a tricky little stretch without losing speed, Popi remarked, "This guy's a pro!"

After a short pause, he picked up the old stories again. "Your grandmother despised the humidity; couldn't keep her beautiful, blonde hair dry for a moment. The language and culture barriers also stood in her way. Your uncles, Roobt and Drake, loved Costa Rica, though. We traveled here together many times before they quit coming."

"Did they lose interest?" Cheyenne questioned.

"No, they loved it almost as much as me. How could they not? It was everything that we lived for; bountiful nature, surfing, and fishing in paradise."

"Then what kept them away?"

"Between the two of them, they were more pragmatic than I am. Their generation, especially those two, appreciate the value of sustainability. They got a sailboat and sailed to the Bahamas and further south, where they found their own paradise. They lived off the grid and swore off of flying because of the huge carbon impact of the airline industry."

Their philosophy turned more towards sustaining the planet and in turn, the family's future. They invested their time and energy into reaching a personal goal of leaving a softer energy footprint. They paid careful attention to more organic production and personal consumption of energy.

They have been using their website and production company to further their ideals. They believe third world countries like Costa should forget about the old energy and delivery systems. They love to say 'BP ... beyond petroleum and off of the grid.' I hope they make an impact. Their approach is at least part of an answer for a successful future."

"Cool! But, you came back once, right?"

"Correcto!" he responded. "And I almost stayed here for good."

Popi's attention turned his eyes to and out the bus' window. A train wreck of fatal thoughts rushed at him, leading him back to where he was the last time he set foot in Matapalo. But before he lost himself completely in the black of the past, he realized Cheyenne was at his side; now he was prepared to face the somber and overcome his hurtful past. Reaching over he took Cheyenne's hand.

Once they reached Mogos at the top of the road they could see for miles under the clearing skies. The air was clean, and the sight of the magical Golfo Dulce and the rugged beauty of her mountainous shores captivated Cheyenne. "This is surely a place where one could be fully absorbed by the beauty of Mother Nature, or even perhaps a place to hide or to find one's self."

"As the long-time Florida treasure hunter, Mel Fischer, once said, 'The real fun is in the quest for treasure!'" Popi replied. "Try to understand; I was lost when I first came to the Osa. Back at home in Florida, life had become dull, so black and white, but here in the Osa life was in Technicolor. That may have been when I started dreaming in Technicolor, too, but I think I always did. Maybe it was more like my dream world, and real life met and fell in love or something like that."

The bus continued tooling downward towards Puerto. By the time they reached the split in the road to Bahia Drake, the bus had nearly reached sea level. The driver swerved onto the branch that led to Ricon and Puerto. After a few miles the road had become extremely rough and dusty, and Cheyenne had no problem imagining her Aunt Irene's discomfort back in her time.

The road, bordered by miles of deep green pastures and fields of rice, was hemmed with barbed-wire fences that penned in Brahma bulls, horses, livestock and other crops. Scattered clusters of houses, people, and activity spread out sparsely along the route with gardens and lush stands of bananas, papaya, and mangos. It seemed like the bus stopped at each of them, but few passengers got off; most of them were obviously heading to Puerto Jimenez.

When the bus finally pulled into Puerto Jimenez and past the soccer field, the sun was directly overhead, and the humidity could be scooped with a spoon. A couple of dogs napped on the main street, a dirt road, like all of the others in town. Two men wearing machetes on their belts and sporting cowboy hats exchanged salutations from horseback in front of the bank on the street, making Popi think if any town in Costa Rica ever felt like a town out of the Wild West, it was Puerto Jimenez.

Cheyenne's eyes were opened wide as she went to buy a phone card at a soda. This was a combination family-owned Tico restaurant and convenience store, where she and Popi shared a casado; salad, red beans and rice was the special of the day. The place was a hole in the wall next to the bus station, but the casado was typical Tico, and was excellent. As Popi finished up his plate, Cheyenne searched for a pay phone to call Jose'.

She had been thinking about him exclusively in Dominical and was hoping to see him for a rendezvous at Matapalo. Sidney had strayed further from her mind. Knowing her whereabouts, Popi waited patiently and struck up a conversation with the two Ticas working the soda.

He asked the younger of the two, the one clearing the table, "Tu hablas Ingles?"

She replied with a sheepish little grin. "Si, a little."

"Have the fishermen been catching tuna?"

Again, with the same diminutive smile, she politely replied. "Si, a little."

Puerto was a fishing community, and you could ask almost anyone for a fishing report and get useful, or at least hospitable, information. As he sat drinking a glass of cold water, his mind wandered back to the time he had spent there. Puerto had two types of weather; hot and wet, or hot and dry. There was no way of getting to Matapalo without traveling through Jimenez, and he wondered if there would even be a Jimenez without a Matapalo.

His mind drifted off, revisiting a fishing trip west of Cabo Matapalo.

They had been very fortunate when, first thing in the morning, they had located a massive pod of spinner dolphin feeding together with a ravenous school of two to three-hundred-pound yellowfin tuna. Irene and her brothers had been extraordinarily blessed, catching a couple of these giant yellowfins. They had eaten sushi and grilled tuna steaks for a week.

Cheyenne returned to the soda with a smile that spoke for itself. Joe had been very happy to hear that they had reached Jimenez. He would join them as soon as he could get away from school and San Jose.

After a walk around town, it was a cinch to see why this place had earned a colorful reputation. Scarlet macaws played together in the trees lining the streets. A pair of toucans squawked over lively Latino salsa music drifting from a Tico cantina. A slow, steady stream of Ticos, hippies, yuppies, hikers, fishermen and Ex-Pats moved in and out of a dozen or so main street venues.

Even though the town nearly sat on the edge of civilization it had many conveniences. The waterfront was active, with simple, but practical pangas, a long dory with an outboard that taxied customers and goods to and from larger sport fishing and commercial boats sitting in deeper water just offshore. Local craftsmen and fish mongers hung their wares out for sale in the shade of giant manga trees. The place was somewhat secretively seductive. It was also the last stop for electricity; the power lines stopped at Crocodile Bay not far from town.

Cheyenne suggested they exchange American dollars for Costa Rican colons, so they stepped into a sun-drenched line of about a dozen Ticos who were patiently waiting for their turn to enter the bank. It was hot, and security at the door was intense and thorough. The line moved slowly and continued to grow behind them.

After a twenty-minute wait, an intensely preoccupied, sanctimonious businessman brusquely shouldered his way ahead of Cheyenne to the front of the line. Immaculately and impressively dressed in an expensive, tailored suit, and perfectly shined Italian dress shoes, his hands were filled with a stack of documents, as he spoke loudly in Spanish on a cell phone, trying to impress the onlookers with his prowess.

Popi gave the man the stink-eye, but Cheyenne spoke firmly to the rude man. "Excuse me, sir!"

Without answering or looking at her, he dismissed her by continuing his cell phone conversation, and leaned forward slightly to emphasize the fact that he was ignoring her.

She glanced at Popi with a shrug and a look of disdain. Popi sensed she was ready to give the usurper a piece of her mind, but he motioned no with his hands and head, and delivered her a look that was easily interpreted. "Let it ride because he isn't worth the hassle."

As Cheyenne thought about retaliating, a somewhat small, furry dog with a whitish-tan coat approached the bank line with a springy trot. While it might have easily been mistaken for a mongrel, it was probably a peekapoo or Bichon mix. It began sniffing the feet of each person as it made its way to the head of the line.

They noticed the dog, but it paid no mind to them. As the dog reached the head of the line, it sniffed the feet of the rude interloper. Popi elbowed Cheyenne and motioned towards the dog. Still on his phone, the businessman sensed the dog's presence, looked down indignantly for a second and shuffled his feet about to discourage its attention.

As if he was for-hire, the dog lifted his leg and showered the man's Italian dress shoes with urine. "Swift justice; Karma's a bitch!" Popi said.

The disgusted businessman howled in disbelief and reacted as if his feet had burst into flames. He fumbled with his phone and papers until they got away from him and landed in the muddy, yellow puddle at his feet. When he saw everyone laughing hysterically at his retribution, he ran after the dog, hurling angry threats and curses. He furiously chased the little cur through a waist-high hedge of blooming gold-dust crotons and hibiscus, and tripped and landed face first in the grimy dirt.

By the time he managed to get up and brush himself off, he was livid with rage and determined to make the insolent little dog pay for what it had done. The red-faced man followed the scampering mutt around the corner of the bank into a side alley, as everyone howled in delight.

There was a sunburned dude in line behind Popi sporting an exceedingly long, red ZZ Top beard, dingy blue jean overalls, and smoking a hand-rolled cigarette. He seemed to enjoy the spectacle more than anyone. When he finally regained his composure, he said, "That was a real LuLu!" Everyone in the line agreed!

With their money exchange complete, they strolled out of the bank. The dog, their new hero, was sitting properly at the door as if it was waiting just for them. Cheyenne spoke first and kneeled down to pat and embrace the animal. "You're an angel of a pup! I couldn't have done that any better!"

Popi scratched its chin and concurred. "A saint; how about a little devil? I believe we'll call you LuLu!"

After a visit to the main street bakery, the three of them, with LuLu leading the way, strutted out of Jimenez past the weathered old metal sign that stood askew at the end of the main street. It read Matapalo 18 km.

They had found a guide to Matapalo...man's best friend!

Within ten minutes the three of them reached a single lane, rusted, steel-beam bridge just past the edge of town. LuLu's nose tilted up as he sniffed the air. Instantly, with an insistent look back and a yank of his head, he led the way down towards the creek bed to the old lower road that was used before the bridge was constructed. Down the road, blazing in their direction, a dust-kicking SUV carrying a load of surfboards came careening over the bridge.

If they hadn't followed LuLu, their fate may have been very different, perhaps with tragic consequences. The runaway rental hit the bridge about as quietly as a Texas tornado and the jolt of the abrupt change of road surface and elevation taken at such high velocity nearly lifted the hood off the rental. The surfboards rattled and shifted, but somehow remained stationary. Through the side windows, two startled faces flashed by in a blur with their mouths wide open and their heads jerked back from the shocking experience. Strains of the Zack Brown Band leaked from the open windows as they sped off in a cloud of dust up Highway 245.

Thankfully, their canine sherpa had opted for the lower road, which provided a perfect escape route from the pending disaster. He led them down to the creek, where its transparent water swirled around their ankles as he skipped onward across a path of smooth river rock.

Finally Popi broke a long silence. "I first came to the Osa to embrace the primordial experience, and also to escape something else. Was it responsibility? Yes, definitely, it was responsibility, but not the conventional kind. I wanted to escape the encroaching culture back home. The more time I spent here, the more I despised the various aspects of American society; the things making us resemble the Babylonian Empire.

We are the world's greatest consumers, or destroyers, if you choose, of the Earth's natural resources. I wanted to distance myself from that kind of irresponsibility; from that kind of guilt. You can't just take from nature; you must give back, too, or sooner or later she's going to strangle ya."

She listened, nodding her head in empathetic acknowledgment.

Popi went on. "Florida was a natural paradise when Europeans first arrived. It wasn't until the 1930's that its population hit the million mark. By the late Fifties and early Sixties we were only thirtieth in population, and then in less than one lifetime we rose to third. Twenty-some-odd million folks live on top of the world's biggest, baddest sand bar now!

I don't believe there's ever been a state in the U.S. of A. that has been as desecrated in the name of progress by greedy development, dirty money, and shady deals than the Sunshine State. All along the way, the state government continually encouraged growth, but did little to protect the integrity of her natural assets as a heritage for the people. Pardon me for grumbling; Florida will always be my first love, but I hate to see her violated."

With nightfall in the wings, their little mascot led them on with the chutzpah of an alpha wolf. He continued on the detour to a neglected side road under a modest sign reading Osa Refuge that was nailed to a mango tree. LuLu was no longer tidy and white, but wore a thin coat of dust from head to toe. Popi looked about the same, and he was getting tired. He began to recollect; he was sure he'd been down this old dirt road before. He leaned down to speak to LuLu. "Where are you taking us? There ain't anything down here but coconuts and empty beaches."

Cheyenne joined in with feigned indignation. "LuLu, what new epic adventure could you be leading us into?"

Popi took the hint. He regained his positive attitude and courageous sense of adventure. His perpetual smirk returned under his slightly bent red beak and barked "On we go!"

Popi realized that the simple fact that the three of them were hiking the Osa, footloose and fancy-free, was the realization of his vision. Now he had the energy and enthusiasm to follow LuLu to the end of the Earth.

Cheyenne responded in kind. With her chin up and tan shoulders thrown back, she marched barefooted behind the determined dog as if she were Cleopatra. Her smile, however, was Mona Lisa's. Her confidence became stronger, and her inner beauty radiated more with each stride.

Popi felt sure LuLu's detour to the sea would take them down for a refreshing swim or a scavenger hunt on the beach. "Bichons were bred and bartered by Spanish and Portuguese seamen for centuries. They're known among sailors as fine shipboard companions who love to go to sea.

Sun Tzu's The Art of War credits scouts and spies as strategic advantages that can ultimately win a war. LuLu is proof positive that the general was correct. According to my bearings, we should be seeing the ocean soon. Our little scout is being drawn by the scent of the salt air; he is taking us to the ocean."

Their scout, however, was not growing excited about the ocean; he was homing in on the smell of food. His scout nose had recognized the scent of vittles simmering over a campfire. LuLu obliviously had his priorities in order, and he picked up the pace. The threesome soon came upon a secluded cove lined with coconut, almond, banana, sangria and ceiba trees.

"These trees are a good omen" he remarked. "The Mayans revered the ceiba tree; they believed it sprouted from the center of the earth, and connected the terrestrial world to the spirit world above. For them, the scent of a burning fire and the aroma of cooking was a holy reminder that food, water and shelter were divine gifts."

They could see a light wisp of smoke rising from a thicket down the beach a bit. LuLu didn't wait; he trotted off with no concern for them. The soft, wet sand pulled at their feet until they felt like flies in molasses. The soft sand didn't slow LuLu down one iota, though, as he picked his way along the edge of the steep beach. Popi grinned as he watched the crazy little dog running like the wind. "That's one smart doggie! He knows exactly what he's doing."

The sun was sinking and the tide was advancing upward to the steepest part of the beach, and in the east a full moon was rising over the mountains. This gave Cheyenne a sensation of freedom; she felt strangely liberated from the confines of civilization. The experience surpassed her expectations as she enjoyed the moment. "This may be the first full moon I see rising over the Golfo Dulce, but it surely will not be the last," she said.

She was anticipating one of Popi's dissertations, and he didn't let her down. "She's an extraordinary place. She's one of only a few tropical fiords in the whole world. She sustains many varied and unique land and aquatic habitats. She's home to a wonderfully complex diversity of marine life, including dolphins, sea turtles, and tropical fish like billfish, wahoo, dorado, parrotfish, red snapper, rooster fish and countless others."

Cheyenne exquisitely tilted her head and asked "She?"

"Yes! She; she is a mother. This is a critical habitat for both humpback whales and the giant whale shark. It's the only place known to man in the entire world where both species breed and give birth. Her beaches serve as significant nesting grounds for hawksbill, Olive Ridley and leatherback sea turtles. She's a nursery for thousands of kinds of sea creatures. She's a topographical freak; her straits have underwater peaks that make them significantly shallower than most of the interior waters. These deep, protected waters explain the abundance of open ocean marine life inside the gulf and why they like to come here to breed."

Cheyenne understood it was places like the Osa's Golfo Dulce that were so valuable to the world that they needed to be protected at all cost. Otherwise, our natural world might not survive for future generations. She shuddered at the dismal vision that the thought conjured in her mind.

As they crossed the dune line they saw LuLu leap into the arms of what looked to be a very old man sitting next to a fire amongst a clutch of dwarf coconut trees. LuLu's tongue swiped across his face like a bartender wiping his counter; quick and complete.

Steam was rising from a Dutch oven that was hung over the fire from a makeshift tripod constructed of driftwood. The old man was sitting on a bench cobbled from a flat slab of mahogany driftwood set atop a stack of river rocks. He had a bundle of banana leaves placed carefully to one side. When the oily-haired fellow saw the smiling pair approaching, he stood up, propelling LuLu from his lap.

In an unrecognizable southern drawl the old man croaked "Have ya' selves a seat and sit a spell. Ya'll er just in the nick of time fer supper! The name's Buckwheat; very kind to meet ya."

As he reached forward with his leathery hand his eyes zoomed right past Popi to fix long and hard on Cheyenne. Popi stepped up to intercept his glare and offered him an introductory handshake. Buckwheat's grip was firm and confident despite his small stature and lowly circumstances. The man was more than well-worn from the deprivation of homelessness and Popi could see an indelible loneliness poorly hidden behind Buckwheat's dancing eyes. His head veered from side to side continually and his body was conspicuously bent. Sporadically, a grimace of pain would flash across his face. The one constant was a sparkle of delight that lit him up every time he looked at Cheyenne. Popi wondered if it was demonic delight. Regardless, something wasn't right.

His campsite was tight and squared away. A five-gallon green, glass jug full of water was slung from a rope harness for easy pouring. There was an improvised shanty with a foyer made of a tarp covered with a sheet of clear plastic suspended by salvaged rope between two palms. Bedding and personal items were tucked neatly under a lean-to roof of woven palm leaves supported by a frame of driftwood posts and palm trunk columns.

One of the palm trunks had been carved out, shelved and pegged to store fishing tackle, tools and toilet items. There were hooks, weights, spools of line, and a couple of old reels, but there was only one stout boat rod that needed refurbishing. Three Cuban yo-yos (hand lines spooled around tin cans) hung from a rusted piece of barb-wire gnarled into slits in the trunk.

Next to the fire, perpendicular to the bench, there was a long, smooth, half buried, driftwood log that made a perfect settee. The guests made themselves comfortable and sat down on it. Their host, with his shoulder-length silver mane, looked like he may be old as Methuselah. It was hard to guess his age in the dancing light and smoke of the fire. Cheyenne marveled that he looked like a grizzled old codger who could be ninety-years old, but occasional flickers of reddish light from the fire smoothed his rugged features to expose for the briefest moment the face of a handsome young man. His once muscular build hinted that one day in the past he could've actually been a surfer. Popi was nagged by a hunch that, perhaps, the old man was a face from his past.

They watched him reach deep into a tall military-style, green canvas duffle bag and pull out a set of coconut shell bowls and mismatched eating utensils. LuLu stayed close to Buckwheat as he peeled back each banana leaf one by one to reveal a large dogtooth snapper. The rosy fish, which must have weighed five or more kilos, had marble-white eyes and savory steam rising from its body.

Buckwheat doled out large portions of what looked like a concoction of rice, beans and who knows what from the Dutch oven into the coconut shell bowls. The spiffy, eight-quart Lodge Logic Oven, with extra thick cast iron walls and super tight lid, was perfect for campfire cooking. Obviously, Buckwheat was a seasoned outdoor chef.

Before he could pass out the dishes, Cheyenne broke the ice by standing up to ask "May I?"

She pointed towards the fish's head. Buckwheat answered with a wobbly, affirmative nod of his head. He watched her every move intently as she positioned herself over the fish, scooped out one of its opal-white eyes from its socket with the nail of her pinkie and plunked it into her mouth. She pealed the whole skin off in one neat, easy piece. She used her fingers to dislodge a healthy chunk of the flaky fillet and placed it on top of a bowl of the rice and bean concoction.

She delivered it to Buckwheat with a mock curtsy. With an approving nod, he dug in as Cheyenne handed Popi his share. She enjoyed serving others, and did it with flair. Before helping herself she prepared a bowl of discarded fish skin for LuLu, who wagged his tail wildly in approval. Like old friends, the four of them sat in tranquil silence, savoring the goodness of their meal as they gorged themselves under the light of the royal moon.

Popi had seconds. Experience and wisdom had taught him to eat heartily in such circumstances; one never really knows when or where the next meal may come from, if it does at all. Buckwheat looked down and scratched under LuLu's chin with his bony fingers. He looked up at them and said, "Cute little dog you've got here."

In perfect harmony, they responded "We thought he was yours!"

Collectively they turned to each other, and then to LuLu. The dog stared back at them, looking a little embarrassed. It seemed as if he wanted to say "Hey, remember, I'm man's best friend!"

They looked over at Buckwheat, who declared "I ain't ever seen this dog before, but he surely is a fine little bicho." A smile appeared on his weathered old face as he patted LuLu's head with one hand, and fed him a morsel of fish with the other. His eyes returned to Cheyenne when he finished with the dog, leaving Popi wondering what was going on.

Cheyenne explained how LuLu had befriended them and then guided them straight to his campsite. Buckwheat shook his head and repeated "Da darn little thang" three times.

Popi sat and watched from the sideline and listened as the other two chatted back and forth. They reminisced about their childhood pets and speculated about LuLu's past as they took turns stoking the fire. Popi forced himself to stay attentive for as long as he could, but after a spell he started nodding off, so he took out his pack and unlaced his Oregon bedroll. He and Cheyenne each carried a self-inflating mattress. He readied his for the night near the edge of the fire.

Once situated, he lay on his back and watched the smoke from the dying flames sending embers up into the endless sky. It had a hypnotic effect, and he began humming Louie Armstrong's What a Wonderful World. As he drifted off he thought he heard Cheyenne saying "I'm tired of all the darkness in our lives. This world is full of injustice."

His eyelids dropped shut as he tumbled into a dream world where he found himself strangely suspended between past and present. He was looking through a porthole-like window, where he saw Cheyenne skipping barefoot down the old dirt road to Playa Dominical. Before its improvement, the road was not much more than a tunnel hacked out through the jungle. Cheyenne was wearing a thin sarong decorated in Rastafarian colors. She was quite alluring, except for a lit cigarette dangling loosely from her lips, a Pall Mall, like Lester's Mom cherished.

From the dream's dankest corner, a familiar voice belched out "I could tag that sweet pussycat!"

Under the surface of sleep, Popi seethed with anger. With murder in his heart, he wrapped his hands around the neck of the nightmare's intruder. He strained to identify the sinner's face throughout the violent struggle, but the porthole in the dream that he was reaching through kept limiting his vision.

He couldn't breathe! The exasperating struggle forced him awake. He was relieved when he realized that he was wringing his own neck and let go. He lay still and drew a long breath. He took a few more, and as his heartbeat returned to normal, he closed his eyes and relaxed.

Then, in a flash, his eyelids sprang open. He looked straight up and was almost blinded by the full moon. He snapped his head around a few times to get reoriented. Cheyenne was sleeping peacefully less than a body's length away by the dwindling coals. Directly across from her, on the other side of the fire, Buckwheat was sprawled spread eagle on a thin mat, with LuLu snuggly tucked between his legs. A chill ran up and down his spine, as he began to realize who Buckwheat was. It was not good.

"No matter how far a man runs or where he hides, he can never escape the past forever." Popi grumbled. He had a feeling that someone from his past was coming back to haunt him. "I think I know this guy from somewhere."

He was surprised when Cheyenne leaned over to quiet him. "Shhh, quiet, Popi. You know him?"

"As far as I know, I've never seen him before, but there is something familiar about him. I can't put my finger on it, but I think it might come to me before too long" Popi whispered. "In the earlier days of the international surf community, there was a criminal element that did business on the black market, mainly illicit drug trafficking. A few were ruthless." It was all slowly coming back to him.

He knew who this S.O.B. Buckwheat was. Back in the day, he was known as Duke Dastard, but behind his back they called him Puke Bastard. Duke was the kind of guy who got what he wanted regardless of the restrictions of law, boundaries or moral conventions. Once, in a seedy bar in Rincon, Puerto Rico, Popi had heard Duke declare that his only regret in life was that he hadn't killed a couple of old friends who had crossed him once in a deal gone wrong. He remembered the man's harsh words. "They got their dumb asses busted and dropped the dime on me! If I ever see either one of 'em agin', I'll cut'em a new asshole!"

Duke had reached into one his calf-high boots, whipped out a big Bowie knife and slashed wildly at the air. Popi got a chill when he remembered how he had warned Duke Dastard that night. "Put that away before some fool gets hurt" he recalled telling the man. Duke didn't like to be told what to do, but after a long, frosty stare-down with a younger Stan Manly, he reluctantly returned the weapon to its sheath.

Duke was a classic case of sociopathic behavior. Like a lot of fifteen-year old runaways, he ended up establishing residence in Florida. He found work on a Fort Pierce shrimp trawler and worked his way up to captain before buying his boat at the age of twenty-four. He had no respect for women and was frequently heard espousing his opinions on them. "Women; they're all bitches and whores. I find 'em, feel em', fick'em and forget 'em."

He was a bad ass who prided himself on getting in a surprise sucker punch at the first indication of a confrontation; the lower the blow and cheaper the shot, the better. The desperado would often get sky high and blurt out his customary warning to all around him. "Don't even try to cross me, 'cause I'm a busy fuckin' street."

Duke had a bitter disdain for most people, but ironically, he had a soft spot in his dark heart for all other living things. He would rather kill three men than one cockroach. Popi had met him while surfing at the Indialantic Boardwalk, back in the mid-Seventies. He remembered him as being muscular and handsome, and he seemed to be a few inches taller in those days. His skin always seemed sunburned red, and his many freckles were dark and patchy across the entire top half of his body.

Stan Manly occasionally cross paths with Duke at some of the go-to surf breaks, like Shark Pit, Boardwalk, Spanish House, Monster

Hole and Reef Road. How could he forget catching that big southerly swell with Duke at St. Augustine's Blowhole before they closed the beach to driving? It was early August, and the waves were perfect six-to-eight feet. Each wave shaped like a horseshoe bowl created a tube breaking both left and right for a hundred yards over an old shipwreck.

He and Duke had shared outgoing, outspoken and fearless personalities back then. They had made a fast connection out surfing in the water, but they rarely socialized for more than a few minutes on land. They traveled in different circles, but these circles touched one another often, since their nucleus was surfing.

Before long, Duke was on his way to Coleman, one of Florida's finest Federal correctional facilities; he had been charged and convicted for smuggling a quarter-ton of marijuana. He had thought his scheme was perfect; he would meet a small freighter out in the middle of the Gulf of Mexico that supplied high quality, meticulously graded and cured red-bud Colombian marijuana.

The Panamanian freighter was on its scheduled route to Tampa with raw textiles, paper and latex. They travelled in opposite directions and stayed at least three miles apart, so as not to look suspicious on the Coast Guard radar. The ship used a souped-up launch to run the load over to Duke and other smugglers, undetected by radar. It seemed no one was the wiser.

Then Duke would start his crew shrimping and slide right in where the rest of the fleet was working until they filled the hold. When finished, the weed would be buried under a few tons of shrimp and ice. Duke had passed more than one inspection coming into port without flinching.

At first he would just head straight into Fort Meyers or Everglades City to download the shrimp by day and the pot by night. He would then run them both up the coast to New England markets and make a killing. He liked to keep his load smaller than most smugglers because he could charge more than twice the going rate for his gourmet Colombian weed than anyone could get for the highest grade of Mexican.

One day, the crew of the Panamanian freighter brought along an unsolicited kilo of cocaine as a bonus. Duke didn't turn them down. He and his team put the product to good use back on shore and sold whatever was left over. Their generosity at clubs and parties paid off, and in no time, everyone who made the scene had to have nose candy. Duke ordered more every trip. It was much more profitable than marijuana and granted him a prized power seat in the realm of the nightlife subculture of Miami.

Once they got a craving for a whiff of the jiff, young ladies would willingly compromise their morals, and even sacrifice their virginity, for a few lines of blow. Duke and his crew took full advantage and enjoyed every excursion into the balmy city to pillage the village as Duke would say. His decadence and downright debauchery were reprehensible; he seemed destined for hell, and he relished it.

As the Coast Guard shut off traditional smuggling routes, Duke adjusted his course up the east coast to stay ahead of the law. He went from Miami to Boca Raton, Ft. Pierce, Sebastian, Eau Gallie, Merritt Island, and Jacksonville, and eventually into the Carolinas. At his peak, he was running three boats, three trucks, and three crews. He knew enough sales outlets to double his business, but he liked to play it safe.

Everyone should have been happy with the money, but a couple of his guys started filching a pound of pot or an ounce of cocaine to dispense of as they saw fit for pocket money. The two men in cahoots got caught doing the stuff with some teenage girls in Myrtle Beach, and after more than a month in jail in Conway, they jumped at the chance to cop a plea to Federal charges levied by the DEA. They could walk with a drug program and probation if they delivered Duke to the Feds. They set up a deal.

Luckily for Duke, when the Feds hit them it was a small load; there was no coke, and they didn't get caught with guns. He made himself right at home in Coleman for the next five years, less 42 days off for good behavior. He seemed to thrive in the prison environment and would brag "I'm the cock of the walk on this cell block!" His cell decorated with Surfer and Surfing magazine contained pullout centerfolds of guys riding giant waves and girls wearing tiny bikinis.

Coleman was where he earned the nickname Buckwheat. Both of the major gangs in the prison, the Bloods and Latinos, liked him and considered him a friend. To them, Duke was colorless, and he had the respect of both groups. He had gladly accepted his jailhouse nickname, and eventually even the prison guards called him Buckwheat.

Duke made several dubious jailhouse connections with some significant figures in African-American and Latino gangs, as well as a couple of serious-minded career white-collar criminals with management skills. He set his mind to take a new approach to business when he got out. It would be an equal opportunity enterprise.

The last time Popi saw Duke was out in the lineup at Manasquan Inlet up in New Jersey. Popi and Virginia had driven up there to visit with her family. Out in the water, Duke bragged about doing business in Thailand, where he had indulged himself with underage prostitutes. "I know a guy who brings 'em in from the farm. I get them sweet chicks fresh, tender, hot and juicy! They don't even have any tail feathers, yet! Ha, ha, ha, hee-hee!"

Popi admonished Duke with a scowl. "Dang, bro! What a pig!"

"That's right, Stan; I pork 'em and I pork 'em good!"

Popi steamed, "I ought to slap you silly!"

Duke just laughed and paddled further out to sit with a group of surfers waiting for the bigger sets. Popi was still burning with righteous indignation when he saw Duke point to the beach, where two 14-year-old girls were lighting up cigarettes. Duke crowed to the crowd "See those young hotties smoking cigarettes on the beach? I know they are freaking sluts. I'll bet anything I can get right into their pants every time. They say if they smoke, they poke!"

Popi knew Duke had said that for his benefit, just to rub it in and make him mad. What a jerk! What a lecherous bastard. Stan Manly had decided not to waste his time and energy; he blew it off and had started catching one wave right after another. He never saw Duke again.

It plagued him to recognize the identity of his friendly host. He hardly looked like the same man. He laid on his back for a couple of hours staring up into the endless expanse of stars. His dire reflections had his mind awash in a flood of concern and worry. He resisted the urge to confront his old acquaintance, or wake Cheyenne to make an escape. He wondered if it was wiser to wait until morning to make sure. He finally resorted to the Serenity Prayer.

God, grant me the serenity to accept the things I cannot change,
The courage to change the things I can,
And the wisdom to know the difference.

After his heartfelt appeal, Popi finally drifted off back to sleep. Before long everyone in the camp was in such a sound slumber that they were dead to the world. Even when a mother humpback and her baby calf surfaced nearby, clearing their blowholes with a remarkable reverberation, no one stirred.

Popi found himself back at the porthole with his hands trembling, wrapped around Cheyenne's throat this time. She was blowing smoke rings into his face and taunting him. "No worries, I love Duke's pork. You should try some! There's plenty for you, too. Have some sauce to go with it!"

Throughout the dream, she was picking a row of rotting teeth with her pinky finger. It was a revolting nightmare. He struggled to wake himself from the appalling battle with Cheyenne. When he finally succeeded, he sat bolt upright and frantically looked around the camp, but he found the perimeter secure and everyone sound asleep. All was well. LuLu was the only one who had been disturbed by Popi's fitful episode. He cocked his head to give Popi a look as if to say "Dude?! Honestly; chill out."

After a pause, the dog laid his head back down on Buckwheat's midsection, which was pumping up and down like a bellow while the man snored up a storm. Muttering under his breath and questioning his very state of mind, Popi felt his own forehead for fever. The moon caught his eye through the thick canopy; it was much lower in the western sky and morning's light would soon arrive. He lay back down, and his heavy eyelids dropped shut before his head hit the air mattress. It was a full hour after sunrise before he could lift them again.

On the other side of the dying embers, unbeknownst to Popi, Buckwheat had kept one eye partially cracked to spy on his guests throughout the night.

Popi rubbed his matted hair, scratched his numb head, wiped the stardust from his eyes, and looked around. Gone! Cheyenne and Buckwheat were nowhere to be seen. Horror struck him. Zen's third precept, the one about sexual immorality, throttled his mind. A young maiden is not to be despoiled! Fear, anger and profound frustration from the abrupt and bewildering circumstances struck his heart like a flaming arrow, burning him with insanity.

Wailing aloud in desperate remorse, tears welled up in his eyes until they flowed down both cheeks in broken streams. His mind was strongly suggesting sinister scenarios, complete with detailed illustrations of insidious images festering in the deepest recesses of his mind. He was so overloaded by pure panic that there was no place for plausible explanation or optimism. He jumped up too fast, got wobbly, and nearly sent himself spilling over into the smoldering remnants of the fire.

He stood there as if he were adrift in a fog and could hear the engines of an enormous ship bearing directly down on him. He fell to his knees, clutched the sand, and sobbed. "Cheyenne. Oh Cheyeeeenne! Oh no! Cheyeeeeeeeenne!"

He was at the end of his rope. Some kind of internal defense mechanism kicked in, and he heard a voice speaking from his soul. "See the light; be the light. The speed of light; nothing is faster than the light, but darkness fleeing before it. Be a man; getup and go. Go!"

His fearful rage subsided, his resolve returned, and his heart sang a new song. He lifted his wet, salty face to the heavens searching for solace. One single beam of intense sunlight cut through the palm frond roof of the shanty. It shined a bright spotlight on the tooled section of the coconut trunk where Buckwheat kept his gear. The barbed wire holder was bare, and the Cuban yo-yos were missing. Light flooded into him, and within seconds, Popi started getting the picture. "They went fishing."

He hung his head in humiliation as LuLu tried his best to lick away the remnants of his tears. He rose up on his feet and started to follow the trail of two sets of footprints that led out of the sheltered nook and down the shady rainforest dune line. The Golfo Dulce glimmered with a thousand hues of turquoise in the morning's resurrecting light.

He saw a pair of anglers out on a spit of land more than a kilometer away. Cheyenne and Buckwheat had walked and talked for quite a ways. They stood together out on a solitary, diminutive headland that protected a cove near the mouth of a slow-moving stream of pure, fresh water which driveled from the floor of a dense portion of rain forest just uphill.

"It's how you twirl the lure and when you release the line that makes the difference. Timing is everything. Here, let me show ya." he suggested.

Buckwheat politely took the yo-yo from Cheyenne. He held the heavy monoline a couple of inches above the swivel of a steel leader that looped through the eye of a dull, silver Gator spoon that had two mismatched, white feathers wrapped in red thread to the treble hook. He began whirling the spoon around over his head. When it reached full speed, he gave it a snap at the end of each orbit until a final whip of the line released the spoon way out into the sea. It landed perfectly along the murky edge of the thin current created by the outflow of the beachside stream.

Cheyenne watched him closely. He stood in the ready, leaned forward a bit from the waist, his face grew taut, and his tongue dangled from the corner of his mouth as he held his head just so. He quickly wound the line around the can as he retrieved the spoon with quick little jerks. Bucky kept missing strikes and silently cursed under his stale breath. It was vital for him to display his prowess before the eager damsel.

His desire to impress Cheyenne was ten times stronger than her genuine interest to learn the subtle art of the Cuban yo-yo and catch some fish. Buckwheat was enjoying himself a bit too much, and it made him look silly. Enthralled with this attractive, healthy, young female, and thrilled that he had found an activity to lure her closer in, that would be good enough, for now. He wasn't sure what was supposed to happen next, but it sure felt good to him to just follow the diagrams of old patterns.

On their walk down the beach to Buckwheat's honey hole, Cheyenne detected that the old geezer was showing some symptoms of Alzheimer's. As a teenager, she had volunteered at a day-care center for Alzheimer's patients where she worked after school at least one afternoon a week for three years. Her great-grandfather, Popi's dad, had died from the dreadful curse. The family knew well the ravages of the insidious disease.

Before leaving camp, Buckwheat had asked, "Cheyenne, will you get them yo-yos ... you know ... the fishin' cans off a' the tool tree and bring 'em with ya? He had reminded her twice more before they left.

Twice she had responded, "I got em,' Bucky."

"I like that. You can call me Bucky."

They had walked about fifty yards down the beach when Bucky stopped short and blurted out "Oh shit! We gotta' go back. I forgot the yo-yos.

"I got them" she had assured him.

"You did?"

"Yep, just like you asked me to."

"I did? Sure I did; I remember. It's all good. Let's go; let's catch some fish."

A little while later he stopped again. "Damn! Where's the goldarned yo-yos? I forgot the yo-yo's for Chris'sakes!"

Cheyenne reassured him yet again. "Got 'em right here, Bucky."

He still wasn't satisfied. "Sumpthin' ain't right! I forgot sumpthin'.

Where's da dadburn tackle box? My little green tackle box. Holy mackerel! We come all this way, and I went and left the lures and all the hooks and weights and everything we need! I guess we'll just hafta' use what's on the yo-yos and hope for the best."

She pointed at his hip. When he looked down, he was perturbed to find his green tackle box bulging from the gunny sack slung over his shoulder. He quickly diverted attention elsewhere. "You know there's no guarantee that we'll take Señor Robalo or Señora Pargo home as dinner guests. They don't always accept an invitation. Ya can't just make'em open up their mouth n' bite no more 'n you can make the sky turn blue."

Unnoticed by the pair on the spit, Popi stopped under some overhanging branches just short of their position to rest and observe. He was still a little bit rattled about Duke. LuLu sat at his feet to reassure him that all was well. He saw Buckwheat hand Cheyenne the line, telling her to "Make it happen!"

She did, too. On her very first toss! The wobbly, flashing spoon must've landed right in front of her quarry. As soon as it hit the water there was a sharp tug at the end of her line. By instinct, she retaliated with a sharp tug of her own. Whatever it was tore off on a jagged line; she worked slowly, pulling it in hand over fist with the yo-yo. Within a few minutes, she was hauling in her first nice fish.

Buckwheat called out "Robalo! Robalo!" A lengthy swordspine snook was soon floundering and taking its last jumps on the hard, wet sand between her feet. In a flash, Buckwheat unhooked and stowed the fish in an onion sack that he knotted to his side. Then, he grabbed the other yo-yo from the beach, waded out deep enough to keep the fish wet, and began to throw his lure.

As they fished side by side, Buckwheat confided in her about how he had done time in prison. Apparently, his long-term memory was still functioning, or at least making a visit. He explained how he had met some influential people in the drug trade there, and how, after his release he went to Amsterdam on a lark, where he had met a Dutchman, who was a legitimate impresario for growers and traders throughout the Orient. It was all legal there, too. He worked for the

Dutchman in his import-export business and was tutored in the esoteric protocol and procedures. He had developed an exceptional aptitude for the business.

"I got to be a liaison man. I connected the sup-ply to the de-mand" he divulged. "I just brokered up miscellaneous deals twixt di-verse biz-ness entities. It was usually up to me to make damn sure ever'body kept things amicable and pro-fessional. I had people for that. It was all about keepin' ever'one happy and gettin' what they wanted."

Cheyenne wasn't overly impressed. "What happened, did you get sent back to prison and go stir crazy?"

"Hell, no! I never got caught with nothin' again. I learnt to cover my ass, and all my bases, too."

He looked for a sign of interest from Cheyenne, but she was intent on fishing. He raised his volume a little to announce "Once, I hooked up my old buddy Razz Munsen with some heroin in Java."

That got a response. "Heroin? My God!"

"We didn't do it; we just got it to sell that one time."

Cheyenne found this troubling. "What about the people who bought it. What about them? What about their lives?"

"I hate to tell you. We didn't even think about them, just the money. I coulda surfed in Indo for six months on my cut!"

He had succeeded in stimulating a little interest. "Who is Razz Munsen?" she asked. "The name sounds familiar."

He was pleased to elaborate. "Razz Munsen was a surfer from New York. That scuzzy city rat won the East Coast Championships and was one of the best a' the early pros. He was always getting in the traveling surf movies. He went on an all-expense-paid trip to Java with an NBC camera crew. They went out there ta' film some top pros and a couple a' TV stars surf in some seriously sick waves for an episode of American Sportsman. Razz insisted that I come along to be a guide. Hell, I'd never even been there in my life!

Razz wangled a ticket and per diem from the network for me, and had me call the old Dutchman for some insight into the area. Boy, if he didn't have some! There was hash, Quaaludes, opium, killer weed, heroin, but not much in the way of coke to be had for next ta' nothin'.

Plus, we learnt' the best places to stay and eat from the Dutchman's business associates. We were there a' month waitin' for a good 'nuff swell.

The heroin was so cheap that Razz, who never did any hisself, bought as much as he could. He planned on jacking up the price but leaving it pure for an easy sale. He could clear 200 grand. I think the producer mighta went in on it, too.

Me and Razz and some other dude stripped the fiberglass off a the bottoms of all of the boards that he brought from his sponsor in Jersey; there were a dozen of 'em. We hollowed 'em out, stuffed 'em full a' the smack, and glassed 'em back up as pretty as ya please. They looked better 'n when we brought 'em, and a K-9 couldn't smell a thing. We got 'em all out clean on the NBC Lear jet with hardly even a sideways look from customs.

Anyway, whenever Razz got back home to New York, he had trouble unloading most of the heroin. He was gettin' paranoid and goin' crazy from holding so much smack. He called me up wonderin' if I knew anyone in Florida who might want it. I only knew one possibility; Sky Watling, a renegade Jamaican Rasta Mon with serious connections in Miami.

I knew him from Coleman. He was a righteous man. We got high all the time in the joint. I asked him if he wanted the junk. He said he couldn't get rid of that much without rubbing shoulders with people he didn't much care for, but on the other hand, he was willing to go up to New York and introduce me or Razz to some Jamaicans he knew in the Bronx. This Rasta dude's cuz', or nephew, or whatever, had got mixed up with some New York gangsta types like the Crips or the Raps, or sump'n. When Razz showed the heroin, they just up and shot him and gaffled Elmo for the smack. Razz was DOA, and Elmo was in the hospital for a month or two from the beating he took trying to hang on to the product."

"That's horrendous!" She was alarmed, but she kept her line in the water and kept fishing.

"Yeah, the War on Drugs got to be no more' n a war on people. The more radical law enforcement got, the more radical the dealers got. Once the ol' time suppliers and networks were taken out of the way, only psycho thugs wanted any part of it. They took all of it over, even the law. They run off or killed off all a' the cool Rastas, Indians and farmers who used to grow the good stuff. They wangled every operation and all the customers. They started melting out coke with acetone and lacquer thinner instead a' ether. It got to where a good bunch of 'em were no more n' out a' work communist guerillas from Nicaragua, San Salvador or wherever. Those boys don't even blink twice at blowin' your dadgum head off.

You know Cheyenne, it hit me after Razz got whacked. It was all my fault. I almost went up there with Sky just to introduce him to Razz in person and make sure ever'thin' was copasetic. I usually accompanied my man on the first trip. Razz said it wasn't necessary, so I stayed home.

After the shootin's is when it sank in; I figured ... just as easy ... it could a' been me. I had enough of it all. I gathered up all my ill-gotten gains, grabbed some clothes and accoutrements and headed down this way. I guess I gone feral since I ran out of money. I'm just livin' on this here beach waiting out those demons 'a death who are sure to come for me any day now. I deserve whatever I get."

Cheyenne calmed him, telling him emphatically that death wasn't coming anytime soon. She thanked him sweetly for teaching her how to catch a fish with a Cuban yo-yo, and reminded him that he still had a lot of living left to do. "God forgives you. Now, you need to forgive yourself. Just make the best of it, Bucky!"

"Make the best of it? I guess so. This wild freedom is the only deity I worship! I loathe computers. Wish't I could go back in time and shove a laptop down the dipshit's throat who invented em'. His family, and all of his friggin' friends can eat one, too! I hate 'em, they are from the Devil; I should know."

She listened as she kept on fishing. She stayed focused on her technique until a jumbo wake turned to hone in on her lure. She let the spoon drop a few inches, raised it up real quick and let it drop again. A white flash attacked like an angry monster, blasting water in all directions as it burst the surface. The denizen of the deep had a broad metallic-green back and long black line running the length of its silver body.

Other details were lost in a blur of action and speed. She squealed at the top of her lungs, evoking a similar response from a couple of macaws watching from the branches of trees nearby. Even though the powerful fish stripped line from her yo-yo so fast that it burned blisters on her fingers, she held on for dear life. The line slowed as the giant fish leaped out of the water.

"Holy mackin' moley!" Buckwheat hollered as the whopper fish leaped and shook its whole body in defiance.

"Grande negra robalo; it's a huge black snook!" Buckwheat cheered as he turned his back to the beast to coach Cheyenne. "Let it have line, but keep some pressure on 'er! Let off, but keep it steady!"

The line continued to tear the skin off of her blisters, but she followed his directions. It peeled off smoothly between her palm and the can as the fish made a mad dash to a deeper refuge. It struggled in desperation, as it rose halfway out of the water and shook like an enormous rag doll. Eventually, only its gaping mouth and open gills could be seen churning the water to froth. When the fish took off on another run, Cheyenne protested profusely as her line spun from the spool through her bleeding fingers. "Owww! That hurts! I can't take much more of this fun!"

Just then, four toucans glided by and landed on a nearby tree. Cheyenne thought she could hear them rooting her on. All of a sudden, she had a powerful sensation of déjà vu. "I've done this before! I know I have."

Buckwheat, meanwhile, was acting like a five-year old at Disney World. He was hopping up and down, flapping his arms, waving his hands, bobbing his head, and shaking his long silver hair all over the place. He was anticipating the fish's next tactic. "Don't give 'er no quarter, she's fixin' to sound. Keep 'er head up. Keep it up!"

Cheyenne's arms, shoulders and back were tense, and she could barely muster enough strength to pull. She grumbled sarcastically "Keep it up? This sucks! This fish just doesn't know when it's beat."

Popi and LuLu watched from their shady cover with great interest.

They could see that she was about to land a big fish on the primitive hand-line. His heart swelled with pride, and the little dog looked on as if it felt the same way.

There are things that nature teaches us; good and bad. Cheyenne's hard-fought battle wasn't over yet. It seemed a stalemate, one that could turn in favor of the fish any moment. The taut monofilament line was cutting into her hands and wrists. The wounds weren't deep, but the salt water amplified the pain. Wet hair pasted across her face framed an agonized grimace, and she was unable to release her grip to wipe the sweat away from her burning, blurry eyes.

Regardless, she grew more determined to win the battle with every passing second. Time was running out for her finned rival as it spent every last dash of energy trying to escape its mortal fate. The mighty fish swam back and forth, as large as a small child, in front of her as she pulled it ever closer to shore. She could feel the hope draining from the weakening fish. Her spirits soared. "She's mine, now!"

When she finally looked into the fish's eyes, her heart burst for her adversary. Under her next breath, she rooted for her opponent. "Come on big girl! You've got it in you; don't give up!"

Unaware that the fish had won Cheyenne's affection, Buckwheat gave her an exaggerated wink and said "In all my days fishing, this is the biggest snook I ever seen. It must be at least 30 kilos! It'll draw a crowd at the fish market; it will fetch a good price!"

She looked even deeper into the big eye of the massive fish. It seemed to look right back with wonder, not fear. It reminded her of the iconic fishing tales that had become a tradition in her family. Along with the legends, a code of conduct had been passed down through the generations as well. This fish was hers; she would decide what to do with it, when and if she landed it.

"It's over. Give the line a double wrap round yer' arm and drag er' up the beach" he implored her.

Cheyenne countered "Not yet, Bucky! This sow's not done!"

Then three explosive swipes of her broad yellow tail sent heaps of white water flying aloft as the finned beast accelerated into one last, desperate run for freedom. Cheyenne braced to stand her ground and let the hook pull or the line break, if it came to that. Leave it up to fate. She wanted the fish to live in recognition of such a noble effort, but her need to triumph overcame her romantic yearning to let her trophy go free. But first she would land the bad girl, somehow.

She managed to unwrap the twisted line as she rushed into the water to give ground and relieve pressure on the bolting fish. She let the fish pull her along with the current in the trough near the shore as she skip-floated along in the nearly chest deep water. Finally, she outlasted her opponent, and the royal snook went belly up. Cheyenne took in almost all of the line and began to pull the exhausted fish gently up to the beach.

Buckwheat came splashing up with the short wooden shaft of a hand gaff gripped tightly in his fist. He tried to push his way past Cheyenne to sink the gaff and secure the fish. But she was much quicker and more athletic. Cheyenne easily blocked and parried his attempt and quickly spun back around to keep control of the tiring fish. "Oh, no you don't!" she protested.

"Oh no, I don't what? I'm just trying to help!"

"You're not killing this fish! Get away with that gaff, or I'll take it and knock a knot on your head with it!"

"Wha'd you say, woman?!" he challenged with scorn.

She had tears of sweat running down her face and shoulders as she turned around to face him nose-to-nose. "You heard me, I'm letting her go!"

"You're what?" Buckwheat burst out in disbelief.

"She's outa here! End of story."

Popi and LuLu jumped out from behind their curtain of dense shade and sauntered towards the debate. From about fifteen yards away, he ended the stalemate with four short words spoken with authority. "Hey! Whatch ya'll doing?"

Buckwheat yelled out loudly. "Stan! You gotta see this snook. It's massive! Come take a look at it. Your crazy granddaughter wants to let it go. It sure will make a stir at the market; we can get a handful of cash fer' this one!"

Popi kept his voice steady and firm. "Forget the market, brother. Cheyenne wants to release her fish. Maybe you'll catch it next time, and then you can take it to the show."

Buckwheat listened and painfully recognized his wisdom. "Hell yeah, you're right! I'll get 'er next time, maybe. For now, it's her call. It's her fish!"

Popi gracefully slid into the water and waded over to them while LuLu ran barking from along the beach. One barb of the treble hook was buried deep into the hinge of the monster's jaw. Buckwheat produced a pair of needle-nose pliers from the pocket of his shorts and twisted it loose without doing any harm. Together, the three of them held the big fish upright to start the next step of catch and release ... revival. In unison, they gently rolled the huge fish over and held it upright in the water. She soon regained her strength and after three or four minutes she swam away on her own accord.

Buckwheat had to get in the last word. "Damndest thing I ever did see! Leave it to a woman to release the biggest snook in all of Costa Rica; it was probably the world's record."

Back on the beach, they walked three abreast over to the stream to let Popi try his luck. Cheyenne had enough of fishing for the day and was content to watch the two old men. Two adolescent Ticos had taken up stations on the other side of the flow to try their luck. Popi caught a nice rabalo and decided to call it quits. The sun was getting high, and they needed to clean their keepers as soon as possible to keep the meat fresh.

Buckwheat kept mumbling. "Damndest thing I ever saw. Let the world record snook just swim off."

They spent the rest of the day helping Bucky shore up his shanty, making repairs to the roof and squaring things away around camp until moonrise. They gorged themselves on a feast of fire-roasted snook fillets, brown rice, beans, and fresh fruit and veggie salad with some of Buckwheat's coconut vinegar dressing.

For dessert, Cheyenne was treated to a smorgasbord of Buckwheat and Popi tales. Popi broke the ice when he surprised Buckwheat by calling him Duke. When recognition came to him, Duke responded "I ain't that man no more. Please, just do like the girl and call me Bucky."

With that settled, the reminiscing was on. It was amusing if not a little sketchy. Cheyenne finally wrapped up the soirée with a question. "Popi and I need to turn in for an early start tomorrow. But first, tell me something. Isn't it a strange coincidence for you two old friends to meet here, on this secluded beach, after all of these years?"

"I don't know if you could call us friends. Your Popi sure could surf back in the day. I saw him out in the water all the time. He did his share a fishin' and guiding, too. Ever'one knew him all up and down the East Coast. He had my respect, not that I had much for anybody at all.

He never did like me much, I don't think. I never had no beef with him, though. Manly never crossed me. I just pissed him off a couple a' times, that's all. I didn't give a darn back then."

Popi chimed in with his version. "He was so self-absorbed that he truly believed that everyone owed him anything he wanted. We sure did catch some good waves from time to time. Bucky had no fear; he would take off on anything."

"True that. We caught our fair share a' waves" confessed Bucky. "I was a holy terror in those days. I loved to pillage the village and ravage like a savage. I guess I'm harmless enough, now, though. I don't bother no one anymore."

Gossip travels fast, even in a land dominated by one dirt road to nowhere through a rain forest jungle and cow pastures. The town was buzzing with the news of Cheyenne's giant snook. The two young Ticos they had seen earlier had witnessed the battle and were also confused by the release of the colossal fish. They told their uncle Alvin Valdez, a well-loved local cab driver, and now the story of the mighty American girl and her strange ways had spread all over town like wildfire.

Alvin was born and raised in Ricon, a secluded enclave on the gnarly nape of the Golfo Dulce; the town is situated on the rugged road from Chacaritas to the splendid vistas of Mogos. He was a member of one of the largest extended families in the region. He had logged thousands of hours carrying passengers between the scattered Osa outposts of Puerto, Drake Bay, Matapalo and Carate for many years. He had become so familiar and appreciated by all of the people that everyone claimed him as their own.

His green van was his true domain, and Tico folks always looked for it with anticipation. He often brought paying customers for their goods and services, and they knew they would soon be hearing fresh news or juicy gossip. He was glad for the opportunity to make extra money by referring fishing charters, surf and nature tours and other tourism services to his customers. If he got lucky, he might even be hired as a guide.

Alvin marveled at the proliferation of people coming from all around the world to visit his humble home on the Osa Peninsula. He was wise beyond his years and adept at establishing an instant rapport with anyone. He had a knack for collecting, cultivating, and embellishing the best stories to recount to his audience. He had found out early on that his charm and talent for storytelling kept his customers comfortable and entertained, and also brought him great tips.

Most of his foreign passengers wanted to fish, surf, sail, go sightseeing, visit a volcano or waterfall, experience wild nature, find a nice restaurant or something like that. However, there were some travelers who boldly sought to satisfy darker desires. He liked to keep his nose clean, so he directed these clients to one of his many cousins, Elvin Valdez. Elvin was the proprietor of a saloon, The Purple Osa, on the back side of the main drag in Puerto Jimenez. The Purple Osa was where these more depraved travelers could partake of anything that their heart desired.

Popi and Cheyenne got an early start after having a quick breakfast of steel-cut oats with mango and a mug of black coffee with Bucky. They quietly hiked on a well-worn footpath, listening to the inspiring sounds of the waking jungle. LuLu followed a couple of steps behind happily. Just as their footpath intersected the public road, the sweet sounds of the forest were drowned out by the coarse mechanical intrusions of society. It was Alvin's green van flying past them.

A recent spattering of rain had secured the dust and dampened the bottom of the arroyos weaving their way down from the mountains into the geometric system of ditches modified by farmers long ago to drain their fields or irrigate crops. The shadows were shrinking as the sun rose above the reach of the towering trees of the rain forest.

As they hiked side-by-side, Popi offered up some local history. "In this area, the land bordering the road has relatively new growth from rain forest replenishment programs. For unknown generations, Tico families cultivated fincas, small, diversified farms, around here. In recent years, Gringo types have bought up all the land so they could create the landscape of their dreams to support their utopian endeavors. Some were extremely wealthy by local standards and claimed huge sections of jungle as their private sanctuary. Some would even guard their new domain jealously from traditional use by the locals. You can say that the newcomers weren't looking for friends."

Most of the Ticos lived to regret their decision to sell their family farms. They went through the money and found themselves displaced. Only a few were able to parlay their grub stake into a livelihood."

LuLu started yelping over the music of the jungle. The concerto reached a crescendo when a troop of Howler monkeys with their long prehensile tails came swinging and swaying up to see what the barking was all about. Popi had to raise his voice to be heard over the wailing. "Howler monkeys! They are the largest of the New World primates and are probably the world's loudest, noisiest animal by far. An adult male can be heard a mile away, no problem."

A few pairs of green parrots patrolling the highway's dense canopy squawked loudly, as if to prove that they deserved a share of the attention. They rounded a curve in the road and came upon a herd of cows grazing on lush grass in a spacious clearing. The pasture had a vivid backdrop of lavish forest, mystical mountains and dazzling blue sky, punctuated by puffs of cotton-white clouds. "Living proof that not every Tico family has sold out" Popi stated proudly.

A traditional scene unfolded before them in the pasture next to the road. There was a hump-backed Brahma bull in the foreground, and positioned resolutely in front of him was a solo sabanero. He was mounted proudly in the engraved saddle on his caballo with a lasso in his hand. The cowboy was one of the five Rodriquez brothers; his family tree and claim to ownership went back to the days just after the Spanish Conquistadores conquered these lands hundreds of years before.

He was short but firmly built. He stood up in his stirrups with a calm, but serious look in his eyes and a slight grimace on his deeply-bronzed face. He twirled the hemp loop an arm's length above his slouch hat and let it fly. The bull dropped his head, and the lasso slipped from one of his well-spaced horns to fall limp in the tall grass.

The rider rolled up the line and reluctantly spurred his pony to move a little closer to the threatened bull. As they have for many generations, the sabanero and caballo worked as one. The caballo high-stepped forward and made a drifting slide to the right to give his partner a better angle for the rope. The sabanero took the reins in his teeth, lifted a bullwhip from his saddle horn and gave it a crack.

When the bull lifted his head, the cowboy sent the lasso circling around his horns and gave it a flick of the wrist to drop it down around his neck. He wrapped the rope around his saddle horn and gave the horse a little nudge. The caballo bowed down, raised his hindquarters and backed away from the unhappy bull. No matter which way the bull turned to make a charge, the pony matched the move, maintaining a distance and keeping the line tight. She faked, feinted and waltzed with the bull until the caballo signaled that the bull had succumbed to their artful synergy. He was ready to be led to another field to breed.

Of course, Popi had an opinion to share with her about all this. "Domesticated animals play just as big of a roll as fossil fuel in stimulating the planet's population explosion. We keep cattle solely to produce food for the masses, and byproducts like leather and glue are a bonus. All cattle need to live is grass and water; grass and water are free, and meat is expensive. That's why so much of the forest around here was cleared. By the 1970's and '80's there was a huge reduction of Central America's virgin rainforest, Costa Rica lost three-fourths of its rain forest to cattle ranching. This changed the ecosystem and caused serious erosion.

It was all done in the name of T-bone steaks and the All-American cheeseburger! Thankfully, much of this land has been reclaimed by the jungle or reforestation projects. Most of the restoration is sponsored by American and European interests. Since then, the Costa Rican government has dedicated itself to treat the unique and diverse habitats as national treasures like Federal parks and refuges. In turn, the government benefits directly from the tourism that they attract. It's a sweet deal all around."

Memories of being raised in a rural agricultural community flashed back to Popi like they had come from a Florida thunderstorm. LuLu worked his way into the lead as they hiked past miles of replanted rainforest and dwindled cattle pastures.

Now and then, pasture land on their left opened up to reveal a stunning view over the bluffs to the emerald-studded Golfo. Hope sprang eternal in those moments, but when they passed the clearing and the forest snuggled back around them they didn't object.

It was in such a place, where the heavy vegetation formed an awning above the road and intensified the sound of her voice that Cheyenne volunteered a change of heart. "I'm not ready to be married, yet. Maybe never, Popi, especially to someone named Sidney!"

Before he could manage to formulate a reply, she silenced him with a sharp wave of her hand. He complied, and once again the clatter of cicadas ceased. LuLu halted.

"Life is too short. I can't live for convenience and security alone."

Popi bit his lip and hesitated before replying. "I see you're not seeking counsel; you are making an announcement." He watched closely as a wave of dread seemed to dampen her demeanor.

She slung her head down low, shaking it lightly left-to-right and spoke softly. "How can I tell him? I don't want to hurt him, but I can't do what he wants and get married now or never. Well, I guess, maybe I could someday. I just know it's not now that's for sure!

"I don't want to tell him. What will I say?" She paused. "Please, don't answer that Popi, it's just rhetorical."

He understood young love and her change of heart. He had been there, and Cheyenne's declaration was giving him another flashback he cared not to relive. He simply took her hand and looked her in the eyes. "He'll live. He'll get over it completely by the time he gets married to someone else who's more convenient." He almost choked from laughing, and she giggled a little, too, through her tears.

"I'm on a different course now, Popi. By changing the way I live in this world, I may be able to influence changes in the way that the world lives on this planet. Conserve! Save what we have today for tomorrow, or there will be no tomorrow like the today we know."

LuLu sat attentively at their feet, waiting for them to move on. When the racket of the cicadas returned, he stood up and started walking away. "We must stop at Ray's ranchero at Rio Tamales along the way" Popi reminded himself as they once again picked up their pace.

They hiked a short distance before reaching Ray's place. They lifted up the rigged loop of copper wire used to secure the wobbly front gate to the barbed-wire fence, and then walked briskly down the path toward his house. Neither of them noticed that LuLu hadn't joined them.

There were a hundred head of Brahmas with their tails brushing away the bugs, and their floppy ears hanging low in the pastures on either side of the narrow dirt road that led down to Ray's house. Surprisingly, Ray was standing at the rusty galvanized gate of the chain-link fence around his yard. A wide grin spread across his face when he recognized Popi. He raised up his hands and rejoiced. "Boy, it has been way too many years since I last seen you Mister Manly! I reckoned you was never coming back. My old dog let me know someone was coming down the road, but he didn't tell me who. By gosh! It's you, ol' Stan Manly, coming!"

Ray had a penchant for punctuating his statements with a little too much enthusiasm. "You look as fine as frog's hair Stan! Speaking of which, who's the young lass you got with you? The latest gold digger? Ha ha! The women always loved Stan Manly!"

Popi introduced a slightly embarrassed Cheyenne. "Ray's got a photographic memory. The man never forgot a darn thing in his life. I bet that hasn't changed a bit through the ages."

"Hell, I sure remember the last time you came walking down that road. Rufus bit ya! Remember? Right on the left ass cheek. Excuse me when I tell you he was one fine guard dog! You were walking down here so sad in the middle of the night that he didn't recognize you. All Rufus does now is sleep. He is as worthless as a preacher in a brothel on Saturday night."

Popi sneered and reached for the very spot while he lifted his left foot and shook it about wildly. "Tell Rufus I'm all the better for it!"

Cheyenne enjoyed the shower of memories. Things like how Ray hated it when people assumed he was from Ft. Lauderdale. He'd proudly tell them "I'm from Broward County, not Fort Lauderdale. I had lived there since before they screwed up the Everglades."

Ray shared the story of how he met his Tica wife, Evette, in Baderia, Texas, while working on a horse ranch. "The night I met Evette I was both dumb and blind. I didn't know shit from shoe polish. What I lacked in good sense, God made up for with Evette."

Cheyenne could sense Ray's honesty; he shared freely and openly with them. "Me and Evette came to the Osa thirty years ago to raise a couple head of cattle, fish and live in peace away from all that crapola back in the States."

I'm getting too old for this now. It's time to sell this spread, and find a smaller place; something more manageable. But who around here can buy this place? There's oceanfront property on the market for twelve million bucks! A real estate lady I know says there's some high-dollar land developers who want it, but I'd hate that. They just want to make a fast buck; they don't give a damn about the land!

But enough about that! Come on in the house. Evette and I will make you as comfortable as we can. You understand? Make yourself right at home."

Popi was surprised by how much Evette had suffered the effects of aging. She was hunched quietly, in a high-back rocking chair. She was mindlessly shifting her dentures back and forth while watching Latino soap operas on a wide screen television that Ray bought for her in San Jose. Ray had put up solar panels and three small windmills and ran wires to a transformer hooked up to state of the art batteries that he ordered online. They always had plenty of electricity to run everything. Ray boasted "BP, baby! Beyond petroleum. I'm off the grid."

Rufus, a dark brown and black furry mutt, possibly a pit bull and Labrador retriever mix, was contentedly sprawled at Evette's side. When they entered the door, Rufus lifted his gray snout and sputtered a disparaging growl. Popi noted that it was only a slight alarm compared to their last encounter that resulted in a bite on the ass. There seemed to be no need to worry; Rufus was already resuming his previous position.

Ray and Evette had shared this home for over thirty years. It was uncomplicated but uniquely creative. It was hand-made entirely from rough wood planks that Ray cut and dressed himself with a portable mill saw that he ran with an old Jeep up on blocks. The bungalow was topped with a cleverly fitted raised tin roof. The tall slatted Bahama windows had no screens or glass. They were propped open with mahogany sticks decorated with hand-carved designs.

When all of the windows were open, the house had the feeling of a pavilion surrounded by a dreamy view of the Rio Tamales valley. The river originated far upland in primary rainforest, and ran along beside their pasture, through the steep hills, and down the bluffs and into a thousand fathoms of purple water to a place called Pavones.

It was the day's final hour of sunlight, and everything but the ocean was glowing with an orange hue. Cheyenne looked at the panorama through the silhouetted frame of a row of tall coconut palms. She saw a procession of perfectly formed waves lining up in the distance. They broke in perfect alignment and rolled one by one up the beach past their house and on and on down the beach forever.

An impressive quiver of surfboards was stacked, leaning and hung in disarray in the far corner of Ray's place. In the opposite corner there was a crazy alcove filled with fishing tackle, rods, reels, lures, and unidentifiable gismos stacked, shelved, hung, or strewn in various stages of repair across what looked like a ship carpenter's table in an old Spanish galleon.

Popi asked "How's the cows? Cheyenne and I checked them out on the way in. They look fat and sassy! You are doing well my old friend. It looks like you've got it made. Ray the cattle baron!"

The distress was clear in Ray's voice as he shared with them. "Manly, I can't believe it's turned out like this. What else can I do? Those are our neighbor's cattle. For years now, we have been letting them use our pastures. They supply us all the meat and poultry we could ever need. Me and the Ticos around here treat each other good and fair; they are the best neighbors. Evette and I can't protect our land or ourselves from squatters, rustlers and thieves all alone out here, and they know it. They speak well of us, check in, watch over us, keep people from messing with us and make sure we are okay. Their family is spread all over and they get a lot of respect. Besides, most Ticos know not to mess with them; they can be some bad mamajamas when they want to be.

"It's getting worse all the time, Stan. Development is to blame. Crime follows the money. There are quite a few formerly honest Ticos who got desperate after they went through the money from selling their property and had no way to make a living. They resent Americans and Europeans who are living on their old homesteads. Desperate people often take drastic measures, and it seems the law never gets there fast enough."

While Ray was filling Popi in, Cheyenne was perusing Ray's extensive quiver. A sleek, yellow East Coast gun hanging on the wall caught her eye. It was 6' 8" x 19 ½" wide, and had a round pin tail with quite a bit of rocker and lift. It was a single-fin Atlantis in almost mint condition. She pulled it down for a closer inspection. She sat the tail on the floor, held the nose in her hand and stared down the length of the board. She flipped it over a couple of times. A master craftsman had sculpted it into a perfect foil. The lines from the thin tail to the tapered nose were so attractive that she couldn't take her eyes off of them.

A hint of a smile returned to Ray as he said, "Haven't ridden' that for years. Never did ride it much; I had already outgrown it before I got it, but I was too vain to admit it. It worked okay for me in bigger waves. It can really hold an edge with that glassed-in fin. If you notice, it's pushed forward more than usual to get that hard thin tail into the action more. When you want to turn or whatever, all you gotta do is think about it and the board will come around. With that fin and the rail transition, it will slingshot your ass right out of a tight bottom turn. You can't do it quite the same with three fins.

Come on Stan, let's knock the dust off of a couple a' these barges and get wet. There's still time for a couple of waves before it gets too dark."

Cheyenne loved the idea. In her gut, she knew this surfboard was made just for her to surf Pavones. She called for LuLu to come along, but he didn't respond. She looked around the house and out on the grounds. No LuLu. Cheyenne said, "He's gone." Semi-panicked, she repeated as she searched. "Where's LuLu?! LuLu! LuLu is gone!"

In the fading daylight, shadows blended into the darkened spaces already void of any light, accentuating the echoing tones that divided the jungle from the Rio Tamales. The streaming water that crisscrossed the shallow slab rock and gravel river bed played a sweet, humble tune that was alluring and pleasant to the ear. It was a melody that was full of life and could never be captured on an instrument or duplicated in voice. The psalm of water rushing back to the source of all life offers no explanation, but somehow is full of reason.

Without delay, Cheyenne, followed by Ray and Popi, had walked about calling for LuLu until they had covered every inch of ground all the way to the bank of the river. The hunt had stopped there, and they silently listened to the soothing chorus of the gentle tributary.

"It's much smaller and gentler than I imagined," Cheyenne said. "We could walk across it without having to catch our breath. I expected to see a fairly mighty river after the reverential way you spoke of it, Popi."

Ray seized the opportunity to join the conversation. "It is a mighty river at times. I've seen it get so ornery that it nearly came and carried my house away. Happens with flash floods early in the rainy season, before the river mouth opens completely, and it can be bad. When the Osa monsoons get going, a foot or two of rain can fall in a few short hours. You wouldn't want to be standing here that's one thing for sure."

They turned towards the beach and walked through two pastures tall with waist-high grass. They opened and shut the three rusty, wire-rigged wood gates one by one until they finally stood on the gray sand of the beach. The air was thick with the rainforest moisture; it smelled of decaying dead debris of past flora and fauna.

Their clothes stuck to them like a napkin sticks to a tall, wet glass of iced tea. There was a barely noticeable effort drawing oxygen from the air, but the tempo of the swells breaking in the distance serenaded them like an ocean lullaby, making them forget about the thickness of the air. They focused their energy on the sounds of the breaking waves coming from the beach.

Ray continued. "Despite being tucked deep inside this fjord, we catch a sweet swell whenever the waves come from out of the south. I love the way it breaks left during mid-tide, when it's incoming. It's rideable weeks at a time, but flat most of the time. No one ever surfed out here back in the day, only me and my amigos. Nowadays, surfer-packed pangas show up whenever the surf's hot. They mainly come from Pavones or Matapalo, sometimes from Golfito or Puerto Jimenez. No matter how far they come from, they come far more often."

Ray proudly pointed towards the water. "There are very few places like this in the world. While sitting on my board here, I've seen a mother jaguar carry her cubs to the side of the river from the jungle for their first drink of water, and then watched as a crocodile nearly grabbed one of them! The things I've seen happen here, no man would believe unless he had lived at the edge of the rainforest and seen it, too."

Cheyenne listened to them ramble on; her attention shifted from their tales of the past to the surf, and back to their lost companion. She missed LuLu so much! It surprised her how connected she had become to the little pooch in such a short time. Or was it someone else she missed?

She loved the way the little dog would tilt his head left to right as if he were seriously considering each word when she spoke. LuLu was smart and compassionate; Cheyenne could tell. He possessed the intuitive ability to nuzzle up at just the right time to help ease frazzled nerves like a mug of warmed milk.

Before the last light dissipated into darkness, the three of them gladly made it back to Ray's porch and out of the thigh-high grass that Ray had warned was snake-infested after dark. Three plates piled with steaming hot rice, black beans and pork sat on the modest dining table. In addition, there were freshly cut slices of tomatoes, pineapple and papaya on a side plate. Ray offered them a seat, and they ate in silence as Evette quietly kept steady time in her weathered rocker like a free-swinging pendulum.

Ray chuckled. "She don't talk much anymore, but she has been a good woman to me. Kept my belly full and my thighs well kept. It gets kind of lonely out here at times. I could have found myself a much younger woman, but training them is as much a troublesome task as keeping them faithful."

Popi let out a little chuckle and said, "Yeah, I guess so."

Cheyenne, incensed by their flippant chauvinistic humor, abruptly pushed her plate aside, stood up, and gave a cold stare to her table mates before walking out and throwing herself into one of the three hammocks hanging from the mahogany ceiling on the back porch. "Those old goats! That's no way to be!"

She tried putting her backpack under her head for a pillow, but it was too lumpy and lopsided to be comfortable, and it was soon shoved to the floor. The day had been very long, and she was emotionally and physically worn out. A solo streak of lightning accompanied by a violent crash of thunder broke the stillness, as it split apart the clouds and opened the floodgates of heaven.

The din of rain pounding on the tin roof continued late into the night, muffling the voices of the two men who were relishing a vintage version of their history. Their tales were mellowed and sweetened by years of storage in the wine cellars of their memories. Even though she was exhausted, Cheyenne's concern for LuLu was robbing her of sleep. There were many very real dangers out there, and her imagination ran wild with worrisome images of the poor little dog that was all alone in the terrible stormy night.

Eventually, she had no energy left even to worry. She turned her head towards the inside of the bungalow. Her last vision was of two old men with a freshly opened fifth of Centenario and two full juice glasses sitting between them on the table, enjoying each other's company. When their conversation grew a bit boisterous, it reluctantly dragged her back to consciousness several times until sleep finally won out. She could smell the sweet, pungent aroma of freshly-plowed earth in her dreams. It vividly took her back to Florida and then on an impossible journey down the road to Matapalo.

The rain tapered off a short time before dawn, and she slowly awoke to a glorious morning. She slipped from her hammock and tiptoed into the house. A nasty ashtray half-full of bent butts was sitting next to a couple of uncorked (one nearly empty, one on its side) brown bottles of rum. The two old men were snoring away on their bent arms and drooling on the table. Evette was asleep in her rocker with an empty glass on her lap.

She realized that there was no need to wake the sleeping household. She slipped out the front door with one thing on her mind; LuLu! She was anxious to see if their little friend had shown up during the night.

She had been impressed with Popi's meditation routines since they'd been traveling together. He was a true seeker of peace, God or whatever, but he wasn't fettered by dogma or protocol. He claimed there was at least an inkling of truth in all religions, and it was possible to glean wisdom from others without compromising your own. He took the time to focus his energy in a positive direction, as taught in Eastern disciplines and philosophies.

In defense of his convictions, Popi once told her "The Bible says that every good and perfect gift comes from God. To me, yoga and Zen are good and perfect gifts from God. If someone doesn't agree, that's okay; the Bible covers that, too. 'One man celebrates a certain day as holy, while another man celebrates each day alike. Let each man be fully convinced in his own mind.' Some folks just don't get it, that's all. I can't let that keep me from a blessing!"

Despite his present condition, she had seen him gain strength and vitality from his morning sessions. She had been studying all that Popi did, and was doing her best to emulate it, but she hadn't had much success. On the way from Tortilla Flats to the beach in Dominical she picked up a dog-eared paperback copy of The Guide to Meditation, by Zen Master Al Rapaport, from Bob the surf guide.

Bob, aka the Bookman, was from San Clemente, California. He told her that she might be able to use more than just a surf guide, and gave her the book. She had no idea how well the old school primer would help to set the foundation and frame the structure of her personal practice of meditation, but she was willing to take a shot with it.

She sat up quietly, straightening her spine, looking forward with her chin parallel to the ground. With her shoulders' back and legs crossed she closed her eyes and touched her fingertips together above her belly button — just like the illustration in the yellowing paperback. She had seen Popi do it sometimes. It took patience to make the various aspects come together. It was like getting directions to a place you've never been.

The anticipation was too intense for relaxation during her first few experiences. Her mind would race, and time passed dreadfully slow; an itch would pop up, her legs would cramp, and she would easily grow restless. But she persisted, and soon began to realize a difference between mind, spirit, and self or being. She understood that presence was the key; just be.

Vacant of clouds and painted with billions of varying shimmering points, a dark sky began to wake around her. In the neutral light of the new morning, she needed to focus her energy more than ever. She couldn't relax, or bear the agony in her heart for little lost LuLu. "Why had he disappeared? What happened? I should have watched out for him! It's my fault. I'll never forgive myself!" The questions flew through her mind, tormenting her with every passing minute.

She stayed seated on the wide, damp, wooden top step of the stairs, still determined to meditate like never before. She sought to disconnect from her selfish side and connect herself with everything else. Her prayers were too deep for words. She felt a reluctance growing within her from too many doubts and fears, mostly centered on a lack of faith. She remembered Popi saying "Just keep it real. No doubt about it, we all have our doubts. It is better to let faith do the driving and leave the doubts in the trunk until you need them to say 'I told you so.'"

As she settled into place, she took several deep breaths like an advanced yogi, releasing an extraordinary exhale before becoming completely motionless. As she corrected her spine's position and dropped her eyelids, the baffling morning call of a howler monkey awakening deep in the jungle enhanced her feeling of connection with the primordial plasma of all living things. The monkey was sending an auspicious prophesy to her soul, wise in the ancient ways of the forest.

She focused on the sound; the monkey mantra helped her to transcend all annoyances. Her rhythmic breathing allowed a feeling of peace and presence to overtake her. When distractions tried to enter, she wasted no energy to fight or avoid them; they flew by like gulls at sea with no place to land.

She ultimately gained a state of tranquil well-being. Her mind began losing its attachment to me, and began to blossom into us, like a crocus springing through the snow in the dead of late winter. She found herself awash in a tidal wave of love and compassion, and in the vast nothingness of the subconscious everything came together in one clear, conscious thought.

"Love holds all things together." Her emotions shifted steeply as streaming images of the two men who had ever owned her heart, Joe and Sid, sped through her struggling mind. Her heart swamped in an emotional typhoon; she watched mesmerized, as vague images of Joe and Sid exchanged a sobbing Cheyenne back and forth between them.

An image of Sidney's face, crying out as Joe snatched her away, filled her mind. Suddenly, in her vision, Joe's face and hers came together, eye-to-eye, and their wet lips melted together in harmony as a wash of bright sunlight blasted under the cusp of her eyelash. Then, and only then, did everything fall into place.

She was overwhelmed with relief. She had an epiphany! She realized, on the deepest level that there was only an end to the fleshly body, but not life itself. The soul, the spirit, life; they were all eternal. She realized her worth was not directly connected to the man she wanted or who wanted her.

A satisfied smile creased her face and tears began to pour down her cheeks. She did her best to stay in the moment, to stay in the presence, but it was gone. "Nothing is the same. Everything is the same" she thought. Her lower lip quivered as she gave up her last bit of doubt. She whispered quietly to herself. "Forgiveness. Forgive. Forgive me. I must forgive myself."

A wet tongue broke her trance as it washed away the flow of tears covering her cheeks. She came back to the present, refreshed and excited. "LuLu, you're back! Hallelujah!"

Later on that morning Ray made sure they had a sweet stash of food to carry with them down the road to Matapalo. He even handed Cheyenne a ration bag of premium American dog food for LuLu. "Rufus insisted" he joked.

Rufus had even stiffly waddled his creaking bones and shaggy fur to the front door to see them off. The old watchdog didn't bark or growl, but Popi kept one eye on him just the same. Ray continued waving from his front steps as they reached the end of his dirt drive and turned west with the sun at their back. As they crossed over the steel-grated bridge, the roar of the Rio Tamales made it hard to converse as the night's flooding rain rushed under them on its wild return to the ocean.

The new day, their reunion with LuLu and the energy of the river fueled a quick, steady pace. They would be in Matapalo before nightfall. Cheyenne remembered some of Popi's tales and wondered aloud "Who is the Queen of the Jungle?"

Popi kept his steady pace but exhaled as if the weight of the world had was on his shoulders. He didn't answer. Cheyenne asked again. "Popi! The Queen of the Jungle! Who is she? I heard you and Ray mention her last night when you were off in La La Land. The way you two were going on, she must have been pretty amazing."

The jungle had vanished again. Popi swiveled his head to look out across a cleared pasture leading down to the cobalt depths of the tropical fjord. Only LuLu noticed a black mangrove hawk perched watchfully on top of a living gumbo limbo fence post. The hawk titled his head and twitched his beak while its sharp, cautious brown eyes relentlessly watched the group pass.

"I don't know how to tell you about the Queen of the Jungle, Cheyenne; the pain remains too raw. I should have vanquished that foe by now. Seriously, at times, it's too much to bear; it won't go away."

It hadn't occurred to Cheyenne that the Queen of the Jungle was a source of Popi's pain. That wasn't the tone in the rum-fueled conversation that she overheard the previous night. She tried to backpedal. "It's fine, Popi. I don't need to know; forget it."

They continued in silence for a few minutes until they reached a section of dense, dark forest that blocked the sun's rays, cooling the path appreciably. Popi opened up a bit. "Pain is too often caused by our rusty recollection of the past and also by guilt. You can truly forgive without truly forgetting. You can't erase a memory, but only time and forgiveness can relieve the pain. Pain withers like a dried up rose in a dusty old box, but the pain of heartbreak persists as a deep, low wave that never seems to end. When you dredge it up, the power can be devastating."

They traipsed along over the dense tropical forest's floor. The canopy continued drawing in around them from all directions like living green fingers. The air became cooler and refreshing, but at the same time, their surroundings became somewhat dark and eerie.

A terrified troop of reddish-brown spider monkeys passed overhead. They were screeching loudly, swinging from branch to branch, hand to tail, with their long limbs, obviously fleeing some unseen threat. Popi lamented their fate. "These monkeys were once abundant throughout the jungles of Central America. Now, they've been over hunted for bush meat, and lost so much of their natural habitat that their numbers have dwindled. Today they are rarely seen outside of the limited areas with enough virgin forest left to sustain their small colonies.

Their collective and unnerving high-pitched screams are an integral part of their complex society. Their noise could probably raise the dead, and it surely serves as a layer of protection for them when threatened by predators. It gives these little primates a sudden sense of alarm, like a shot of adrenaline, which annoys and confuses their hunter. It's like jamming radar with disruptive electronic signals, or like a squid blowing a cloud of ink; it works for them."

At first, it seemed as if they would zoom right by, but monkey curiosity stopped them dead in their tracks, where they hung by their tails and feet, staring inquisitively from the trees above. Cheyenne anxiously stepped closer to Popi, and he put his arm around her tense shoulders. They didn't notice that a startled LuLu was hiding behind Cheyenne's legs.

Their mighty little mascot recognized the crazy primate culprits from the day before, and even he knew there was no telling what they might do. The monkeys could be pesky, mean, and hard to deal with, especially in numbers. It had taken him all night and a good bit of swimming to lose them and get back to Cheyenne, and now here they were again.

Popi, too, bristled with expectation from the encounter. He held Cheyenne possessively for a lingering moment while he looked around for a branch that would make an excellent club. The monkeys felt his vibe and moved away until they soon disappeared back into the jungle.

Enlivened by his little rush of adrenalin, he needed to push through his pain. He placed his hands gently in Cheyenne's hands and looked earnestly into her eyes. "The Queen of the Jungle lived at Tres Montañas, a sort of unprocessed imperial villa at the top of the hill above Matapalo. We were tight; very tight, more than just friends."

His voice trailed off as he let go of her hands and turned away. They resumed walking. After a long wait, she asked, "Lovers, Popi?"

"More than friends," I said. "More than just friends doesn't leave just one option." His tone had an air of finality to it.

They moved along in silence. LuLu led the way as if they were on a pilgrimage of epic proportions. He cut a gallant figure as he seemingly took personal responsibility for the collective security of those in his charge. The noble canine enthusiastically encountered every obstacle with a total lack of hesitation, fear, or regard for his own safety. The spirit of their grand adventure filled them with confidence, even as the terrain got a bit steep, and the tangle of vines, branches, stalks, leaves, and rocks grew denser and closer to their path.

Despite the previous night's deluge, the rivers they encountered later in the day were only up slightly and crossing them was no hazard. The tropical downpour must've been localized. If it had been upstream, it would not be running clear and free of debris. These smaller rivers had no bridges, but these places were easy to cross when the rivers weren't swollen.

LuLu stopped at the next traditional crossing, even though all seemed well. It was. The sun was peeking through the jungle at just the right angle to slice the mist from a waterfall tumbling from a ledge that emerged through the boughs and vines above them. The sunbeam split into a dense, miniature spectrum of light that formed a rainbow fan all the way across the river. It was intoxicating.

"They said a pot of gold awaits you at the end of the rainbow. It could be true, Cheyenne. I have never made it to the end of the rainbow. They just keep on moving away in front of you. When I was a kid, I'd look around on the ground to see if any of the little people dropped some coins in their haste to escape. I had heard that on a movie or somewhere, and hoped it was true."

Popi said no more as he tenuously followed LuLu over a path of glistening cobblestones and coarse sand leading them to the creek's opposite bank. Cheyenne and LuLu negotiated the path with grace, making it look easy. Popi made it across alright, but with barely a trace of his old smoothness and style.

Now and then a vehicle would pass by them. It was easy to tell the difference between a tourist and the Tico farmers or transplants. Tourists would almost always stop and hesitate before crossing any flowing water. The locals and Ticos knew the drill. They only slowed down when someone else was approaching head-on, or when the water was just too high and fast.

There were a lot of water crossings in the area. The cab drivers racing the clock in their bright red compacts were hampered by the crossings the most. The majority of local farmers drove small trucks, like Kias, Toyotas or Mazdas, with jury-rigged, extended beds and high sides to maximize their load. Labor and service workers traveling back and forth between Jimenez and Osa's outer edge eco-lodges favored dirt bikes to minimize fuel cost, maximize accessibility and save time. Now and again, wealthy Ticos, professionals or cash-rich farmers who had sold their Osa land to foreign investors would pass by in brand new, shiny, all-wheel drive SUV's. These untarnished trophies were few and far between on the road to Matapalo, but they were there, nevertheless, as a constant reminder of the ever-evolving world of the have's and have-not's.

A couple of taxis went by as they made their way along the road. The cabs packed with wide-eyed tourists seeking the quintessential Costa Rican experience, was all Popi needed to see to get a bit worked up again.

"That tells the real story. There it is! Smart phones, laptops, iPods, Banana Republic, Club Med, disposable income and yuppie subculture routines that include trips to paradise on a regular basis. Everyone in paradise has a Nike T-Shirt! Leave that crap at the border! Do they slow down long enough to realize where they actually are or know what's going on around them?

Paradise is inside each of us. Eastern philosophies seek spirit, and Christianity teaches us to be like Christ. Take a look at what he said, and you'll see they aren't so different after all. It's all about essence. Isn't it?"

"Is it not easier to live an Eastern Philosophy with a Western paycheck?" Cheyenne asked.

"You sound like Confucius. Yes, money is important, in one way or another, but sustainability, health, and well-being are also important. The difference between the East and West is more about God's role in our lives, and who has the final decision on our destiny. Is it an unseen deity, we, or a combination of some sort? Virginia believed that it was our ability to communicate that creates God in our midst."

"Back in the states we're all screwed up, thinking only of ourselves from our particular point of view," Cheyenne replied. "Politics? One side put us in the outhouse, and the other side pushed us in. The

Right call themselves Conservatives when they have a tendency to be radical. The Left say they are Liberals, but they tend to be close-minded and judgmental towards people with divergent opinions. Both sides cultivate a system deeply rooted in bigotry of one form or another. We need a new direction that will be by and for the people and do what's best. We know right from wrong. It should be pretty simple, but it's not!"

"Amen! You're preaching to the choir, girl." Popi nodded briskly in agreement. "I think I hear the Holy Ghost up in there!"

Something caught LuLu's attention. He leaped along behind three electric-blue butterflies, as large as sedge wrens, as they glided through the jungle with ease on gossamer wings. To their amazement, the butterflies cut across their path. Like magic fairies, they crisscrossed into the deep caverns formed under the draping arms of a giant strangler fig standing at the side of the trail. It was a Matapalo tree.

Only two of the three butterflies could be seen emerging from the dark shade on their way back to the jungle backdrop from where they came. LuLu dashed to the tree's hanging roots followed closely by Popi and Cheyenne. There, hanging in a mammoth spider's lurch was the gilded fairy creature with its wing caught by merely the outer thread of the spider's web. The butterfly twitched frantically in an admirable effort to escape, but the thread held. It seemed even more vivid and captivated, if possible, near death as it attracted the attention of a huge, golden silk orb-weaver.

Much kinder than a house cat who toys with its prey, the yellow-bellied arachnid scampered across the thickest of its silk net to apply the instantaneous death bite. Eight eyes, eight legs and a throbbing thumb-sized orb all moved in the same direction, with one purpose; sustenance.

"Death comes quickly to those who drift too freely in the jungle" noted Popi.

In a swift fit of screaming terror, feathers and talons, a screaming shrike swooped down out of the hanging canopy of the Matapalo tree to strike the spider squarely with a death blow of its own. The captive butterfly dropped from the web, fluttered, and almost landed in a wet, tangled mass of peat, decaying leaves and rotting deadfall on the jungle floor. It seemed nearly wasted, but astonishingly the radiant insect began to flutter its wings and flew off in the direction of the other two. Cheyenne stepped out of the way so quickly that she tripped over her own feet. Popi caught her by the nape of the neck and helped her regain her balance.

"Can you believe it, Popi? That was amazing!"

"Death for one; life for another. That's the rhythm, but I don't know the rhyme or reason. Is it destiny, or is a choice involved?""

"Popi, what about your choices?"

He didn't answer right away. After returning to their walk, he explained again why the two of them headed for Matapalo, and how he envision her savoring the beauty of it. The same beauty that captured him in the enchantment of his youth — back when finding Paradise was his passionate fixation. At the time, Matapalo was as close to Paradise as he could find. Now together, they had found their way back.

He needed to tell Cheyenne why it was all so important. "Can you miss your destiny, or is it set in stone? Back in the day, when Florida had lost its luster, and my heart broke because of it, I came here looking for peace. It was before I realized that Paradise can only be found in one's soul. One can only judge themselves on how they make others feel not matter where they are mentally or physically.

I'd heard some vague stories of Matapalo's spectacular surfing and fishing, its untouched rainforest and clean water, and the Pura Vida attitude of the locals. I was compelled to make the trip, and when I finally made it down here, I thought my search was over. I had found Paradise until it slipped away in a heartbeat."

Cheyenne listened, but didn't get the drift "In a heartbeat?"

"Money! The love of money is the root of evil. It's true; it fouled Costa Rica's Pura Vida, and changed most everything.

In high school, we lived in a working-class neighborhood; we suffered through the chaos and confusion of busing and desegregation and the urban sprawl that reached our rural neighborhoods. There was an explosion of people, development, drugs and petty crime. Our once quiet and peaceful rural community swiftly became a redneck ghetto!

Most Floridians accepted the fact that they were being groomed by the powers that be to be low-wage, working-class heroes. It seemed to me they were happy to fill their days with hard work and their nights swilling beer and watered-down house drinks in nondescript, road to ruin bars.

Very few Florida folks tracked trends like the Punk Rock Movement. It was Rage Against the Machine refuge for some, but by the time the locals got around to it, it was past its prime in the hotspot cities of the world. Hearing the Sex Pistols play Anarchy in the UK changed my life. I started to hate the bloody Queen, too, and the establishment she represented.

I decided that the comfort was the reward for capitulation to their manipulation. I didn't need to lead a life of convenience. I had found my direction, and it pointed me straight into an uphill battle. This music, with such a raw, defiant edge and a call to anarchy energized me and served me well. I disregarded social conventions and ignored barriers erected to confine us.

Their forward motion had been stopped by Popi's ranting. Cheyenne and LuLu stood by, watching his message expand as he used his hands and arms to express more of his feelings. Sensing that it could take a while, she reclined against a large rock by the roadside.

"There are ways to escape the gravitational pull of the blue collar. Get an education, find a good-paying job and move up the corporate ladder, or you can deal drugs. I hung with both types, but I wasn't either. Vietnam, one of the weird American wars, had finally ended, and there were no jobs for a kid who had dropped out of school. As I told you before, I changed high schools five times before I finally took the high school equivalency test and got my General Education Degree.

There was no money or scholarships to pay my way to college and selling drugs wasn't for me. Over time, I found my mother's advice was true; she'd preach 'Be a jack of all trades.' She was right; I learned how to parlay my abilities like fishing, gardening and writing to support our family and our outdoor lifestyle.

Our family lived by a creed; Less is more, more is less. We xeriscaped our yard, grew organic gardens, worked off the grid and changed our values and outlook. We shared cars, rode bicycles, traveled by sailboat and worked on extended environmental education programs. We were trying to effect a change, but we were running out of time. We watched as our Sunshine State was being exploited all around us by the money movers; the developers, realtors and government.

In Florida, the only thing that slowed development down was when the real estate bubble broke. It gave us some time to rally the troops, but we were up against an army of outside investors who were chomping at the bit to get it going again.

During the money crunch after the slowdown, there was no telling when the bank you had a loan with would get shut down by the FDIC. The Department of the Treasury was divvying up assets to Bank of America, or BB&T or some other TARP favorite. These big banks would take over your loan and jump at the first chance to enforce the small print option to demand full payment immediately. Of course, no one could do that, and most everyone had missed a payment. It was the most successful bank heist in history. I can't wait to read the book How to Acquire Property and Assets Without Investing Your Own Money.

Meanwhile, people obsessed on the economy and jobs, and they worried about their losses and the price of gas. The whole corporate culture is skewed. Somehow, American industrialists think they can't turn a profit and provide a healthy work environment and still be able to make money. They could pay employees a whole lot more, provide insurance and other benefits and still be rich men. How much does one man need?

And get rid of stockholders and CEO's; CEOs are a joke. Stockholders are a financial drain on any business, and they don't contribute anything beyond their initial investment. Pay investors off once and split the profits with the employees. If you go public, the stockholders can kick you out anytime they have a mind to.

Anyway, I saw NBC News one night, and they were all euphoric in New York about a sign of an improving economy. Florida real estate was back on the move; ground had been broken for a massive condominium community on a huge block of foreclosed property near Daytona. Rick Scott was governor, and he had to sign an executive order to approve the project.

They blew right by the environmental protection statutes and made it all look legit. He finagled private funding to repair the old rail lines to Orlando, where there was fatal gun play in the streets on a daily basis, but was home to Sea World and Disney. By adding in the toll road construction, there would be six thousand jobs created by the administration!"

Cheyenne was amazed by his energy and concern. It wasn't so much like Popi was lost in his speech; it was more as he was found!

"Never mind that the land for the project was classified as wetlands by the EPA, and restricted from development. They didn't mention that on the news. It didn't register with the public that they were applauding the destruction of the natural environment that sustains all of us for a temporary fix to an appalling situation.

Everywhere around me I could see how Mother Earth was being overwhelmed by the idea that the natural world is here for us to exploit for profit. Americans have an unsustainable appetite for stuff! Our culture was totally consumed by the desire for more stuff, but my family wanted to be more like the Native Americans and leave a soft footprint on the face of the Earth. The Earth is sacred."

His hands stopped waving, and for the first time in ten minutes he looked around and took a step towards continuing their journey.

"We were frustrated by the lack of state and local government support for wise conservation measures. The establishment brainwashed us; from our first day in elementary school we were taught to be proud of the rapid growth of our state. They teach land-scraping and pre-fab as the model for development techniques at the University of Florida, for crying out loud!

That's how construction projects maximize their profits; Florida's a giant outdoor building factory. That's why half the houses in the state come with the same cabinets, counters and Berber carpets. Some people in high-end condos would be surprised to see the same counters and insulated window frames in their homes used down in the low-rent government-subsidized apartments situated next to the bus stops. That's real world community planning. That's progress?"

Cheyenne half listened to his rambling as they made their way down the road. "How could Popi have so much anger pinned up inside of him?" she thought.

He continued and didn't miss a beat. "Until I found Costa I was spinning my wheels and sinking deeper. Then I saw a chance for a new beginning in a pristine refuge away from all of the madness in Florida. Hell, you could still drink right out of the streams in Costa!"

She noticed that Popi's tone had finally become a little less frantic and more upbeat. He seemed to be through the worst of his tale!

"Alina was a dynamo! She took turns as first mate for all of the best captains running the largest of the Crocodile Bay charter boats. They fished mostly for marlin and yellowfin; the big boys. It was surprising to see someone so petite and attractive swing a flying gaff, as well as any man. She could haul in a hefty tuna without a whimper, and dress it for sushi with her eyes shut. She could open your eyes when she was dressed up to go out for sushi, too. Most of the Tico men respected her, but some were jealous of her skill set and unavailability; know what I mean?"

"Wait a second here. Alina's the Queen of the Jungle?"

"Yes, Alina was the Queen of the Jungle. She was a big advocate of catch and release of billfish, and aligned herself on the side of conservation. Alina got it; being totally immersed in the New World's greatest coastal rain forest taught her many lessons. She became absorbed by it as well and felt called to be a zealous advocate and protector of it. She was an influential figure around here, that's for sure. Alina was a strong-willed woman who didn't put up with any bullshit.

Destructive exploitation of the rainforest and wildlife riled her up. More than once she stood in the way of crews with chainsaws and heavy equipment which were ready to clear jungle for development around Matapalo. She saw herself as a bastion of reason and enlightenment in a war against the sheer stupidity man. She also understood that others wished to live in a nice house in the jungle, just as she did, and they were bound to pursue their vision, just as she had. While she accepted the inevitability of population growth in the area, she insisted that everyone use the least invasive methods possible to pursue their dreams.

She could talk a cop out of his donut, so she usually only needed to have a heart-to-heart dialog with the land owners to help set acceptable parameters. Almost all the new land owners were receptive to her way of thinking, and under her guidance they became more receptive to becoming stewards of the land and water.

The Ticos listened to her and grew to share her gusto for the natural aspects of their homeland more and more. They became very motivated to preserve and restore the rainforest and the animals that depend on it. She made them feel proud to live in such a wonderful place.

But there were guys like Julian, the Butcher, and other unscrupulous, money-hungry Me First developers slash trust-fund babies, who didn't appreciate Alina's interference. It affected their bottom line. Their opposition to her stance caused everyone a world of concern, fueling fear amongst the Ticos with their open hostility. The Queen of the Jungle had the courage of her convictions, and was willing to put it all on the line for what she held sacred.

I'll never forget how Alina reacted when she found out that her family had cleared part of the forest to build cabanas. 'Dammit, I can't believe it!' she screamed at me. 'The monkeys and the trees are one. To them, every leaf, every branch, every trunk counts!"

"Popi, it seems as if your Queen of the Jungle forgot how they cleared rainforest for the dirt road to Matapalo, or how her cabana sat where a small bit of unmolested tropical rainforest once sat."

Cheyenne's strong point struck home. A somber shadow formed around his eyes, shaded by his downcast brow; the look matched his tone. "So it seems we must all become somewhat blind to our cause in the end."

She tilted her head slightly up and down in concert with his message. "This is easy to understand seeing how we all think of ourselves first."

Popi continued, barely missing a beat. "She had been away on an extended visit to the States to raise awareness and funding for her cause. She was torn between the love and respect she had for her family and her duty to save every bit of cherished jungle. It was her fiftieth birthday, and she spent part of it sobbing like a baby in my arms."

"Alina surfed, fished and loved nature ... sounds like your type, Popi."

"In many ways, but not all; Alina and I were kindred spirits for sure. Like me, Alina was a born and bred Floridian. Florida was all about nature and the outdoors for both of us growing up; we loved hiking in the woods as much as we loved the ocean. We saw firsthand how rapid progress overwhelms nature. But like me, Alina was a river, not the rock of granite that my dear Virginia was for me. Yes, from the moment we met, it was like Alina and I were lifelong friends, but not lovers, you hear me?

I must admit that I loved her. There was an undeclared magnetism between us. I wanted her, but I never pursued her. It may have been the same with her." Popi turned away and pretended to scan the horizon so she wouldn't see the tears welling in his eyes. "I'm sure it was."

"Aw, Popi, are you alright?" Cheyenne tenderly touched his arm.

"We spent a lot of time together. There were rumors, first in Matapalo, and then back home. The internet will never replace the grapevine."

Cheyenne understood. "I can remember the family talking about how you ran around with some other woman, Popi. It wasn't true?"

"Faithful to your grandmother, even to this very day." He looked down, kicked at the dirt, and a growing grin chased his melancholy away. "No other human could ever stand in the way of what Virginia and I had; what I still have for her."

She was impressed. "I hope I can find love like that, Popi. How could your family doubt you?"

"The family had every right to misjudge me the way they did. I didn't communicate my intentions as well as I should have. They didn't appreciate my direction at the time, and I was too driven to care about that. It was quite stressful for them to deal with my wandering ways. They thought I should stay home tending to business and such, not away in some exotic foreign land, where English wasn't the first choice. They didn't realize I was fearful of a calamity in our backyard, and was looking ahead for their future. Hell, I was just trying to find a better place for them, and you, to live, Cheyenne."

"Where's LuLu, Popi? Did he sneak away again?" Cheyenne felt more confident now when the little dog disappeared, but she did enjoy following LuLu along their path.

"I guess he's over listening to this old man's meanderings" Popi conceded.

He was glad to quit talking and escape the limelight for a while. He marched boldly into the lead like a soldier. Cheyenne struggled to keep up with him and his renewed sense of purpose. "What about LuLu?" she pleaded.

"He's up ahead, guaran-dam-tee it! That dog has a mind of its own, and I can almost read it. Don't worry; I know the way. LuLu knows we've got to keep up our pace if we want to beat the afternoon rain to Matapalo. He's one fine dog!"

They easily made their way across the rivers of the parched Rios Sombreo and Carbona. There wasn't much water trickling over the dry patches of white tombstone bedrock in either one, so the crossings were pretty simple. Passing the two rivers brought them closer to their destination.

In Carbona, they came to an aqua-blue, blocked-wall, primary school that sat at the foot of a steep, rocky incline surrounded by rainforest. Out front, three boys sporting blue plaid uniforms were kicking a soccer ball through ankle-high grass. The boys' attention turned from the ball to the odd couple walking by giving them a friendly wave. The boys waved back and mirrored the couple's warm smiles for a moment before returning to the ball with a heightened sense of urgency. One lad pushed another boy down to block his compadre, absconded with the prize and scored a goal with the purloined ball. They all rolled on the ground giggling.

"The people of the Osa are like these children. They are proud, but also humble, good-natured and very kind. Just like you and me, Costa Ricans also love futbol."

Popi and the boys watched as Cheyenne placed an imaginary soccer ball on the ground, took a couple of paces backward, lifted her hand above her head as if she was approaching a corner kick, and followed through with a technically flawless air kick. She jumped up; fist pumping and cheered for her success, screaming "Goal!" All four of her male spectators broke out in a chorus of belly laughter.

As they made their way back down the road, she took the offense. "Popi, you almost act as if Ticos are different than us. DNA knows no borders; it can hook up with anyone's, anywhere. Governments have borders, not DNA. If we were only a slight bit more aware of this, we'd have less war. The men who lead governments start wars, but never fight them."

Ignoring Cheyenne's jab, he looked out ahead as he continued the march, and replied "Some men believe war is the way to peace. They sold World War I as The War to End All Wars. Can you imagine winning that war and getting called up later to fight in World War II?"

Popi, wasn't it Jimi Hendrix who wrote 'When the power of love overcomes the love of power, the world will know peace?"

"Jimi wrestled with his own demons; maybe now he knows peace." Popi fell to his knees, mimicking Hendrix on an air guitar; he threw his head back just like Jimi, and broke out in a frail rail.

"You know you're a cute little heartbreaker. You've got to be all mine, all mine... Ooh, foxy lady!" and then continued with a convincing guitar growl, hammering out "Gnut-gnut gn-eow, gnut-gnut gn-eow, gnut-gnut gn-eowie-oww! Foxy Lady!"

They laughed so hard that it confused the newly returned LuLu; the poor dog didn't know whether to wag his tail or run for help. The road flattened out, and the jungle began to recede a little. Popi was anticipating the sight of Martina's Buena Esperanza. Martina, a German immigrant, ran a sort of hostel that became a haven for travelers. It was the closest thing Matapalo had to a town center. The school was the only other building that was visible from the road.

They were only a short way from Martina's, and then it would be on to Matapalo Point and farther west to Cabo Matapalo. Matapalo, wedged between this trio of landmarks surrounded by cloud-shrouded mountain peaks, skirted the only remaining tropical rain forest found on the entire Pacific coast of the Americas.

There is a handful of point breaks, the kind that produce rides of a lifetime, strewn out across the coast like a royal flush. "Because of the very nature of Matapalo's geography and environmental abundance, the bodies and spirits of these local people grow strong. Their spirit is a burning ember that's impossible to extinguish."

Martina's had not yet come into view, but in spite of it being siesta time, an alluring melody of jolly voices floated through the jungle to reach out like a warm handshake. As if they did it every day, they took a sharp left off the beaten path, dipped through a hibiscus-garnished archway to the open patio, and peeked in the door. The bar was empty, except for four men playing dominoes at a far table.

Three of the men were obviously Tico farm laborers. Each carried the tools of their trade; machetes were sheathed in dark leather scabbards to their sides. Two fresh rossimos of green bananas lay between them on the hard dirt floor, and empty shot glasses crowded the edges of the table.

The dominoes in the center of the group held every bit of their attention, and nothing else but slapping down the next numbers seemed to matter. The outside man could pass as a Tico laborer, but he was way too tall and broad in the shoulders to match the type. He noticed Popi and Cheyenne and hung a worn dish towel with a traditional flower pattern over his right arm as he got up and slipped behind the counter. In Spanish, the moose of a man asked them what they would have. Popi replied "Dos cervezas frias, por favor."

The bartender smiled haplessly, and like a seasoned pro, reached under the bar to pull out two icy, cold Coronas from an ancient Igloo cooler. He popped the caps, squeezed a slice of lime through the necks, and tapped the tall bottles on the bar in from of them. Before Popi could get his money out to pay, the big man waved him off. "You can hold off on that for now. I might trust you to run a tab, if you are who I think you are, that is. Stan Manly, is that you?"

Popi's inscrutable mug was betrayed by a wide grin. "Tomas?"

With a booming voice, the bartender proclaimed "Stan Manly! It is you! It's Stan Manly!"

The bear of a man nearly pulled his lost friend over the counter with a Kodiak hug. Tears fell as fast as back slaps. Chest to chest, eye to eye they greeted each other as if they were twins separated since birth. "Tomas, I thought I'd never see you again my old friend!"

"Manly, I figured you would be back one day to defend your name, if nothing else. I know you are no murderer. A day never passes that I don't think of Alina and you, Stan Manly. There has been an empty place in my heart ever since that dark day. She was a fearless General; Matapalo's bravest steward. Queen of the Jungle and the jungle and all of its creatures cried out when we lost her." Tomas tried but could not stop the tears streaming down his contorted face. "Why has it taken you so long to return? How could you stay away from the place you loved so much for so long, mi amigo?"

"I am back, now." Popi calmly assured him as he looked away.

Back at the domino table a dispute had arisen, disrupting both the friendly game and interrupting the reunion. One of the Ticos had thrown down a domino and grabbed the pot. Another one threw his down and started scraping as much as he could his way. The third stood up abruptly and started fumbling for his machete.

"Thank God they're too drunk to hurt anyone," Tomas said as he puffed up his chest and closed the distance, towering over the discontented gamblers. "Lo que pasa mis amigos? Chill out! How about a round on the house? Name your poison."

That much English the repentant muchachos clearly understood, and peace was restored to the group.

While Tomas occupied himself with a new game of dominoes, Popi felt the urge to hand the baton to Cheyenne. He felt she could handle knowing the full story. She needed to experience some of his destiny to carry on his legacy, like the stories of the Cracker settlers who hacked out a free existence in the howling wilderness of Florida.

He knew the significance of his experiences, and he knew that Cheyenne was also a dreamer like him. Hadn't LuLu homed in on her beacon? Not many understood the ways of animals in this day, but you couldn't fool him. He knew the little booger would have been lost if Cheyenne hadn't willed him back to Ray's place. She was special, and he felt strongly that she should know his heart; he was finally ready to share it.

Tomas threw the pair an approving glance and a wave of the hand to suggest that they grab another Corona. Neither of them had finished their first one yet. Thomas turned back to keep his customers on task for a pleasant game. Sensing that Popi had something to say, Cheyenne turned to him. "Did you want to say something, Popi? I'm listening."

Popi tried his best to cut to the chase. "Tomas was the Queen of the Jungle's real lover, not me. While she and I loved each other, and had a certain level of desire to be together, we both loved and respected Tomas, and I loved my Virginia, more.

Early on, I was a buoy in choppy seas. For quite a few years, Alina was self-absorbed and narcissistic. She had quite an appetite for the fast lane; men, boats and controlled substances. She was skidding out of control. That's when we connected. I was safe; she knew I could be trusted from personal experience.

When she decided to straighten up and fly right, there was nobody else she could trust to not press the issue. Alina could trust me; it was a first for her. She saw the foundation of love and respect that Virginia and I had between us. She loved to surf; I loved to surf. She loved to fish; I loved to fish — it was what we shared the most. There were no affairs between us; for Alina and me it was our love for Matapalo and all the things connected to it that resonated between us. When she sobered up, she immersed herself in the ocean and jungle, and it drowned out her cravings for her darker side. Naturally, her life took a turn for the better.

Sure, we had fun; we were secure in the safety of our relationship. You should have seen us dance, right here on Martina's dance floor. For such a dangerous, headstrong and independent woman, she could be carefree and sexy when she wanted to. I guess it wasn't such a good idea for a happily-married man to be out with an attractive woman in public like that, even if it was a million miles from home.

Alina played into the idea that we were having an affair because it kept her father from being suspicious of Tomas. Her dad had his share of run-ins with more than one of Alina's former suitors — and in his eyes, none of them were good enough for his princess! He was probably correct, until she met Tomas. She loved her dad immensely, but she did not want him involved in her business with Tomas.

Anything fun came first with Alina; there was always later for seriousness. She led the lifestyle of a naturalist and a versatile waterman; excuse the gender bender, but she deserved the title.

Her passion for the Earth enthralled her with every aspect of its beauty and primitive danger. While she traveled and explored the world's surf breaks, fishing, and dive spots, she became more aware of the world's problems. She realized that we, collectively, were standing on the edge; her concern for the environment increased and she was compelled to act, which made her vulnerable.

Her circle of concern maxed out her circle of influence and then some. Perhaps her notion of personal responsibility was unrealistic. She took it to heart that she hadn't been able to keep everything in check. She took every infringement personally, and she got to be a bit fanatical. This obsession of hers led to some serious confrontations. She shouldn't have tried to manage threats alone; she should never have been left alone to do that."

"What are you getting at, Granddad; spit it out. What happened?"

Keeping his eyes connected to Cheyenne's eyes, he lifted up his beer bottle to finish it off before he started. "Okay; I came here to stay at Alina's cabana to finish a manuscript I was writing. It was the start of the rainy season. Alina planned to leave the same day I was to arrive for a dive trip to the Keys with her dad and sisters, who all live in South Beach. She and I planned to surf Backwash Bay together sometime in early August when she came back home.

His tone deepened. "Exactly like we just did, I rode the bus to Jimenez, then caught a ride to the bottom of the hill, and started up the stairway path leading to Tres Montañas. Many of the wood slab steps had been washed away by relentless rains. It was tough going.

For me, it was always a grueling trek up the trail. It left nearly everyone gasping for breath, dripping with sweat, or with a mild case of vertigo. Everyone that is, but Alina and the Tico children. I can see her, fit as a fiddle in her bikini, scurrying up the steps, springing on the tiptoes of her bare feet like a wood sprite on her way back to her fairytale castle of Tres Montañas. Unfortunately, an ugly troll lay in wait to put an end to this story.

For Alina, it was always 'Can't you keep up with me? I thought you were Manly. Ha ha ha! I'll pass you on the way back down before you are halfway up! Vamonos, you old fart ... andale'!' She could be demanding, but she demanded from her heart. She had a tremendous amount of patience with most people. She knew when to back off, or when it would be best to extend a helping hand to her fellow man or woman. But negligent disregard for the rainforest of Matapalo or its inhabitants lit a short fuse to a volatile spot within her. Alina was the type who ran towards trouble, not away from it. Her heart was too big for her own good.

Remember, monkeys ruled the trees around Tres Montañas. Alina knew them, and she treated them as her family. They were so close that the capuchin mothers would bring the newborns down for her to see. Some locals called her the Queen of the Jungle because of the way she had with the birds and animals, as well as her confidence, strength, and authority. Others referred to her as the Queen of the Mountain, because Alina usually rose to the top!

In her day, she reigned over a portion of this rain forest. She viewed exploitation of its resources as sacrilege. It was her dedication to the sanctity of the jungle and all its creatures that earned her my adoration."

As his story unraveled, Popi avoided eye contact with her. He could feel that her patience was running low because he still hadn't come to the point, difficult as it was. He lifted his Corona to his mouth once again and drained the lukewarm brew. He pointed to Tomas and said, "I see my old friend, Tomas, has made it all good with his compadres."

On cue, Tomas broke away from the table where everyone had just polished off a round of rum shots. He opened his arms and smiled broadly. "Stan, as you can see, not much has changed around here. I'm waiting for my replacement to show. You can put your stuff in my bungalow; mi casa es su casa.

"You want to go surfing? Go on; grab a board from over there. There are a couple of antiques that might fit your style. There's a bar of wax on the shelf above the board rack. I'll meet you at Pan Dulce before sunset and run your old ass off the peak." Before they could comment, Tomas turned on his heels and headed back to monitor the domino desperados.

Popi turned back to Cheyenne. "Things don't change so much; people stay the same. Tomas stood by me when I needed a friend the most — the day I found Alina."

Cheyenne was almost beside herself with curiosity. She had waited patiently as Popi conducted his concerto to a crescendo, and now it seemed there was an unscheduled intermission. They followed a narrow gravel path bordered with white coconut-sized cobblestones that twisted past a maze of tropical hedges and flower beds. Neatly trimmed rows of yellow crotons, pink hibiscus, and white periwinkles obstructed the client's view of the empty crates, trash cans and other trappings that littered the back of the bar. At the end of the path, they found Tomas' round bamboo shanty. "It's been a while, but this is it! Like I said, things don't really change that much; no, they don't."

He dreaded revealing the details of Alina's fate and his involvement to Cheyenne. He dreaded speaking it aloud, so he welcomed the diversion.

Tomas was a minimalist; you could walk right through his house on your way to the beach. The wide-open door frames covered with sheer, off-white lengths of cloth wound around bamboo rods felt more like a pavilion than a house, when you stood in the middle of the one big room. The top half of the hut was nothing but a window that stayed open all the time. The overhanging palm-thatched roof extended so far out that it provided a beautiful patio that circled the dwelling and kept all but the driven rain out. The Osa rarely had this type of weather. Four hand-hewn, teak bed frames, fitted with mosquito nets and thin foam pads positioned near the walls, with a single yoga mat sitting in the middle of the room. "A few of the tree forts we built as kids in Florida were as sophisticated as this. This is what you call Spartan" she remarked out loud.

They stowed their backpacks under one of the beds, and stepped outside to peruse the inventory of surfboards lined up in a driftwood rack that was built to fit the arch of the porch. She examined the display for a while before commenting on the collection. "Not much of a selection here. A handful of ding-riddled long boards, one

California beach-break board, two tall pintail single fins, a funky old fun shape, and a Ben Aipa, Rocket Stinger Fish; these look pretty old school to me. I was hoping to try a more modern high-performance board this time around."

"I'm not surprised. I think they might be the same boards I went here when I left this all behind. It doesn't look like Tomas added anything new to the quiver. He can ride any of these just fine."

She examined the upper deck of the sun-stained fun shape. It had a nifty logo of a dancing Rasta Man high stepping and throwing his shoulder length dreadlocks back over his head. Above him in roots lettering it said Soul Man. Underneath that, she noticed an inscription written on the foam with indelible ink. "To my friend, Stan Manly, a Real Soul Brother, man!"

"Wow. Who shaped this for you, Popi?"

He picked the board up gingerly with both hands to scrutinize the inscription. He feigned ignorance as he held it closer for a better look. He shook his head. "I have no idea who shaped it. I suppose he was pretty good, though."

She was perplexed. "Come on, Popi! It says for Stan Manly right here!"

"You asked who shaped it. Ed Town made Soul Man surfboards; he was the best glasser around, but no telling who shaped it. It could have been Ed, or maybe half a dozen other guys. No matter who designed it, they were all at the top of their game. They were East Coast shapers who made boards for the early Florida pros that came out of nowhere to dominate the scene.

Ed could get blanks shaped from all of them. Sometimes, some big-time shaper from out of town would stop by for a visit, and Ed would have him in the shaping room working all day before he knew what happened. That's how much love they had for the craft and each other. Surfers were like a tribe or something. I'm pretty sure Ricky Carroll shaped this one; he liked to do the fun shapes."

"By the way, that board is magic. It's probably the loosest one in the rack, but those three fins will help you hold your edge. The waves have a lot of power here, so that board will be high-performance enough. It's fun to ride. That's why they call it a Fun Shape."

"Cool, soul brother. I'm stoked. I'm a real Soul Woo-Man with a 6' 8" high-performance fun shape. I'm ready to do the Rasta Man Boogie in the barrel, Popi. Can you hang?"

The idea of surfing in Matapalo with his granddaughter nearly overwhelmed him. "Yes, sunshine, I can hang — hang ten! Let's go check Pan Dulce, first. You'll like that wave. It's an awesome right-hander; breaks for hundreds of yards!"

Enchanted with the dreamlike scenery, Cheyenne watched as a pair of scarlet macaws dragging lengths of blue and red feathers, hovered face-to-face just above the tree line. She wondered about their loud squawking. "Are they bickering, or declaring their undying love for the world?"

"It's hard to tell, sometimes. They mate for life."

At play under the macaws, were a dozen or more neon black and yellow-striped zebra butterflies, fluttering about, like a well-tuned ballet on an open stage. But in the serenity of the moment, the devil's time had come. Popi mumbled "I'm reminded of the cold-hearted humans I've encountered during my life of folly on this planet." His head hung low as Cheyenne looked back to face him.

She knew she'd be stepping into a jagged trap like a clawless crab, but she went ahead anyhow. "What reminds you, the Zebra butterflies?"

"Yes" he whispered.

"I'm sorry, Popi, I was being facetious" she confessed.

"No worries my dearest. Yes, they did remind me; they're the banner of Matapalo, my paradise. But back to that awful day; I held Alina's cold, lifeless hand, and since that day an empty place in my heart has been filled with dread. I ran away, but now I'm facing it, again. Maybe I'll come to regret it, but I can't turn back now."

"Take it easy, Popi. You don't have to do this."

It was time to lance the boil. "Her cold hands ... I can still feel them!"

He dropped to the ground with his head in his hands. She sank down next to him and wrapped her arm around his collapsing shoulders. He released a mournful sigh and held his tears back behind a levy of willpower as he relived his last dreadful journey to Matapalo.

"Harmony was my thing, so it didn't take much time back in the hectic States before I was itching to return to the Osa. I was totally stoked to be back in Matapalo and couldn't wait to see Alina. It made climbing the hill a breeze. Like the sign on the road to Carrates says, Bienvenido Osa - La Verde a Azule Suenos.

About halfway up the steep trail, I took a puff of ganja from a papaya stem and sat a bit. The cabbie who had given me a ride to the bottom of the trail from town had tossed me a hockey puck-sized wad of sticky local bud as I exited his van. 'I got more if you want!' he had yelled out to me as I started my way up the steps. It seemed harmless at the time."

He hung his head in disgust and wrung his hands to keep from trembling. "Maybe I would have been in time to help her if I hadn't stopped to puff and take in the day."

Cheyenne was at a loss for words. She placed each of her hands on his shoulder blades.

Popi glanced up. "Pay no mind to me; I walk this bridge every day since. Sometimes long, sometimes not, but I cross it just the same.

When I made it to the top of the hill, I crept out wide behind the big house where all the meals were served. I had to be stealthy. There was an unwritten rule of the property; personal visitors were to avoid disturbing the privacy of Tres Montañas clientele. No problem here, I wasn't eager to meet anyone at the time, especially if I didn't have to.

The last third of the climb is pretty vertical, and it can be difficult to negotiate if you aren't used to it, so I was a little winded. There is a flat ridge near the top. From that vantage point, I could catch my breath and scope out the big house and the pool area for signs of life. I was in a hurry to get settled and go out to surf before dinner, but I sure wanted to be careful and make sure Alina's paying customers were happy. One look at me might ruin their whole vacation."

Seeing Popi had regained his composure, she gave him a hand up and urged him on. "Please, continue," she asked as they started walking again.

Popi obliged. "I could see fresh flowers arranged all around the main house, telling me guests must be registered, but I hadn't spotted any.

I worked my way along the western edge of the property where there is a lot of cover and plenty of dark shade. A family of white-throated capuchin monkeys was napping in the low limbs of an enormous carambola tree. Usually, they make pretty good watchdogs with all of their screaming and yelping at the slightest disturbance, but oddly, they just sat there, like they had been through hell and back. They looked wiped out, and it wasn't even that late in the day.

I should have known something was wrong from the blank stare that I got from the matriarch of the troop; she was usually bold and vocal. I should have been paying better attention; she was in shock. Alina favored the capuchin monkeys. I think, maybe, it was because she was a kindred soul. She needed the Rain Forest to survive, too. They loved each other's company.

The name capuchin is derived from a cloister of monks dubbed the Order of Capuchin Friars Minor and offshoot of the Franciscans. Damn, Alina could have used a Saint's protection that day! It has caused me much sorrow that there wasn't any protection for her that day. My faith since then has been tested.

I made my way up the driveway to the cuidador's home. No truck, no barking dog, no cuidador to greet me; it was unusual. Tres Montañas is an immense property of many hectares; they could've been off anywhere. I thought maybe they went up the mountain to check their water system; it was critical to the lodge to keep it working.

I was disappointed not to meet the new caretakers. I had brought them a few conveniences and goodies from the States. Alina had told me good things about her new husband and wife team. Alina managed Tres Montañas, while the caretakers maintained it. I had wanted to get off to a good start with them, but I figured it could wait; there would be plenty of time for formal introductions later.

Alina kept a set of keys stashed under half of a coconut shell in the garden near her front step. It had been a long day since leaving the house for the Orlando airport at 3:30 am, so I was ready to get settled in. I was beat, but being a kid at heart, I prioritized play time over rest and chores, which Alina would be keen to point out.

I anticipated catching a few waves before dusk after I got my stuff squared away. Even with the threat of possible chores, I was ecstatic to take the short walk up to Alina's cabana. I wondered if she made her plane alright, and thought how nice it was of her to let me write all alone up here while she was gone.

Walking up her astonishing garden path reminded me that she would leave a list of labor-intensive tasks for me to accomplish during my visit. Alina loved to plant gardens, and they were everywhere. She also like to put boarders to work on them. She would probably assign me some weeding and trimming right away, but, like she always said 'All in good time.' I would let it go for another day. Surfing couldn't wait.

Her free spirit and passion for Mother Earth was evident in the passive layout of her modest estate. She had a three-sided outdoor shower that was open to the world on the side of the property where the jungle dropped down the steep side of the mountain, leaving a clear view of the sky. I guess she was hidden from the eyes of men, but stood naked before God.

Her home was a simple, but accommodating, one open room Pacific cabana. Florida folks we hang with wouldn't consider it adequate, but a Tico family would never turn their noses up at it. It would be more than they were used to. It was all Alina needed to call home."

"As I reached her place, a lightning flash of biblical proportions lit up the sky. Thunder cracked and rumbled simultaneously through the mountains of Matapalo as if the Pearly Gates had crashed and fallen into the sea. I'd never seen or heard anything like it. It was so loud and long that I imagined it was heard in Hell; the demons felt it, and trembled in fear.

"Alina's door was cracked open ever so slightly. There was a lethal black and green dart frog, a harlequin, at the base of the clay steps — the kind the aboriginals used for their poison blowgun darts. When the frog saw me coming, it was his cue to hop inside, which he did. Like a lead-in actor, the lethal frog followed the script as a messenger of metaphor. Death entered before me."

Popi stopped again. He set his board down in the sand and sat on the nose. "A pot of warm water sat there next to a cup, waiting under a coffee sock full of fresh grounds. Something was fishy."

He looked up at the heavens as if talking to the sky, and muttered "Virginia believed God is our ability to communicate. Perhaps, if I was listening closer, I would have heard the Devil speaking to me at that very moment.

I pushed the door open wider with just my finger. There, against the opposite wall, was her luggage, all opened and jumbled up. Alina had not gone anywhere; someone had ransacked the place. My heart started pounding out of my chest. There was a picture of us holding a pair of yellowfin tuna on the floor with a few other things knocked off her little vanity. There was a letter started on some fancy stationary with gold trim still unfinished on the writing pad. My head started spinning as I saw what was written on the pad. It said 'Manly, my love.'

That was all she had written. It hit me in the stomach like a cannon ball. It was like a bad acid trip. The room started moving in and out, and losing its shape. No matter how hard I tried to fill my lungs, I couldn't breathe. It was bad! Something drew me to the ladder to her sleeping loft, where I climbed up. When I hit the top rung I could see her form; she looked like a sleeping child spread out over her bed. I turned her to face me and nothing, but her two pale cold, eyes stared back at me. They were empty of life; she was gone.

I pulled her to me, held her close, and then I started weeping like never before. I could hear loud voices and a barking dog. I prayed for relief, but it wasn't my day. At first I sat there waiting with Alina in my arms, but something or someone, maybe it was Alina told me

I should move! I hesitated; I wanted to tell them for her sake, but my gut hollered 'Run!' and I did.

I bolted out the side door through the thickest part of Alina's yard. I stopped and lay flat, catching my breath, trying to figure out what was going on and what to do next. I spied two men running towards Alina's place. I realized that I had left my backpack in her cabana. What could I do? As I escaped down the hill, I distinctly heard one of them yell 'Stan Manly es solo."

He exhaled deeply as he lifted his creaky body up. Cheyenne reached out to assist him, clasping his arm. He didn't need the help, but he welcomed it. He led her methodically into what seemed to be an impenetrable wall of vegetation, but they leaned through it to find a shoulder-wide footpath. She stopped and raised her palm with emphasis. "Hold it, Popi! What happened? Did they catch you?"

He drummed his fingers on his expanding breastbones and replied with bravado "I'm here, am I not?"

He hastened down the damp forest path. He stopped abruptly at a fork in the trail, hesitated a moment, and then scratched his sweaty brow. "As much as I'm prepared to complete this story, one of us should be there to meet Tomas. You wouldn't know it, since he is never on time, but he hates to wait. We should split up here. The short track is rough and rocky, but better to take the long, easy way up to the road and cross down. You're fair-footed, so you'll be fine on this shortcut straight to Pan Dulce. You can't miss it, young lady.

Go past Pan Dulce Point around to Backwash Bay. No matter how good the waves are at Pan Dulce, don't stop! I'll see you at Backwash Bay. I'll be under the Matapalo tree. Don't go out if no one else is there yet. Adios!"

One moment, she was looking right at him, and in an instant, he was gone; he had vanished into the brush. She recalled hearing once that you should never say goodbye to those you love, only see you soon, catch you later until we meet again; anything but goodbye. If you say goodbye, it might be forever.

"I didn't have a chance to say anything." She shrugged and started on her way. She was walking as fast as she could when she suddenly realized that Popi's last word was adios. She stopped short. Did he slip? He said, Adios. That means Goodbye. Is that a bad omen?

Her mind started slipping, and she nearly stumbled at the base of a huge manga tree when she thought one of the twisted roots was a snake poised to strike. She needed to calm herself down. She bit her lip, made the sign of the cross and kept on going. Seconds later, she was encouraged by the refreshing vibration of breaking waves; they sounded like they were calling to her. When she came skipping up to the edge of the jungle and got a clear look at Pan Dulce's rocky point, she got confused. It didn't seem right. She watched a set come through, and the light came on. "Oh wow!"

The surf was breaking perpendicular to the shore. The sea had deposited piles of neatly twirled, ocean-smoothed driftwood trees, logs and boards to create an intricate, multi-level set of front row bleachers. They were positioned perfectly on the beach for seats with a view of Pan Dulce's main attraction. She took a place directly in front of the main take-off point to watch the show. After a few waves had come through, she saw the surfers who were out ripping it to shreds. "Matapalo, Surf-utopia" she gasped.

The geographical setting was perfect for a surf feast. Symmetrical waves broke along left to right for hundreds of yards, into a sparkling bay. A Bahia was so magnificently dreamy that people might not believe it was real on a postcard. The bigger set waves bounced high off the farthest end of the point's bizarre, volcanic rock formation that jutted out from the shore to the ocean and north.

The white water would get sucked down and folded under by a blue maelstrom as the wave receded, leaving the ominous rock high and dry. The retreating wave formed to go back from where it started and ran head-on into the next precision wall. The colliding forces sent a monstrous peacock tail of water fanning out high over the drink. She assumed Backwash Bay must be around the point.

Such luscious surf; it was seductive and almost dreamlike for her. Nothing remained of her former measurement of what a surf break should look like. This was it her spot —her Eden. If she was ever to raise a family, at that moment she decided it would be here. She knew it, deep inside of her, like she knew she needed to draw her next breath. As fast as this vision arose, she tucked it back away, safely hidden for her future.

"I buy into Popi's 'every star is a setting sun' theory," she thought. "Kharmic wind can push people together as well as tear them apart. Hoping for something secure around the corner when you have wild perfection in front of you just ain't my thing. I don't need to see anymore or see anyone.

Why not go out here at Pan Dulce? There're other people out there. I'll go to Backwash Bay, but not until I taste one of these sweet morsels."

She picked up her board and tried to ascertain how she was going to paddle out through the puzzling thin maze of exposed volcanic rocks, and turbulent channels. She heard Tomas' unmistakable, autocratic voice coming up behind her.

"The surf's looking pretty good this afternoon. Wish I didn't have to pick up these folks at Carate. Can't those idiots find their way to Corcovada without me holding their hands? Well, the tide's a little low for my liking anyway. I don't have much of a taste for eating rocks! I saw a couple of newbie surfers pay the price here just the other day. It certainly ain't no place for the weaker sex."

Thomas' flippant remark incited her to paddle straight out even though it was meant as a serious warning. There was something conclusive about the way he said, "Please don't go" as she headed off, so she turned around.

"I have a letter for your grandfather. It would be a shame if he was to not read it. My cousin Lukas, who worked closely with the Federal Police, gave it to me many years after Alina's death. He helped me keep Stan out of their reach until he could get out of Costa Rica.

Lukas knew the Federales were off the track, searching for Alina's murderer. He knew it wasn't Stan Manly who killed her. The Federales were following a cloudy trail of gossip, false reports and fairy tales. Stan Manly was seen nowhere and everywhere at once. It was crazy! If a chicken was stolen, Stan Manly was the culprit. Meanwhile, the real Stan Manly was nowhere to be found."

Tomas handed her a leather-bound journal; in it was a thin plastic sleeve covering three pages of gold trimmed bond paper. She took it and nodded. "Of course, thank you for all you have done for my Popi."

The big man reached out with his broad hands, took hers, and knelt down to kiss them. She felt a tear land on her wrist. "It was for Alina. She was the only woman, besides my mother, I've ever loved. We love your Popi, too."

He stood up, gently let go of her hands and turned to head off and give those people a ride.

She watched him go and wondered "Where is LuLu? Did he go with Popi? I hope so, then the adios won't count.

Without opening its pages, she slid the journal into her backpack, picked up her board and started walking in the only direction left; to Backwash Bay.

Again, her thoughts drifted to LuLu, and she wondered where he was. She hoped he didn't go off too far. She had quickly grown to love the princely little pooch. He filled a void in her life, and they were a good match. They were independent, but connected.

This reminded her of Joe. It was starting to soak in that her meditation had cleared out a lot of static and clutter, even though at first it hadn't seemed like it was doing much good. She was becoming increasingly aware of her real feelings; she didn't just admire Joe, she desired him. It was a strong yearning; one she was growing accustomed to for the first time.

She could feel Joe's presence in her heart. She knew there would be, as the Haitians say, mountains, beyond mountains, but in her heart and soul, she knew they would be good sojourners together. She was ready to see him again.

Then there's Popi; what about him? Would he fulfill his quest? There she was, all alone on the beach, thinking about the three men in her life; LuLu, Joe and Popi. "Where the heck are they?" This thought cycled though her mind for a moment until the ocean caught her attention once again.

Out of the dozen or so surfers in the water, one was taking off on a set wave that ricocheted off the last rock. He slipped down a steep wall that met another deflection coming from the oblique. The result of the convergent forces was a standing wave that tripled up to give him an elevator ride up and discharged him into the perfect position to speed through a hurling barrel.

Cheyenne's heart jumped at the sight. "I'll be back to try that, but first I'm off to Backwash Bay." To reassure herself, she shouted over her shoulder to Pan Dulce and the crew "See ya soon!"

She walked on and prayed that Joe and Popi would be part of her life forever. It would be great if they could all just stay in Matapalo forever, too. She loved it. As she rounded the bend, the sound of waves seemed to diminish. She found herself looking down from the point over a small, tranquil bay. The lack of surf caught her off guard. "There's no way this is Backwash Bay; where's the surf? It's dead flat here."

As if on cue, a flurry of action commenced center stage in the middle of the bay. There it was. She got it. "I see, now. Those guys are way out there! Wow!"

She rooted for the surfers; several of them were chasing a wave that was welling up on the invisible ridge below it. Up, up, and up it went, reaching for the sky from the deep bowels of the Pacific. The lip started feathering all the way across the wide pinnacle of the rogue peak. Cheyenne howled at the monster wave. "Hawaii Five-O!"

When the wave finally pitched over, it lifted three dwarfed riders up for a heart-stopping push down the vertical face. Two of the three riders carved hard down the line, while a guy about thirty yards out in front of them dropped in only far enough to dig a turn and kick his board out over the top. All-out speed was the only hope to make the next section walling up ahead; you'd better have a good board, she thought to herself.

The pack outside were all jockeying for the next set wave rising up from the freakish impact zone, and it wasn't long until every surfer had ridden a wave all the way across Backwash Bay. It was a thrilling sight, one that alleviated any longings for Pan Dulce. The more she observed, the more she liked this wave and approved of the captivating beauty of Backwash Bay. The Bay was a hidden jewel tucked between two rocky points, with a lush jungle backdrop; what could there be not to like?

In her heart, she knew she had found a place she could call home. No matter how clear her mind had been a second earlier, it now snapped away from the surf back to the man. "Oh, the choices a girl must make in Matapalo."

She looked in every direction, but Popi was nowhere to be seen. She began to worry, and thought to herself "Where's Popi, I don't see him around, anywhere. Shouldn't he be by one of these trees with Lulu by now? I took my time getting here. I hope everything is alright. This isn't good."

She caught herself. "I need to get a grip; he can find me. I know he will. Something tells me I should stop here to pray and meditate like I did before."

She planted the board in the sand, placed the journal atop of it, and sat down, taking a meditative position on the beach. As she took her first deep breath, her eyes drifted toward the leather journal; she found herself fighting off the temptation of reading it. After chasing her mind for a spell, she slid into a place of peaceful awareness. Her peace was once again interrupted by a wet nose and a sloppy tongue completely covering her face with a loving doggie smooch. LuLu's licking power was so vigorous that Cheyenne's face slid up and down with each lick, and she had to keep her eyes shut. "Not again! How I've missed your hairy sweetheart kisses!"

"I've missed yours, too!" a funny little voice replied.

Cheyenne had to open her eyes. "Joe!"

LuLu struck a proud pose and watched as Cheyenne leaped to her feet and threw her arms around Joe's neck to deliver a seriously long kiss. After a couple of more delightful smacks, they stood back to admire one another. Joe pulled Cheyenne close again and savored a full helping of her honey-coated lips with what Nat King Cole would call shafafa on the side!

The Road To Matapalo

Cheyenne was bursting with exuberance over her newly found independence, and it intrigued Jose. She told him "I've got so much to share!" then she placed her hands against his chest, setting him back a bit and scolded him. "But first, what took you so long to get here, buster?"

This placed Joe on the defensive. "Do you have any idea how much trouble it is to get here from San Jose?" he stammered a little. "The last bus stop is in Jimenez, and from there it's a Hail Mary. Finding my way to you was an act of faith; maybe even a small miracle!"

She gently lifted her pointing finger to his mouth. "Can't take a joke, huh? Hush now. Lo siento!"

Before he could grab her for another caress, she stepped back, put her arms out and did a free-spirited triple twirl that ended with an exaggerated curtsy. Then she hurried back to him, snuggled up close and whispered in his ear. "Have you ever seen Eden?" There was an undeniable twinkle in her eyes.

LuLu wouldn't be denied and from his hind legs he did a couple of happy twirls of his own. Cheyenne was tickled. "Look at LuLu, he's all full of it!"

Joe was puzzled. "Do you know this dog?"

"He is my friend, guide and protector; my shining knight who protects my honor. My LuLu!" Then she spoke directly to LuLu. "I was just wondering where you had gotten off to."

It was Joe's turn to be perplexed. "When the cab dropped me off at Caboneras, he came running right up to me, wagging his tail, like he had been waiting there just for me. The driver, Alvin Valdez, said his name was LuLu, and he belonged to Ms. Alina, the Queen of the Jungle.

I called him by that name, LuLu, and the little dog stuck right by me like an old friend. As I began walking along, it seemed like I followed him, and he brought me straight to you. I think I like him! He's certainly smart and adorable." Then looking down at the dog, he added "and maybe clairvoyant."

Apparently, there was much more to LuLu than met the eye. "That's weird" she marveled. "There's no way that this dog is old enough to be the same LuLu that the cab driver was talking about. What's up with that?"

With that, she began to download like a zip drive. She had been holding so much in for so long that it all came out at once. She blathered incessantly about love, passion, human nature, surfing, the rainforest, the planet, war, life, family and murder. The twinkle in her eyes became a bit wilder, almost a little crazed, and her energy level erupted. Everything was happening too fast, but there seemed to be no stopping it.

Joe ran the back of his hand across his forehead. "Whoa, sensory overload! Slow down and give me a chance to come up for air. Where's Popi?"

The sun was slowly starting to collapse below the horizon. Cheyenne had all but forgotten Popi in her excitement. She took stock for a minute. Almost like divine intervention, a hint from Popi floated up from her subconscious like bubbles from the bottom of a pond. LuLu touched his wet nose softly on the back of her calf, and Cheyenne smiled.

"Of course! Popi is at the Matapalo tree standing over Backwash Bay! He told me it was the biggest one around, by far. That's why he said he would see me at Backwash Bay, but never showed up here. He said he would be under the tree. This is where Popi has been headed all this time. Not just to Matapalo, the place, but to this particular tree. I don't know what, but something is waiting for him there." LuLu once again put his damp muzzle to the soft back of Cheyenne's knee.

"Did you know Matapalo means strangler in Spanish?" Joe asked her.

In a loving, but commanding voice, Cheyenne ordered them to follow her. "To Matapalo we go!"

They turned towards the jungle together and began to trot off towards a likely spot. LuLu had charged ahead, taking the lead thirty yards out in front, directly on course for the Strangler. But before they went too far, Joe reached out to stop her.

"Cheyenne, wait a minute! Before we go any further, I have to tell you! It can't wait another second. I love you. I came here to tell you, I love you! I want to be with you."

Cheyenne's reaction wasn't quite what Joe had imagined. Without losing stride, she raised the journal and secret letters in the air. "Good, Joe. That's great, but for now I have bigger fish to fry! This is for Popi; I think it will clear his name and lead us to Alina's killers." Without any further questions or words, Joe followed Cheyenne and LuLu toward the spiritual tree.

There he was, like a geriatric Tarzan, secure on the timber of the flying buttresses of God's phenomenal universe, the ancient Matapalo. The old-growth tree had wrapped itself around a prehistoric mahogany tree that was decorated with patches of white and blue fungi. On the forest floor, scores of vivid neo-orange, buttercup-shaped mushrooms supported the base of the pair. The mycelium could feel Popi's intense energy too, as he ascended the branches.

Together the trees must have been 70 meters tall and 10 meters wide. Standing high on the top of the forest, they ruled like they were hip deep in water. The Matapalo was so tightly wound and had enveloped the big tree for so long that the two behemoths had completely transfused into one enormous spear. All the locals knew of this ageless Matapalo; in pre-Columbian days, the tree was considered a wise soul, but today it was now known only as the Strangler.

Popi was leaning way over from a natural platform of tangled, gargantuan roots and protuberances, some as big around as most trees, sixty feet above the jungle floor. LuLu circled around a couple of times and looked up at Popi's podium expectantly.

Through her heavy breathing, Cheyenne asked in a low voice "Did he come here to die?"

Surprisingly, Popi replied "I came here to live!"

She ignored his statement. "Popi, please! This isn't such a good day to die, is it? No! Please, come down." She lifted the bag that Tomas had given her to pass on to him. "Tomas gave me this journal and these letters. I'm not sure, but I feel they'll clear your name and expose who murdered Alina!"

Popi answered matter-of-factly. "I'll come down shortly to look at that, but first tell me your answer to my question. If man has the Word of God, who then speaks for this tree?"

Thinking fast, Cheyenne shouted back at Popi. "You do, my revered grandfather; grand elder of Matapalo."

Joe fought the urge to laugh and climb to get Popi down, but in a strange way he believed Popi's time may have come. He prayed under his breath for God's protection.

Cheyenne couldn't contain herself, and finally clambered up to escort Popi down. Joe knew better than to try to stop her. He felt for his rosary and turned up the heat on a spiritual appeal.

Cheyenne made it up to Popi in a jiffy, and sat on the branch next to him. When she turned to look down, she was taken aback by how high up they were. Popi continued to lean out over the edge, securing himself with one arm around a thick vine. "The day that Alina was murdered, this is where I hid. The Federales stopped right underneath me, right there where Joe is, to set up a temporary command center for the search. I stayed perfectly still here for hours, in fact, so long that the tree spoke to me."

Cheyenne humored him. "And what did it divulge, Popi?"

"I can't tell you exactly what the Matapalo said on that frightening night, but I'll try my best. At first, it was nothing more than a gentle breeze rustling pass the leaves, but then words seemed to form in the zephyrs.

'My roots grow deep under the rios in the Montana Valley and my limbs caress the clouds. I need not travel to find wisdom. The past is set in stone, but the future is a primed canvas and all of the colors are waiting for you to mix and use them.

You yearn to understand what can't be understood. Your search for meaning means nothing and is worth even less. One day bring Cheyenne here, but not until the time is right.'

"I was astonished, and asked the tree 'Who's Cheyenne?' I waited for a long time and asked several more times, but I never heard an answer. I had been up all night without sleep, but I had to keep moving now that the Federales had moved on. It was misty and hard to pick a direction. From somewhere in the jungle I heard the tree; it seemed like it came from somewhere else, maybe in my head. 'Cheyenne is a dreamer.' I just kept moving."

Losing her fear, Cheyenne came to her feet, stepped closer to the towering wall and said "I'm here, now."

A strange sound emanated from the highest branches; at first it was like a gentle breeze rustling through the foliage. Then a message began to form. It spoke in a barely discernible, quiet voice. "The one you crowned 'Queen of the Jungle' will always be here. Someday, we will all be together, and there will be no remembrance of former things. No one can hide from what is coming.

Until then, children, you were created to tend the garden. Your people have gone astray and their ways are ignorant and vain. Life is sanctified. Revive your love for your Earth, where your creator brought you forth and provided you a place to live. I remember; it was perfect and it was good before you arrived; there were no storms then. This is the center of the universe for you, at least on this side of the grave.

This life is a seed that must be planted to blossom in greater glory. Do not stop your ears; do not close your eyes. There is no defense for disregard. You are yet called to tend the garden; do not despoil it. You know in your heart what is right, so do it with all of your might. Go now, find your paradise. It is within. Let peace and good will rule your heart and your home.

God is us. God is love. Love sustains all. Sustain all in love. Think it, live it, do it! Amen!"

Awestruck, Cheyenne whispered "Did you hear that, Popi?"

With a knowing grin, Popi shook his head as he started thinking about returning to the ground. "I did once, a long time ago. That's why we came here today. Doubting already, darling?"

Joe had only heard the wind and the sounds of the ocean from where he stood; he was still giving it everything he had with his rosary. He had no idea how well it was working, since we don't always see every answer to each prayer. "Hey is everything okay? Maybe you should come down now."

Cheyenne and Popi started down, and when he only had about six feet to go Popi sprung out of the tree like a mad wizard tossing his cape, and landed square on the ground. He planted his feet, jumped left and right, ready for anything. "The tree just told me to surf Backwash Bay and Pan Dulce en la manana. I will be glad to oblige. He said you should come, too, Joe!"

Popi reached out to Joe and said "Hey youngster! It's good to see you, once again! Think ya might be staying in these parts for a while? Get my drift? Around Matapalo? Around me and LuLu and maybe even Cheyenne over there?" Cheyenne was making her way down the tree more carefully than he had a minute before.

Joe and Popi started catching up on school news and talking sports. Joe surprised Popi. "The SEC is by far the best conference in college football. But how about Florida State, they weren't supposed to have a good team this year, and yet they are still undefeated."

Popi was delighted. "I see you get ESPN on cable in your dorm. The Gators play Georgia next; that's my favorite game! All the Crackers show up for that one in Jacksonville, Florida. Crackers, get it? I guess you probably don't. Let me explain."

As she reached the ground and heard their conversation, she laughed. "All that rhetoric about modern culture being from the devil and you two end up talking football?"

She dropped in behind them next to LuLu, and she bent down to address the contented little dog. "I heard the old tree today. It said 'God is us. God is love. Love sustains all. Sustain all in love. Think it, live it, do it!' just like it said to Popi so long ago."

LuLu let out a joyful yelp.

"You heard it, too?"

Epilogue

Later that night, after spending hours at the bar catching up with Martina, Popi plopped his head dead-center on the pillow setout on his teak bunk in Tomas' bungalow. For the first time in years, he felt like the old Stan Manly. Just thinking of Joe and Cheyenne, who had left for Cabo Matapalo to wade in the tidal pools under the full moon, gave Popi's heart a reassuring tug.

He couldn't help but think back to when Cheyenne had been the apple of his eye, a little girl who tugged at his heart each time he saw her. He knew she was in good hands hanging with Joe. Popi wasn't surprised his old friend, Tomas, had not returned. Tomas had no concept of time and always lost track of it. Some things would never change.

Before saying his prayers, he revisited the day. "Oh, my heavens. . . the letters!" He lit an oil-burning hurricane lamp positioned above his bunk, and pulled the gold-trimmed sheets from the journal and out of their protective sleeve. He read:

"My Dearest Stan,
"Once again our paths run parallel, but do not intersect. What a shame I'm not at Tres Montañas with you; we could race down the trail to Matapalo. You would end up trudging along with your head down, and I would have my head held high with a spring in my step, running along just fine! Ha, I know I can tease you. You love it! Seriously, this is one of the reasons you and I get along so very well. I can be myself without being judged. But now, I'm being judged by the outside world. I see a new element here in Matapalo, infringing on our simple lives. They're not here to live peacefully with nature, but here to buy and develop Matapalo. I have spoken my peace to them, and if I'm not careful, the peace here will soon turn to push and shove. I hear an eerie cry coming from the trees."

"Yes," he thought, "she was right!" He could see the changes in the short time since he had been back. He could smell the smoke of the burning jungle, see the new rooftops springing up along the mountainside and he noticed the powerline poles being erected along the roadside outside of Jimenez. A touch of resentment darkened his heart, and he continued to read.

"Regardless, my life has never been better. I'll never forget how you saw me through my roughest times. My father and my entire family carried me, too. I survived my many blunders, thanks to everyone's help. Now, I walk on my own two feet; head up, ears and eyes wide open, and my mind clear. At least it seems that way to me.

I love Matapalo; it has completed me. You and I are much alike in that respect. The love of Mother Nature guides us both.

But now it's time, after this trip, for you to go back home and share more time with your family, and help repair your community. Go on, love Costa Rica, but not to the detriment of your loved ones or your community. Your tribe needs you. Grow where you are planted."

As long as I live here there will always be a place for you in Matapalo.
Peace! Hug a tree,
Alina

P.S. I have compiled a list of Stan chores for you. I certainly would not want you to get bored. I have also included a summary of some details and particulars concerning the property's new cuidadors. As nice as they seemed at first, and coming with such high recommendations, I am now having some misgivings about our arrangement. Keep an eye on them for me. I'm glad you are around while I'm not; I have concerns.

Catch a wave at Pan Dulce for me and keep me in your heart always. Save a dance at Martina's for when I see you again; a Corona, too."

Stan's hands dropped like rocks to his chest and the pages fell to the floor. He pushed his reading glasses aside, wiped tears from his eyes and slightly lifted his head back, peering at the thatched ceiling.

He knew in his heart who had killed Alina, and he was going to see to it they paid!

About The Author

Outdoor photojournalist and author Rodney Smith is a Florida native who writes and captures images to entertain and inspire his audience. While his subjects touch on a plethora of topics, Smith's focus is mainly trained on outdoor centric topics including, but not limited to surfing, hiking, sports fishing, paddling, camping, beach-combing, and adventuring. His strong efforts address current issues affecting our collective quality of life.

An ardent observer of Earth's climate change and the decline of our planet's bio-diversity, including the steady decline of his backyard waterway, the *Indian River Lagoon*, Smith works tirelessly on conservation issues as both an advocate and educator. His highly successful program, *Hook Kids on Fishing*, has taught thousands of children and their families the value of a healthy environment and the benefits of an outdoor experience. He also motivated the start of *Anglers for Conservation*, a group of environmentally concerned citizens that promote stewardship of our local waters.

Through his many appearances and speaking engagements Smith has displayed a unique and in-depth understanding of the economical and environmental impacts of Florida's poor politics and rapid population growth. A longtime fishing captain and founder of *Coastal Angler Magazine*, Smith is spiritually connected to the history, progression and evolution of Florida's culture and its people.

Rodney Smith is also the author of two instructional books, *Catching Made Easy* and *Enjoying Life on the Indian River Lagoon Coast*. For more information on these books or the other services Smith provides, please visit **rodneysmithmedia.com** or email **irlcoast@gmail.com**.

Made in the USA
Columbia, SC
08 August 2017